Taylor's Law

Jennifer Raines

Taylor's Law
Copyright © 2022 Jennifer Raines
All rights reserved.

ISBN: (ebook) 978-1-958136-03-4
(print) 978-1-958136-16-4

Inkspell Publishing
207 Moonglow Circle #101
Murrells Inlet, SC 29576

Edited By Yezanira Venecia
Cover art By Fantasia Frog Designs

DEDICATION

Thanks to my Canadian mentor, V I Peace. Without V's tough questions and constructive feedback, I wouldn't have made it this far.

CHAPTER ONE

Taylor Law

Ella Anderson exited the train station, her gaze captured by the imposing glass and chrome high-rise squatting diagonally opposite. She pressed a hand to her nervous stomach. The few mouthfuls of dry toast she'd forced herself to swallow at breakfast refused to settle. The stylish sign mounted on the front of the building on the other side of the concourse left no room for doubt—Taylor Law. A prestigious location and a blatant statement of wealth and power.

Ridiculous to think a building could gleam malevolently, but in the weak rays cast by an autumnal sun, it looked as menacing as it had eight years ago. Ella had first-hand experience of the company's ruthlessness. Taylor Law had represented the crook who'd legally swindled prime farmland from her father. Her sworn statement about the verbal agreement and hand shake between the two men had counted for nothing. The icy dread that had seeped into her bones when she'd learned of this appointment returned. She shivered.

Wealth bought power. To hell with justice.

Releasing the hand of her curly-haired niece, Ella

scooped the toddler high in her arms and smiled at Tessa's delight.

"That's my girl." She blew noisy kisses on the bridge of Tessa's nose before settling the giggling child on her hip. With a conscious straightening of her spine, she navigated her way through the throngs of Monday morning tourists crisscrossing the foreshore concourse.

Nine fifteen was too early for workers to have emerged from their offices for a coffee break. Perfect timing for carefree travellers to head to the ferry wharves for the tourist destinations on Sydney Harbour—Taronga Park Zoo, Manly Beach or Watsons Bay. Their easy-going laughter was a sharp contrast to her edgy apprehension.

Within minutes she'd walked out of the brisk wind through automatic entrance doors to the lobby. Quieter here away from the noise of the street, but the marble tiles were equally formidable, symbolising clarity and control when she had neither. She'd come to this meeting in place of her sister, Chrissy, who could no longer attend anything. Ella swallowed the lump of tears in her throat. A command—she'd hardly call it an invitation—from Jacob Taylor, who wasn't just any lawyer; he carried the building's name.

The letter had been in the innocent-looking pile of mail she'd collected from her neighbour when she'd returned from the family farm to the apartment last night. As Chrissy's executor, she'd opened the letter addressed to her sister, the weight of the stiff cream parchment ominous even before she read the missive. The company name in bold print and the typed, blunt sentence stating the time and place for this meeting had confused her. The next paragraph mentioned Drew Browning, paternity and custody in carefully crafted sentences—an implied threat that had left her struggling to breathe. *Custody!*

Entering the elevator, she let Tessa press the button for the tenth floor. She slid the child to the floor and took her hand. Smooth, silent, fast, the glass cube rose through the centre of the building. A disembodied-elevator voice announced each floor: three, then seven, then nine, cutting her connection to her own world with breathtaking speed. The doors opened into a foyer three times the size of her office in the community justice centre she managed, and was more opulent than a five-star hotel. The ripe fragrance of Oriental lilies was another assault on her senses.

"Can I help you?" inquired the elegant blonde perched behind an oversized reception counter. The crimson and white lilies spilled from a vase on her right, plucked of their stamen, presumably to prevent the sticky orange anthers from staining the countertop and marring the perfect image being created. The company name was emblazoned on the reception wall in letters half Ella's height.

"Ms. Anderson to see Mr. Taylor." She'd only explain Chrissy's absence once. She didn't have the strength for more. Every bone and muscle in her body ached at the injustice of Chrissy's early death. Saying "my sister is dead" offended her sense of right and wrong. The words becoming harder, not easier, with each retelling.

"Please take a seat, Ms. Anderson." The woman gestured towards the ox-blood chesterfield positioned against the opposite wall. The colour seemed fitting for this antechamber to hell. "I'll let Mr. Taylor know you've arrived."

The firm instructions reinforced all of Ella's impressions. *Power!* The word reverberated through her head. Drew Browning—a man whose name didn't appear on Tessa's birth certificate and whom Chrissy had never named—had hired Taylor Law to represent him. Potential father! He was a stranger to Tessa, to Ella and her family. Choosing Taylor Law to represent him was a brutal demonstration he had the money and power to buy the result he wanted. Panic rose like bile in her throat.

She dropped onto the couch, settling Tessa beside her.

"'Ootles." Tessa reached out a hand, her grey gaze full of trust. Ella knew zilch about genetics, but no one in her immediate family had grey eyes.

She pulled a soft bear with a chewed ear from her bag. "Here's Tootles." And wished for her own brown bear to stand sentinel at her shoulder during this meeting. Tessa began a private and unintelligible conversation with the raggedy toy, while Ella leaned back against the expensive leather, a false comfort. This time yesterday her path had been clear, raising Tessa as if she were her own child because she loved her. She'd promised Chrissy to give her niece the best upbringing she could.

Ella had never questioned the rightness of it. Tessa was the child of her heart, her nurturing love built on a million small memories—bathing Tessa when she was a baby, sharing mealtimes, comforting her when she was teething, and waiting to give her a hug when she let go of the security of the coffee table to take her first steps. When Chrissy's health stopped her from doing simple tasks, Ella had accepted she'd be a single parent.

"You can go in now, Ms. Anderson."

Ready or not, here I come. The words from a children's game echoed in her mind. She had no idea what had precipitated this meeting, but her need to know outweighed the anxiety pounding at her temples. Outweighed her concern at bringing Tessa. With her regular sitter unavailable and the doctor's advice to keep the toddler close until she established new routines, her options had shrunk to zero.

"Tessa." She waited while the child scrambled off the sofa, the bear clutched in one hand. She held out her hand and the child took it.

The secretary threw the panelled teak door wide. A sense of unreality swept over Ella as she approached the office. Today Tessa might have a father. *Dear heaven.* She struggled to get her head around the idea. An absent, anonymous man who'd abandoned Chrissy, a man Ella and her family hadn't factored into Tessa's upbringing.

Taking a deep breath, she stepped into the lion's den.

Two men—where Ella had expected one lawyer—

dressed in stylish dark worsted suits, crisp business shirts and silk ties, stood when she entered. They'd been sitting in low, burnished gold, leather armchairs, but broke off their conversation to rise at her arrival. The similarity between them ended there.

Her attention skittered away from the face of the older man. She assumed he was the lawyer, Jacob Taylor. Her quarry became the younger man who'd stepped towards her. With his body encased in a minimalist, form-fitting Lanvin suit, he looked as sleek and lethal as a bullet. His face could have been carved from marble—classic lines, strong bones and a determined chin. The russet brown hair pulled back into a stubby ponytail and the gold stud in his right ear shattered his veneer of sophistication. A pirate king.

The friendly interest she'd programmed herself to display at this meeting evaporated as their eyes met.

And held.

His steel-grey gaze probed deeply, demanding access to her closest held secrets. Her instinct to share was physically and emotionally shocking. This close, his subtle scent, sandalwood with a dash of something spicy, teased her nostrils, undermining her resistance and offering a giddy temptation she struggled to understand. Her greeting caught in her throat, and she took a step back. Her nerves stretched tight, her body responding to him even as the blazing intelligence concentrated on her shifted into suspicion. She couldn't look away.

"Who are you?" he demanded.

The tension in his liquid chocolate voice rippled through her. This man couldn't be Tessa's father. The ferocity of her denial rattled her. Every cell refused to accept he'd been her sister's lover. And some remnant of reasoned thought nagged at her. He'd have eaten Chrissy alive.

"Eleanor Anderson." With an effort, she gathered her professional poise. "Chrissy's sister. Ella. You must be Drew." She reached out a hand.

"You know damn well I'm not Drew."

"If you aren't Drew, who are you?" Off-balanced by his instant attack, she tried to steady her jumpy nerves. Withdrawing her hand, she turned to the older man, who was staring at Tessa. "Mr. Taylor, your letter requested Chrissy meet you here about Drew Browning's paternity and ..." She stumbled to a halt over the word "custody," then shook her head as a bizarre idea formed. "You can't be Drew?"

"I'm his father, Peter." His presence confused her further but confirmed the identity of the pirate king.

She stretched out a hand for a second time. "Then you must be Mr. Taylor. Good morning."

"Where's Chrissy?" Taylor demanded.

Before she could answer, Tessa's soft voice ricocheted around the room. "Mama's in heaven."

Ella gathered Tessa into her arms, hugging her tightly. She buried her nose against the child's neck to hide the tears threatening to spill over. "That's right, my darling," she crooned. "Mama had to go away."

"You must be devastated," said Peter gently. "A sudden accident?"

"An illness," Ella responded to his genuine sympathy. After a country funeral, sympathy was familiar territory. She'd learned to handle well wishes from near strangers.

"We should have acted faster." Peter turned to the silent lawyer. Taylor monitored her every move, cataloguing her sins. "Chrissy didn't say she was sick, did she? When did she die?"

"Ten days ago." The longest two hundred and forty hours of Ella's life.

"I'm sorry I didn't meet her. If we hadn't delayed ..." His distress obvious, Peter glanced at Jacob Taylor.

"I don't know when Drew employed Taylor Law, but Chrissy wasn't often conscious in her final days," Ella admitted. Those relentless days, when hope was gone and her sister's spirit had unwound like the spring in an old-fashioned timepiece. "You wouldn't have been able to question her."

"You've misunderstood. Jake's representing my wife and I." Peter stared at Tessa where her head rested against Ella's shoulder. "And this is Tessa." His voice softened, his mouth stretching into a smile as he studied the little girl.

"'Ootles fell," said Tessa.

Peter swooped to pick up the toy and handed it to her. "Ms. Anderson, Eleanor."

"Call me Ella," she said automatically, while she struggled to fit this new piece of the jigsaw into any kind of coherent picture. "I don't understand. The letter mentioned 'Drew Browning.'"

"Please sit down." Peter Browning opened his arms in welcome.

Taking a steadying breath, Ella scanned the sparse but elegantly furnished room, choosing the two-seater sofa, leaving the armchairs for the pirate lawyer and … Tessa's grandfather? Peter's presence reminded her there were other players in family disputes. A mistake not to anticipate who might be present today.

She settled Tessa beside her, placing her bag on the low central table. A single bark to bark piece of cedar, prized in her stretch of country above all other timbers. Beautiful, rare and very valuable—a timely reminder she'd entered an alien universe. Presumptive grandfather, not father, had chosen wealth and power to guard his back. *What the hell was going on?*

Tessa tucked Tootles safely between them, even her childish instincts recognising danger and seeking to protect. Ella rubbed Tessa's cheek and patted the bear.

"How can we help you?" Jacob Taylor interrupted.

"I received your summons." *Less than eighteen hours ago*, but Ella's mind still whirled with the speed of having her world tipped on its axis.

"Chrissy asked *me* for this meeting."

"I don't understand." Ella fell off the edge of a cliff she hadn't seen coming; Taylor's words tipping her into a spinning vortex. She turned to the older man. "Your son didn't initiate this?" Her voice cracked. Her vision blurred.

"Ella … Eleanor, are you okay? Can I get you a drink—tea, coffee, water?" Peter's face held concern.

Returning her gaze to Taylor, her mouth went dry. More than wealth and power—a history of ruthless elimination of opponents. Any sign of weakness on her part would be an open invitation to take advantage of her. *Chrissy, what didn't you tell me?* "I don't think I'll be here long enough for a cup of tea. But, thank you."

"What don't you understand?" Taylor studied her with the intensity of a lepidopterist examining an exotic butterfly on the end of a pin.

"I assumed Drew contacted you," Ella said. Maybe he'd heard from a mutual friend that Chrissy was dying? Maybe he'd finally bothered to check if there'd been consequences of his relationship with Chrissy?

"Drew's not in Australia."

"London's not another planet." She was babbling, trying to distract them both.

"You know Drew's in London." Taylor pounced on her admission.

"Chrissy said he was. She followed his blog." With the dedication of a true fan, and she'd never once mentioned he was her lover. Ella had listened with half an ear to her sister's gushing adoration and never guessed he was Tessa's unnamed father. Did that make her gullible or an idiot? Or had she been selfishly content when Chrissy insisted Tessa was hers alone, and she wanted Ella to look after her when Chrissy died? "She knew some of the people he wrote about. I had no idea they'd had any kind of personal relationship until I saw your letter."

"Yet you assumed I was Drew?" Taylor challenged.

"Based on your age." Ella hadn't anticipated the direction of the conversation, leaving her floundering. "Celebrity gossip doesn't interest me, and essentially he's a gossip columnist." *Why had her sister contacted Jacob Taylor of all the lawyers on the planet, and why hadn't she told Ella?*

"You didn't check what he looks like?"

"No, I had other priorities last night." Ella hadn't cared until he was linked to Chrissy in Taylor's letter. Disbelief had pinned her to her chair, until a desperate anxiety had driven her to check her niece was safely asleep. She'd stayed to keep guard, fighting sleep as long as she could. In her dreams she was arguing with a faceless lawyer. She insisted she had custody of Tessa. He laughed, and said, *"You have nothing in writing."* She'd woken, dripping with sweat. "I ran out of time this morning." She straightened Tootles in her niece's slackening grip.

Taylor's penetrating gaze narrowed in speculation. "When I received her letter, I talked to Peter."

"Not Drew?" His hesitation gave Ella a possible answer to the question most necessary for her sanity. "Drew denies paternity?"

The older man interrupted. "When Jake told me, I asked him to arrange a meeting."

"Why did you agree to a meeting, Mr. Taylor, if Drew denies the claim?"

"This isn't about me." Taylor waved an impatient hand. "What do you want?"

"I want to see Chrissy's letter to you." *To know what Chrissy asked for. What she offered in return. Then I will wake up and discover this is all a bad dream.*

"Why?"

Because I only have your word that she wrote to you! was the answer she ached to give, but she had no power in this place. She was the supplicant. "Your letter mentioned custody." She licked her dry-as-a-dirt-bowl lips. "Chrissy lived with me. As you can imagine, I talked to her often about Tessa's upbringing. I'd like to confirm if her letter to you is consistent with our conversations."

"She asked for money. Lots of money," he replied.

Ella's brain simply shut down. *Dear heaven.* Lots of money?

"Blackmail is an unpleasant business." Taylor seemed to relish the accusation.

"Chrissy was dying, not a criminal." Terrified was a better description. Adrenalin surged through Ella's system, and she welcomed the anger. "You're twisting her meaning. Seeking child support is not blackmail. It's a child's right." She'd explained the concept more times than she could count to absent fathers resentful of their obligations. Working alongside the community justice centre lawyers brought her into daily contact with family disputes.

Tessa tugged on her hand. "'Ootles doesn't like fighting."

"We're not fighting, darling." Ella ran her fingers up and down Tessa's back in a soothing manner, although she needed the contact more than the child. She met Taylor's smoky stare over the child's head. Her outburst hadn't tempted him to hand over Chrissy's letter. *Was the claim for cash in exchange for custody?*

"Stop upsetting Tessa, Jake. And look at her. I have a photo at home that could be her twin. The family resemblance is uncanny," Peter beamed.

"A physical resemblance isn't enough." Jacob Taylor's unreadable stare rested on her niece, and Ella held her breath. "At its heart, this is a paternity claim issued more than two years after the event."

"Bron will love her," Peter said simply.

Ella was lost, but the words had a powerful effect on Taylor. He looked tired, the lines around his eyes in sharper relief, before he shook off whatever emotion had battered him.

"We need to fully investigate," he insisted.

"That's your job. Ella, do you believe your sister?" Peter asked.

The direct question had Ella reassessing him. Grey hair and a heavily lined face gave the impression life hadn't always been easy for Peter Browning, but the glint lighting his eyes suggested he'd lived, loved and survived with his sense of humour intact. Under her intent examination, his smile broadened.

After reading and re-reading Taylor's letter, when she couldn't pretend it was some kind of macabre joke, she'd scoured her memory for any references Chrissy had made to Drew. She'd recalled off-hand comments and unfinished sentences starting with "Drew said" or "Drew wanted" and was amazed at her blindness in not working it out for herself. Combined with her sister's direct approach to Taylor Law, they added up to a plain truth.

With her heart pounding, she said, "If Chrissy said Drew is Tessa's father, then he is."

"Tessa's my granddaughter," he whispered, with a dazed smile.

"Hold on." Taylor's words snapped with the force of a whipcord through the room.

"Jake, please." Peter's answer was a quietly spoken plea. The old man's defencelessness triggered more alarm bells for Ella. Was he, like Tessa, an innocent?

The younger man's shoulders hunched in exasperation, but his expression offered endless tolerance for the older man. Another possibility for Taylor's hostility occurred to Ella: concern. The pirate lawyer recognised Peter Browning's vulnerability and was doing all in his power to protect an old man from false claims. She remembered her father's joy when he'd first seen Tessa. The promise of a grandchild was a very big claim.

His patience gave her a different insight into Jacob Taylor. A noble knight with his auburn-tinted locks caught in a leather thong. Disciplined in body and mind, the danger lurking in his eyes a warning he'd defend his own. Knight or pirate, he was displaying chivalrous instincts.

"We agreed on this, Peter."

Ella hadn't expected care beneath the toughness of the ruthless lawyer.

"You talk to Ella. Over there." Peter indicated the windows on the opposite side of the room. "If it's okay with you, Ella, I'll stay with Tessa. I imagine she doesn't like to be away from you at the moment?"

"She's extra clingy. I'm not leaving her alone with anyone she doesn't know yet." But she didn't want Tessa to overhear her conversation. Small ears picked up surprising details.

Peter nodded, moving to sit on the other side of Tessa. "How did Tootles get here today?"

"Tess, honey, I'll be over there." Ella pointed before crossing the room, forcing Taylor to follow her. She stopped, her position giving her a clear line of sight to the child.

"On the train." Tessa answered her grandfather, her gaze following Ella.

"Did he like the train?"

"He's a girl."

* * *

Given Peter's immediate fascination, it was madness to leave him with the child, but Jake had expected Chrissy Anderson to walk through his door. A known entity. He'd prepared for meeting her.

Eleanor Anderson represented a Pandora's box of problems. She stopped and swivelled to face him. Her sudden halt and the colour flooding her cheeks revealed her unease. A sure sign of guilt. Looking for more signs, Jake found what he searched for. Her crossed arms, her rapid breathing, the turbulence in her large, softly-fringed green eyes, and the hasty brush of her hand to tuck some stray honey-gold curls behind her ear were a play for time. All evidence she'd miscalculated badly, and now needed to change tactics.

Tall, slender to the point of thinness, her subtle curves held an appeal he found disconcerting. Under his relentless scrutiny, the colour faded from her creamy complexion to accentuate her high cheekbones. Without intending to, his gaze lingered on her mouth.

Her teeth tugged on her full lower lip, the action shooting an unexpected judder of awareness through him. *A practised trick*, he told himself, while fighting the urge to step closer and rub his thumb where her teeth had been, soothing any ache. He imagined her lips would be soft, yielding. The temptation to prove he was right in this as well jolted him out of his racing thoughts.

Jake ruthlessly suppressed the unwanted reaction. There was a better than even chance she was responsible for the ugly blackmail attempt in the letter. He wouldn't allow some huckster to steal from his uncle. Peter would have been a soft touch for a grandchild at any time, but since his wife had been diagnosed with a degenerative disease, he was more vulnerable. And Peter was right. His aunt, Bron, would love this child. She'd open her arms to Tessa as she had to him when he'd arrived on their doorstep all those years ago—an orphan at nine. He owed them too much to let them be exploited while he did nothing.

"Let's rewind, shall we? I received a letter claiming to be from Chrissy Anderson." He'd been prepared to listen to Chrissy, despite the incoherent threats of blackmail and offer to sell the child for a price. It wasn't in his DNA to turn his back on a child in need.

"You said Chrissy wrote to you."

"I've never seen her signature." The letter had been desperate, Jake recalled, more like the Chrissy he remembered than the woman in front of him, who didn't look desperate. She possessed more intelligence, more poise and more backbone than Chrissy ever had, or sheer rat cunning if she hoped to con him.

"You didn't question Chrissy wrote it until I arrived," she responded. "It can be easily verified. There are more important questions to answer this morning."

How could a little thing like her stiffening her spine churn him up inside, make his fingers itch to walk up that backbone to see if her resistance held? He pointed a finger at her. "Can you prove your identity?"

She turned on her heel and headed back towards her bag.

Jake wanted to get this charade over with. He'd called Drew when he got Chrissy's undated letter a fortnight ago. The details she'd supplied made her claim possible. Plus, Jake's own memory of her. The last night he'd seen Chrissy, she'd been inconsolable, her despair taking on a life of its own. Her letter provided a belated reason for her anguish. Pregnant to Drew.

The call was Jake's first contact with his cousin since Drew's move to London. Drew's mocking voice had conjured a clear picture of Jake's treacherous, self-indulgent cousin. Seemingly open and confiding, his cousin had expressed surprise at Jake's call. Drew's dismissal of paternity was too fast, and his outrage too staged for Jake to be satisfied. The conviction Drew was lying festered like an ulcer in his gut. Abandoning an innocent child to Drew's indifference and Chrissy's messy greed wasn't an option. He'd broken his cardinal rule of not carrying tales about Drew to his aunt and uncle. He'd asked to speak to Peter privately and told him there was a possibility Drew had fathered a child.

Only a possibility.

Peter had appeared without warning this morning. He'd insisted on being present at this meeting and was fast becoming too besotted with Tessa to think straight. Approaching his uncle was a mistake. Peter's enthusiasm had scuttled Jake's plan of meeting Chrissy privately, of testing each detail of her story, of demanding a DNA test. He'd been alarmed by his uncle's growing excitement before a stranger had walked into his office and played on Peter's sympathy and compassion with an ease that infuriated him. Messenger or instigator, he intended to find out.

She strode towards him, indignation in every step. Rifling through her wallet she produced a driver's licence. The photo was unflattering but accurate, although she looked thinner in the face now.

"I'd like to see her letter, please." The "please" had cost her. The fact she'd used it when she was angry and frightened, made him award her grudging respect. She wasn't a coward.

"Do you have authority to speak on her behalf?"

"I have—had—power of attorney and enduring guardianship." Her stricken expression said she understood the futility of her answer—both powers expired on the death of the person named. "I'm her executor."

"We aren't making a claim against her estate." He wasn't prepared to share the letter, a letter Eleanor might have written or dictated, until he'd researched Eleanor Anderson. "Do you have any other authority?"

"I have moral authority. If you even understand what that means." She pushed a strand of hair behind her ears, drawing attention to the elegant line of her neck.

You're in no position to accuse me of lacking moral authority." Although Jake's suspicions rested largely on the letter's claim for money. She looked as if she'd like to say something but shut her mouth, her lips pressed firmly together. She smelled of honeysuckle and summer days. And he was as crazy as his uncle to be attracted by a woman who could be running an elaborate scam. "Her death *does* complicate the situation."

"My niece has lost her mother, and I have lost my sister." Her voice trembled. Either she was as accomplished a performer as her sister, or she was struggling to contain unspeakable distress. He'd refused to speak for weeks after his parents' death in a light-plane crash. She exhaled a slow breath. "That's more than a complication."

"It makes it harder to get to the truth," he persisted, refusing to accept responsibility for her situation when his uncle and aunt deserved his loyalty.

"What truth do you want to find, Mr. Taylor?" Her emphasis on the word "truth" implied he was a peddler of lies.

"I chose neutral territory to discuss Chrissy's claim."

"Hardly neutral." She glanced around the room, sniffing the air with the disdain of a temperance preacher in a bar. She wouldn't be the first client to assume the deliberate informality was a trap. His office stood in such stark contrast to the rest of the building. His first move to stamp his style on the physical space of his business.

"I invited you to bring your own solicitor, Ms. Anderson." He'd expected Chrissy to come alone. Like he'd expected Peter to wait at home to receive his verdict.

* * *

Ella had answered so many insensitive bureaucratic inquiries about her sister in the days since her death that she'd developed a scab over the wound. Taylor's hostility ripped the top off, leaving her with no protection from the cocktail of anger and fear and loss possessing her.

His gentleness with Peter had lowered her guard, so she'd lost sight of the crucial fact. Jacob Taylor was the mercenary, the gun for hire. Based on her family's experience with this law firm, ethics was a non-starter in any contest between them.

"Do I need one, Mr. Taylor?" She could have called one of the lawyers from the centre last night when she'd opened the letter, but initially she'd been frozen in place, sitting with the missive spread out in front of her. When she'd tried to move, she'd ached—body, heart and soul. Being with Tessa was all that had mattered.

"Not for the preliminary chat I planned to have with Chrissy."

"*You* planned to have?" This morning Ella had foolishly believed her knowledge of the law and her experience at mediation would be enough for this first meeting. Another mistake. Her first had been her forlorn request to see Chrissy's letter. *When on earth had Chrissy written it?*

"When I sent the letter, I didn't expect Peter to be here this morning." Frown lines between his eyebrows marred the classical beauty of his face. "Can I see Tessa's birth certificate?" He held out a hand. "Birth certificates can be illuminating documents."

"Don't be so patronising. They weren't married, and he didn't claim paternity at the time, so his name isn't listed." *Chrissy could have named him but repeatedly refused.* Ella's focus had been getting here on time, not searching files to prove Tessa's existence. The meeting wasn't supposed to unravel like this.

"Don't you want me to see it?" His voice dropped to a husky drawl, dragging across nerve endings exposed by Ella's unexpected, edgy response to him. His swift antagonism was electrifying. "Does it have someone else's name?"

With the deliberate insult, something inside her snapped. Selfish, impetuous Chrissy. But she hadn't deserved to be left pregnant, sick and alone; she hadn't deserved to die so young. Ella surrendered to the red-hot rage ripping through her and zeroed in on the nearest target: Jacob Taylor. "I find your accusation offensive, Mr. Taylor."

"I don't like to see vulnerable people taken advantage of."

She was tempted to laugh out loud. Taylor Law had worked hand in hand with a lying cheat to crush her father without compunction. "You expect me to believe you."

He checked over his shoulder to see if Peter was within hearing, then dropped his voice another octave. "I won't allow you to play on an old man's desire to be a grandfather."

Ella clenched her hands into fists, the sincerity in his voice punching a hole in her anger. If concern for an old man was motivating him, it handicapped her ability to fight him. Justice was her passion. "I didn't know Peter Browning would be here."

"You haven't brought any evidence to support your claim."

"I came to see why Chrissy received a letter from a

lawyer regarding paternity and custody for a man who hasn't once bothered to visit Tessa. Not when she was born, not in the loss of her mother." Her pre-dawn decision was looking increasingly reckless. "But you don't want to believe that."

"You must think I'm an idiot."

"Just incapable of empathy." *Except for his client.* "I'm the idiot. Custody is an ugly word. It reeks of uncertainty for a child who's just lost her mother. I received your summons last night and obediently showed up here. My mother taught me keeping appointments was basic courtesy. A mistake where you're concerned," she continued. His attack implied only one conclusion, and she hated him for making it. "Why would you send a letter suggesting paternity if you think there's another man?"

His eyes flashed fire, and he took a step closer.

Adrenalin rushed through Ella's veins, making her heedless of consequences. "Or men. Is that how you live your life? Chrissy Anderson the pretender, Drew Browning the saint."

"How I live my life is irrelevant." His voice was steel encased in velvet. "You're the person who needs to prove your bona fides here, not me."

Her attack was illogical and his response biting. "I'd like to see her letter." Her desperation shamed her. *Why had Chrissy written to him, not Drew?* At least it explained why she hadn't told Ella. Her sister had remembered the Taylor Law name and knew Ella would never willingly deal with anyone associated with the company. Ella's satisfaction at challenging Taylor dissolved. Another mistake she shouldn't have made.

"I didn't bring the birth certificate with me, Mr. Taylor. My excuse is my late notice of this meeting. I'll ask my lawyer to get in touch. If Peter"—she glanced across to Tessa and Peter and gathered her long-ago legal training as a shield—"or his son would like information, my lawyer will facilitate an exchange of views."

"Did you expect Drew to be here?"

"I didn't know what to expect." She'd been blindsided by the official summons from Taylor Law. When he peered down his aristocratic nose at her as if she were something unpleasant stuck to his shoe, her instinctive response was to stand up straighter, square her shoulders and spit in his eye. Instead, she stared into unfathomable slate-grey depths.

"Did Chrissy expect *me* to get Drew here?"

"I have no idea." Ella couldn't lie. Nor could she expose her sister's flaws to this unsympathetic man—her essential naivety, her desperation to party, and the terror she'd hidden behind bravado when the final deadly diagnosis was made. Unless you'd known her and seen her disintegration in the last few months of her life, Chrissy's behaviour appeared unbelievable.

In the early hours of this morning, an old conversation had danced just out of reach in her mind. A conversation where Chrissy said she'd told Tessa's father and he'd laughed at her. Chrissy had been slipping in and out of consciousness at the time, so Ella couldn't be sure. "Did Chrissy's letter say anything about telling Drew he was Tessa's father when she discovered she was pregnant?"

"No, and it's the first time I've heard her claim." He kept his voice low and his back to Peter.

"You knew her." Ella was convinced he was hiding an essential clue to the puzzle. As he eyeballed her, she opted for a wild guess. "She wrote to you. *You,* not Taylor Law."

"I met her a few times." His tone was non-committal.

"With Drew?" She swallowed her surprise.

He nodded.

"Then you know more about her relationship with him than I do." The fear in her belly expanded, threatening to paralyse her. Her sister had sent Ella unarmed into the battle of her life.

"Drew met her when she arrived in town from the country. She had a boyfriend in tow. They split up soon after she met Drew." He shrugged with elegant indifference.

Ella flinched, recalling the hurtful cascading consequences of Chrissy's unannounced flight from home. "How long did you know her?"

"She and Drew were together a few months," he continued. "Her beauty won her some top modelling jobs. She stood out. I saw them at occasional social functions."

"Were you around when they broke up?"

"Yes." His long lashes dipped to hide his expression.

Ella would swap a month's supply of *tarallucci*, her favourite Italian nibble, to know what he wasn't telling her. "What did she say then?"

"Chrissy didn't tell me she was pregnant."

"But you remembered enough of that time to contact Peter Browning." She studied him closely, trying to find a crack in his facade of seeming detachment—a lawyer's trick. "What changed your mind, Counsellor?"

"Drew denied all knowledge," he said smoothly.

"You knew that when you arranged this meeting." And the only change in plan was Ella's arrival in place of Chrissy.

"Are you sure coming forward was Chrissy's idea?" he asked. "The Browning name appeared in the *Business Weekly*'s top one hundred list about a month ago."

"And Chrissy's letter asked for money?" Ella's stomach churned with nausea. He'd known Chrissy, maybe he would have given her a fair hearing, whereas Ella was instantly suspect. "Two and two make five in your world." *Dear heaven.*

"Peter has more money than Drew."

"You're saying she knew that?"

"Chrissy was dying when the letter was written. You were about to be left holding the toddler. Literally. An unwanted, inconvenient child. You wouldn't be the first to try and make some money from a situation like that." His assumptions revealed cold calculation while painting Ella as the heartless schemer. "Drew's in the UK. Peter's here. The letter was sent to *me*, not Drew. Did you think his family would be an easy touch?" He stepped closer, blocking the light from the window, his shadow pitiless.

Chrissy had been restless and unhappy in the last weeks of her life, her actions not always logical. Ella's best hadn't been enough. The knowledge of her failure to comfort Chrissy blunted the impact of Jacob Taylor's accusations.

"No answer, Ms. Anderson?"

"I will say this as many times as it takes to get it through your thick head." Her hands formed fists at her side once again. "I will never sell access to Tessa. I will *always* welcome family who love her into her life."

Shock, fear and grief. She'd dealt with them all before presenting herself and Tessa in this shrine to wealth. Ignorant of Chrissy's demands, she'd anticipated a cold exchange of questions and answers. Things they both wanted to know. Not open warfare. Jacob Taylor suspected she'd hatched this scam. And scam it must be, considering his reaction.

Ella had responded like an automaton to the letter, dangerously trusting her knowledge and her instincts. Evidence, if she needed any more, that she wasn't functioning normally. She should have done her research, spoken to her parents, brought a solicitor with her. To an outsider, her behaviour was as bizarre as Chrissy's. She drew a steadying breath. Time to start again, draw on her training.

"DNA is the only way to confirm she's a Browning," he stated. "Then we can talk about '*love*.'"

"You make Drew sound like my sister Grace's prize stud bull." Ella had never questioned her paternity. Her father had been present every day of her life. She held up a hand when Taylor started to speak. "But I agree. The stakes are too high for everyone not to have a test."

"If paternity is confirmed, will your conditions remain the same?"

"Conditions?" She was pleased her voice didn't tremble. He was smart enough not to talk money again. The bogeyman she'd refused to face during the night whispered in her ear. Taylor's letter had linked the words "paternity" and "custody." "I haven't seen Chrissy's letter."

"Tell me your conditions." A cold implacability lurked behind his inscrutable expression, yet he smelled invitingly warm, of sandalwood and spice. The contradiction rattled her.

"If ... when Drew is confirmed as Tessa's father, I'm prepared to grant access to Peter and his wife." She swallowed, her mouth dry with fear. "Unless they intend harm, I believe grandparents should be part of a child's life."

"The letter offered sole custody. At a price."

Blood roared in her ears as the horror of Chrissy's betrayal hit her with the force of a battering ram—the reason his condemnation ran bone-deep. And she couldn't blame him.

"I'll make arrangements with your lawyer," Taylor said.

"For the DNA test?" Ella matched his icy neutrality, when rage against the obscene suggestion Tessa was for sale, that any child was for sale, burned through her. Her nails dug into her palms. She half-lifted her fists, ready to pummel him until he stopped telling her Chrissy had kept secrets from her ... *again*. Except he was the messenger. Her sister was offering Tessa to the highest bidder.

CHAPTER TWO

"Of course." Jake absorbed her frozenness, recalling her outstretched hand on arrival.

She looked stunned, fragile enough to snap in two. Was it possible she'd been sucker-punched too? That something other than avarice had brought her here. He couldn't afford to consider her needs. Concern about his aunt and uncle was riding Jake hard. Offering them a grandchild was potential dynamite. Hell, Peter was three-quarters of the way in love with Tessa. If Bron saw Tessa, he didn't like his chances of preventing them from being hurt.

Expecting Chrissy, he hadn't run any checks before this meeting. Eleanor Anderson made him want to possess even the smallest details of her history, current living arrangements and bank balance. Within twenty-four hours he'd know everything.

"If you want me to believe you knew nothing, tell me how and when you found out about Chrissy's plan?"

Her head lifted like an animal scenting danger. "I received your letter about today's meeting."

"Nothing else?"

She hesitated for so long he thought she wouldn't answer. "Nothing else."

27

Their eyes met for an eternity. Before she turned away, Jake imagined he read pain beneath the defiance. The sense of her vulnerability lodged deep in his gut. The competing compulsions to ravish her, protect her, and keep a possible cheat the hell away from his family warred within him.

"Who's your lawyer?" he asked.

"I'll ring the details through to you." She waved a hand dismissively. "Your number's on your letter."

A play for time? *Did she even have a lawyer?* The sense she was finished with him took hold. She glanced over her shoulder. Peter had won Tessa's confidence enough so she'd crawled into his lap with her bear. A fist squeezed Jake's heart.

"Tessa." The child's head turned at her aunt's call. "Time to go."

"So soon?" His uncle sounded disappointed but stood to pass the little girl back to Ella. "Goodbye for now, Tessa. We'll see each other again soon."

Ella tilted her head but didn't respond to Peter's comment. Absently, she smoothed out the creases in Tessa's overalls; her hand capable, her touch holding affection. Tessa rested her head on her aunt's shoulder again—a habitual pose? A sign of complete trust. "Goodbye, Peter."

"Stay a bit longer, Ella. You can't have worked out all the details yet." Peter stared longingly at the child. "Tessa and I were just getting to know each other."

Bloody hell. The genie was well and truly out of the bottle. Jake could read the resolve in Peter's voice. His uncle had decided Tessa was his granddaughter. "Ella and I have agreed a DNA test is the essential next step."

"I need to get Tessa to another appointment now." Ella extended her hand to Peter Browning. Jake was prepared to bet there wasn't another appointment. She was offering a sop for the disappointment in Peter Browning's eyes. *Hell! Did that add weight to the idea she was kind or conniving?* His uncle turned and walked towards the windows. "Don't forget to ring through your lawyer's details," Jake said.

"As soon as I can." She bent to collect her bag. With it slung over her free shoulder, she hoisted Tessa more firmly onto her hip. In a moment she'd be gone.

With no conscious plan in mind, Jake blocked the doorway. He didn't want her to leave without looking at him. Her agreement appeared to give him the victory, but he could smell defeat. He waited until she reached him. "A DNA test is the simplest solution."

Her chin lifted. Jake was in front of her, so close he could almost taste the subtle fragrance she wore. He had to fight not to lean closer.

"That should have been your first suggestion, Counsellor, not your last. If you'd been doing your job."

"I was waiting for you to suggest it." Jake registered her indrawn breath, her green gaze scorching him. "You won't convince a court of law without it."

"Unlike you, I believe Chrissy, but scientific proof will protect all concerned." Her teeth caught her lower lip.

As Jake's eyes helplessly followed the gesture, he knew she was hiding something. "We can organise a DNA test without Drew." If he hadn't been watching so closely, he'd never have guessed she was shaken. "The Browning family will never turn away from one of its own, Ms. Anderson."

Something flared in her eyes, but she lowered her eyelids, and he couldn't read her. Jake wanted to ruffle her, provoke the huskier tones that had marked her anger. Her honest rage cut through the jumble of demands and counter demands, of the truths and lies that had brought them here.

She wrapped Tessa more closely against her side, holding the wretched bear like a guard in front of them, and lifted her head. Her fine skin and delicately drawn features, her sleep-deprived bruised eyes counted for naught against the determination in her squared shoulders. The lady was in adversarial mode. His resolve hardened. Still, part of him responded to the stiff-backed stance and hint of resoluteness in her gaze. The contradiction in the tough, tender image she embodied stirred his curiosity. Crazy to be curious about a potential blackmailer.

"I'd like to resolve this as soon as possible, Ms. Anderson."

"I'll make your wishes a priority," she promised solemnly.

Jake didn't believe her. Couldn't escape the conviction he'd handled the situation, and her, badly.

* * *

The memory of his speculative regard lingered as Ella retraced her steps to the elevator, along with the sense of his tenacity. The reaction between them had been explosive—his instantly negative, his animosity personal when objectivity should have been his goal.

Before the meeting, she'd been like an old woman working her worry beads, each roll of a bead between her finger and thumb another reminder of Taylor Law's past duplicity. Her usually reliable gut had said the company, and all who worked for it, wouldn't recognise justice if it bit them on the bum. Now she wasn't sure what to believe. While she didn't trust Jake Taylor, his concern for Peter Browning mirrored her view of family breakups. Grandparents were too often sidelined when their children's relationships broke up. She shivered in the temperature-controlled hallway.

"Ellie cold." Tessa patted her cheek.

"Just a little." She held the child's hand against her cheek before planting a kiss in the tiny palm. "Now, you've made me warm."

Ella's clear-headed approach to crises was a byword in her office. Pity she'd blown her reputation this morning. Criticising Taylor for not asking for a DNA test immediately was sheer bluff. She should have raised it first, should have worked from the list of questions she'd prepared for the meeting. Except, caught between Taylor's suspicion and an animal magnetism he took for granted, her brains had leaked out of her head.

Move on, Ella. He's an attractive beast. You stuffed up. He made the first move; you can control the next.

"Me push." Tessa tossed herself towards the buttons in the elevator, a game she never tired of playing.

"You push." Then Ella slid the child to the floor.

Jacob Taylor wouldn't have held the meeting if he hadn't already decided there was a strong probability Drew was Tessa's father. *What game was he playing?*

As the elevator descended, she studied the little girl holding her hand. She'd promised Chrissy she'd raise Tessa as her own. Possession is nine-tenths of the law—a dangerous truth. She had Tessa. She could walk away, apologise for the misunderstanding, claim Chrissy hadn't been rational in those last weeks of her life.

Dear heaven, she was tempted. But that would be a lie.

"Want to take Tootles shopping?" She scooped Tessa up as they exited the building, glancing over her shoulder, half-expecting Taylor to be tracking her from his lofty position. She shouldn't have provoked him at the end. By making it personal, she feared she'd roused the hunter in him.

Collecting her car from the station carpark near her home, Ella drove to the supermarket. Restocking the kitchen qualified as a formal engagement and absolved her of her white lie to Peter. Once home, she deposited Tessa with their downstairs neighbour, Mrs. Panygotis, Mrs. P to her friends.

Twenty minutes later she was still unloading the car and transporting boxes and bags. Her arms ached. The defiance invigorating her as she'd sailed out of Taylor's office had trickled away. After grabbing the last box from the back seat of the car, she climbed the single flight of stairs from the street to the front door of her apartment block. She nudged the door open with her hip before turning to face the next two flights to their first-floor flat.

Setting the final box on the kitchenette bench, she opened the fridge intent on storing the perishables and was confronted by a huge round farm cheese occupying the entire top shelf. A wedge was missing from one side. Hot tears ran unchecked down her cheeks.

Chrissy's funeral had been held in the country town near their family dairy farm. Remembering her family's unconditional love and support, the tears came faster. Ella riffled through the shopping for a box of tissues. Blindly, she pulled the seal open but couldn't see the tissues she used to mop her flooding eyes.

"*Take it. Eat it.*" Her mother had hugged her before she'd left the farm at dawn yesterday, tucking one of her sister's prize-winning cheddars in with the luggage. "*You love cheese, and you need to gain back some of the weight you've lost. Think of it as comfort food.*"

"Ella, are you ready for Tessa now?" Mrs. P's voice intruded on her brooding. "Mr. P needs me."

Ella blotted her tears and turned with a smile to the woman coming through the open doorway, Tessa on her hip. Ella met her neighbour halfway, her arms outstretched to take the toddler. "Thanks again for your help. I don't know what we'd have done without you over the last few months."

"There's no need to thank us, lovey." Mrs. P ruffled Tessa's curls. "We're sorry you've lost her. But you have this little one to love. Call if you need anything."

Ella locked the door behind her neighbour and turned back to survey the silent room. Chrissy had a way of filling an empty room—the light danced differently. "I'm sorry we've lost her too."

Despite all her preparations, her practical approach to crises, she'd been numb when Chrissy died. Helpless in the face of a grief she'd thought she was prepared for. Like receiving a knock-out punch in a bruising heavyweight bout; she'd developed a boxer's unsteady gait, dazed expression and groggy grasp on reality. She knew she was wounded, but until this morning, she believed she'd been coping.

"Na na." Tessa's tiny fingers closed on Ella's chin.

"Hungry?" Ella planted loud kisses on Tessa's cheeks. "Hungry for kisses?"

Tessa pulled harder. "Na na."

Keeping Tessa propped on one hip, Ella boogied her into the kitchenette, peeled a banana and mashed it into a bowl with some milk. With Tessa in her high chair, and hopefully occupied for a few minutes, Ella finished stocking her cupboards.

"Bath time, honey." Ella tried and failed to reach the child before a handful of mashed banana missed Tessa's mouth and was smeared across her cheek and into her hair.

Bath time and bedtime. Rituals her little girl loved. Later Ella prepared Tessa's bag to take to the child care centre the next day, sorted out her own clothes and put on a load of washing. Anything to put off the moment when she allowed herself to review what had happened in Jacob Taylor's office.

Finally out of excuses, she collapsed onto the sofa. Another second-hand piece of furniture; its many flaws hidden by a bold multi-coloured chintz spread Chrissy had found online. Ella let her head fall back. With only a table lamp beside her, she could distinguish the tiny fluorescent constellations Chrissy had bought her for her birthday. Ella had stuck them to the ceiling, amazed Chrissy had recognised she missed the star-filled country skies of home.

"Oh, Chrissy, I wish you'd told me what you planned," she cried aloud. *Except you knew I'd stop you.*

Pulling an old shawl from the back of the sofa around her shoulders, she slid further down into the chintz-covered cushions.

"*Tessa's my granddaughter.*" Peter's regret at her departure had exposed the higher price of her sister's last escapade. Tessa had family on her father's side, who deserved to know her, and Tessa deserved to know them.

Ella pictured Peter Browning's face amidst the ceiling

stars of the Southern Cross. She read the trouble in his expression and heard again the excited discovery in his voice as he said the words. Her father had walked around for days with a silly smile on his face after Tessa's birth.

Denying Tessa access to her biological father and grandparents if they wanted to get to know her was cold. She wasn't cold.

Her eyes drifted closed. The image of Jacob Taylor appeared—strong, determined, waiting—piercing her with his brilliant slate eyes. Her earlier tension returned, making her shiver despite her warm covering. She'd met the speculative glint in his gaze with assumed indifference, when her body vibrated at his nearness. An accident of chemistry. It had to be, although she'd never experienced anything like it.

"Custody—at a price." Taylor's disgust had been clear. Lots of money. Ella's eyes snapped open. Taylor Law was a commercial and property law powerhouse specialising in contract law, not family law. How could she not have made the connection? *What was she missing?*

This wasn't a simple case of inviting the Brownings to spend some time with their granddaughter. They came from money, and "custody for a price" remained a threat until she could unravel this mess. Would filthy-rich grandparents object to a small, cheaply furnished apartment, public schools and farm holidays as a lifestyle for their granddaughter?

"Start with the known facts, Ella," she chastised herself. Another test she'd failed this morning.

Chrissy knew Jacob Taylor, knew he was a lawyer, and must at some point have worked out his connection to Taylor Law. The company's name was a battle cry for unethical practice in her family. Had Chrissy taken a punt on Taylor using his company's ruthlessness to prosecute her case?

"Did you ask him to be your hired gun and instead he's backing the Brownings?"

A dangerous miscalculation. Or had Chrissy acted on impulse, recklessly ignoring consequences? Expecting Ella to manage the fallout because she always had. She hugged a cushion to her chest.

If she could see her sister's letter to the lawyer, she'd know more. "Did you offer custody of Tessa to guarantee she'd be raised with wealth, or did you want your baby to know her father?" She could live with that but couldn't deceive herself. Chrissy hadn't been coherent enough to argue either case at the end. She pushed herself up straighter on the sofa.

With Jacob Taylor clouding her judgement, the truth in all its searing ugliness was her only option. She knew her role. The solid, no-nonsense sister, too responsible to take risks because too many people depended on her, had always depended on her. Fact one, she'd had no time to establish legal custody for herself or protect her parents' rights. Dread made her heart quicken, panic snapping at the edges of her good intentions.

Tomorrow she'd start again, check the relevant legislation, establish her own rights and do some research on Jacob Taylor. Get more advice to protect them all, including a lovely old man who'd partnered with an abrasive representative for his family.

Until she'd assembled all her facts, and regained her balance, she'd ignore the demands of the pirate king.

* * *

Four days later Ella grimaced as she climbed the stairs. The satisfaction she got from managing the privately funded community justice centre was as important to her as the paycheck. But her last client had lingered and lingered. The elderly widow had craved company as much as advice. Tending to her had tapped into Ella's diminishing store of energy reserves. More importantly, it made her late.

Four nights of Jacob-Taylor-induced insomnia weren't

helping either.

Brushing her forearm across her forehead, she caught sight of her watch. Nine-thirty. She'd promised Mrs. P she'd be back by nine, updated that in a text to nine-fifteen. By the time she'd locked up and reached the car, it had been quicker to drive straight home.

"Mrs. P, it's me." Her neighbour must have risen to her feet as soon as she turned the key, because she was halfway across the living room when Ella entered. "I'm sorry I'm late."

"Don't worry, lovey. Traffic, I suppose."

Ella didn't explain, already anticipating the moment she'd shut the door and crawl into bed. Seeing Mrs. P's mind was elsewhere triggered another spurt of guilt. Mr. P, her invalid husband, was alone downstairs.

"A man came to see you."

"A man?" Ella's brain went into overdrive, considering and dismissing any number of innocent males who might have called.

"Had the look of a pirate. A bit like that gorgeous Irish bloke, Colin O'Donoghue. Remember, he played 'Hook' Jones, the kind of pirate you fantasise having his wicked way with you." The older woman sighed and fanned her face with one hand. "And his smile ... the glint in his eye promises endless pleasure."

"Jacob Taylor was here?" Her body stilled. Mrs. P had voiced her recurring dream.

"Said his name was Jake. Said you were expecting him." The woman shot her a canny look. "I said it was funny you were out if you were expecting him. Very reliable you are, I told him. Although it's lucky I told him I had no idea what time you'd be home tonight." She laughed with delight at this new joke. "Otherwise, he might have hung around and discovered you're late."

"Thank you, Mrs. P." Ella kissed the older woman on the cheek, loving her for her staunch protectiveness of those she termed her "brood."

"Trouble, love?"

"I don't know yet." Not knowing what she was fighting magnified the threat, knotting muscles already clenched tight.

"We're downstairs if you need us." She stopped in the doorway. "Tessa went to bed good as gold. She's a darling little mite."

Some of the tension created by the mention of Taylor's visit leaked out with the assurance Tessa was safe and well. "Our very own treasure."

Ella closed the door behind Mrs. P and rested her back against it. Jacob Taylor here. He'd introduced himself as Jake. Somehow the diminutive reinforced her image of him as a pirate. Undaunted by her defiance, tracking her to her home harbour. She glanced around the room. Cheaply furnished, but it was her sanctuary.

The authoritative knock on the door reverberated through her body, bringing with it an instinctive knowledge. Jacob Taylor had grown tired of her avoidance tactics and opted for a direct attack, unaware Chrissy had lobbed another grenade at Ella from beyond the grave. Tucked in the top drawer of the sideboard was Chrissy's letter of explanation—apology—self-excuse. Swinging the door wide, Ella kept a firm grip on the knob.

"Good evening, Eleanor Jane Anderson." His low-pitched drawl wrapped around her name, raising tiny hairs on the back of her neck. Her hand tightened on the doorknob until her knuckles shone white. "You're late home, aren't you?" His accusation tapped into her own guilt.

"I'm sorry." Unsure if she was apologising to him for being late or for ignoring him, she bit her lip in frustration. Damn him! No one else made her babble like an idiot.

* * *

Jake's gut tightened when she caught her lip between her

teeth. From his car on the other side of the street, he'd seen her park and head for the apartment block. She'd hurried towards the door, but her shoulders had drooped. Tired? Up close the impression was confirmed.

The lady was having sleepless nights.

So was he, but he bet lurid dreams of tumbling him into bed weren't keeping her awake, whereas the idea of tracing his palms over her slim curves had woken him four nights in a row.

"I've been working."

"Can I come in?" Jake asked, but he'd been edging forward since she opened the door. His investigator, Murphy, had been busy, but he wanted more information. Specifically, answers for her elusiveness of the past four days.

"Is that necessary?"

As he stepped forward, she released the handle to step back, a slow dance allowing him entry into the small living room.

Jake scanned it in a glance. Painted in blue and white and furnished with comfortable-looking second-hand furniture. An armchair upholstered in dark-blue velvet and a sofa covered with a multi-coloured chintz throw faced a small television. Behind them stood a dining table and four chairs with cushions in different colours. A few feet beyond them was a tiny kitchenette painted sunshine yellow. A kaleidoscope of colour that worked, but clearly came from inventiveness and hard work rather than a generous budget, verifying Murphy's assessment money was tight.

The cosy warmth briefly distracted him from his purpose. It offered a sharp contrast to the black and white sterility of his waiting penthouse. When his engagement to Julia ended, he'd taken the first convenient apartment offered. He'd made a mistake. With her and it. Several mistakes, truth be told. And he tried not to repeat his mistakes. He rarely thought of his ex-fiancée now, but this business had raked it all up again.

"Aren't you going to ask why I'm here?"

"I'm sure you'll tell me."

Jake had anticipated more stonewalling. She'd ignored phone calls, texts and emails and would ignore more. "I'm a busy man."

"Don't let me keep you." She infused more sass than sarcasm into the five syllables.

"I guess I asked for that." *But he hadn't asked for her to fill his head and senses to the exclusion of all else.* The inconsistencies in her story and character had buried themselves in Jake's brain until his goal had subtly shifted to solving the puzzle of Eleanor Jane Anderson as much as establishing Tessa's paternity.

Tension bounced between them.

"Let's start again," Jake said. "I'd like to talk to you."

She didn't answer.

"And you should talk to me. I called earlier."

Skittish as a cat on a hot tin roof, unsure whether to spring or retreat, she shucked her coat, draped it over the back of a chair, then eased out the creases with fingers Jake ached to have on him, easing out the tensions of his day. Tonight her clothing was more conservative than in his office: an emerald green sweater and dark straight skirt, both a little loose. Too big, like the outfit she'd worn previously. She either liked loose clothing or she'd lost weight since she'd bought her wardrobe.

Would she tell him if he asked? If he traced his thumbs over the dark circles under her eyes, would she tell him he was the cause of her sleepless nights? The effect she had on his libido was instant. He refused to let it cloud his judgement.

"Mrs. P told me you dropped by." Another message she would have ignored.

"Mrs. P?"

"Mrs. Panygotis is the babysitter," she explained.

"She behaved as if you have a closer relationship. She was very inquisitive," he added, responding to the question in her eyes.

Jake should have said loyal. Which added to the riddle of this woman. Brazen impostors didn't usually make friends with garrulous old ladies with invalid husbands. More evidence of Eleanor Anderson's reputation for compassion and straight dealing?

"She asked if I was your boyfriend." Jake sauntered towards the chair she was using as a barricade. "From the look in her eye, she wanted to know if I was your lover." The flash in her eyes as she met his brought some satisfaction. He unsettled her as much as she unsettled him.

"I imagine it gave you a lot of pleasure to deny the charge," she snapped, but her hand crept to her throat. "What do you want?"

"Don't you have a boyfriend, Eleanor?" he queried.

She bristled at his far-too-personal inquiry. "I'm looking after a two-year-old child and work full-time. Until a short time ago, I was also caring for an invalid. Not an attractive prospect for most men."

"And you resent that?" He could almost hate himself for the cross-examination, but ambushing her on her own territory was his best chance of confirming Murphy's interim conclusion.

"I'm explaining the situation because you appear to have trouble grasping simple facts." She sighed. "What do you want, Mr. Taylor?"

"Jake," he replied. "You're not a fool. You must have expected my visit. You haven't contacted my office. You said you would." He rocked back on his heels. "I thought it might help if I called here. Peter's been asking after Tessa."

Expressions chased across her face, incomprehension, anger, pain, and she waved a hand as if warning him to stay back. Awareness of her fragility sliced through him. She was holding herself upright through sheer force of will, but her needs had to be irrelevant when his aunt and uncle were her potential victims.

"What do you want me to tell him, Eleanor? That you're a fraud? That you're trying to extort even more money from an old man who wants a grandchild?"

"I've told you I don't want your money." Her voice was flat. The sense something had happened since they'd last spoken was a splinter burrowing deeper under a nail.

"You haven't made any effort to clear the air. Just held Tessa out as a lure."

"I'm considering my options." Her fingers curled around the back of the chair.

"I thought you might hit me in my office." Jake's gaze dropped to her grip on the chair.

She released her hands and forced them to hang loosely at her sides. "Scared you, did I?"

"Like now ..." he continued. He marvelled at her capacity to seem relaxed when her temper simmered. "You showed amazing self-control. Your fists were white-knuckle tight, yet you unclenched them, stretching your fingers along your thighs."

As if conscious her hands were again fisting at her thighs, she raised one to tuck a tendril of hair behind her ear. "I was brought up to believe violence solves nothing."

"It must be a terrible handicap on occasion." He watched her hands form firm fists again.

"Apparently not one you share?"

"I'm a pacifist, too, but it means you feel powerless sometimes." Jake had found self-respect counted more than power, or even public humiliation.

"I have a clear picture of the Taylor Law *edifice* in my mind." She mocked him. "I doubt you've ever been powerless."

"Keep thinking that and you make it easy for me to win."

"This isn't a personal battle, Mr. Taylor. We're talking about a human being, a precious child."

"Indeed, we are, Eleanor. So, let's start with the truth."

A murmur on the baby monitor gave her an excuse to escape. "I must check Tessa."

* * *

Ella closed the bedroom door behind her and stopped, letting her eyes adjust to the dim light cast by the baby lamp in the corner. After a few deep breaths, she crossed to the cot. With unsteady hands, she pulled the cover over the sleeping child, then when she could trust herself not to disturb Tessa, she stroked the tousled hair back from the small face. "You're my baby girl." Touching Tessa centred her, reminded her what she was fighting for. "And I can't hide in here all night."

She listened to the sounds of the invader in her home. Moving around the other room, stopping beside the mantelpiece. *Was he looking at the photographs? Moving towards the kitchenette?* Each step reverberated through her as if she moved with him.

She reviewed the conversation she'd had with a trusted colleague yesterday.

"Do you know Jacob Taylor, Taylor Law?"

"That buccaneer." Tony had grinned.

"Pirate came to my mind," she'd answered, feeling her way. *"Is he a friend of yours?"*

"A close one. I told him the earring and ponytail made him look like a lawbreaker, not a lawmaker." He'd sobered. *"What do you want to ask me, EJ?"*

"I've heard about some questionable practices at Taylor Law."

"Recent?"

She'd shaken her head in response.

"And you won't. Jake's dad died when he was a kid. Jake's a very private guy, but in the last few years before he took back the company, one of the partners engaged in some shady deals. Jake got rid of him when he worked out what was happening. Does that answer your question?"

"I'm not sure."

"I'd trust him with my life, EJ."

A lot of lives were at stake in a custody case. The ripples from any judgement stretched over years and could harm extended family members as well as the child. Drew was the wildcard. A potential rocket released into an enclosed space, wreaking havoc with each ricochet around the room. He could appear at any time and refuse any kind of a relationship with Tessa. If he rejected Tessa, would that be worse for her than not knowing he was her father?

With a last caress of Tessa, Ella returned to the living room. Standing with her back against the door, she drew strength from its solidity, while he stood near the sofa. "Why are you here, Mr. Taylor?" His silent stare forced her to amend her question. "I'd like an answer to my question … Jake."

"Me too." His quick grin was a distraction, offering a truce when he'd been poking at her since he'd arrived. "I want answers to my questions."

"The DNA test will provide the critical answer." She was committed to finding the truth.

"There are interim steps we can take, barriers we can clear." He waved a hand in the air. "What do your parents think?"

"They've just lost a daughter. They're grieving." And she'd added confusion to their pain by telling them about Drew Browning. That Tessa's unnamed father had been identified.

"You haven't told them?" His disbelief raised her hackles—she didn't hide from facts.

"I told them Chrissy wrote to a lawyer naming Drew Browning as Tessa's father. I said I'd met her paternal grandfather. We'd agreed to a DNA test." But they'd lost *their* baby daughter. She couldn't add to their distress by telling them Taylor Law could upend their lives again.

"Did you say I'd be in touch?" He sauntered towards her.

"There's no need for you to get in touch." A pulse throbbed at her temple. His pushiness was ratcheting minor irritation up to major annoyance.

"Chrissy may have discussed her plans with them, shown them the letter. They may have insights into her wishes, for herself and for Tessa." The distance between them offered scant protection from his low-voiced provocation. The anger that had hovered beneath the incomprehension and pain whenever Ella considered what her sister had done, hit with renewed force.

"They don't know she wrote to you." Ella was a voodoo doll he poked with relentless questions. When he would have continued, she held up a hand. "I mentioned a lawyer. I didn't give your name."

He closed the gap between them. "And you expect me to accept your word?"

"I imagine trust is a scarce commodity at Taylor Law."

"Careful, Eleanor. I've been patient until now."

"Patient!" Her temper strained at its leash, spewing sparks she didn't want to contain. "When you see plots everywhere? My family didn't contact you."

"Someone in your family did," he corrected her.

"Are we all under suspicion? Do you want samples of our handwriting, logs of our movements, transcripts of our conversations? It was Chrissy." Ella's stretched budget had obsessed her sister at the end. Ella had never been able to convince her sister that money couldn't buy health or happiness. Ella made a last effort to steady herself. "I'm not prepared to go further without talking to Drew about his intentions."

"Are you sure your silence over the last few days isn't an attempt to force up the offer? Enhance Tessa's attractiveness on the auction block?"

Her blood reached flashpoint. "You blind, arrogant idiot!"

Ella swung at him, surrendering to the fury burning through her. She'd never felt the need to smash her fist into a brick wall. Until tonight. Until Jake had lanced the blister of her grief. His words showed her she hadn't taken even the shortest step towards accepting her sister's death. Fighting him was more cathartic than struggling with her denial and anger alone. He caught her arm, stilling it.

She tried to beat him off. He captured her other hand, their bodies pressed close in a scuffle where she could smell him pressed close against her—musky, male, a mate. Her anger burned fiercely, hot, red, flashing. She refused to yield to his greater strength, drawing a leg back to kick. With savage satisfaction, she recognised his dilemma; she'd hurt him unless he defended himself.

JENNIFER RAINES

CHAPTER THREE

He lifted Ella's body from the floor and plonked her down on the sofa, then pinned her hands and leaned over her. "Stay there."

"Get off me, you oaf," she gritted, her face inches from his.

Ella registered his strength opposed to her slighter frame and was aware he could crush her as easily as he'd swat a mosquito. She wasn't afraid. She revelled in the battle, a respite from the crazy place where Chrissy had hung her out to dry. His hands were gentle. She hadn't expected forbearance. Probably didn't deserve his care. Heat radiated off him, fuelling a different heat in her, and an unwelcome flash of respect.

"If you stop fighting—"

"I'll stop when I've thrown you out." She lashed out with both feet, bewilderment compelling her to continue the fight.

"If you hit me, Eleanor, you'll hurt yourself." He held both her hands above her head with one of his, and manoeuvred her until she lay lengthways on the sofa. He sat pressed against her thighs.

"Get off me," she repeated. But he'd already released her

hands.

"When you remember you were brought up to believe violence solves nothing." He echoed her earlier claim without a hint of sarcasm.

"You're the one using brute force!" she protested. But he wasn't. *He hadn't.* He'd held her while she attacked him, absorbing her angry hurt.

"I'll admit to provocation," he said.

Their gazes locked. Seeing the determination in his matched her own, Ella accepted the inevitable. Her rage trickled away, replaced by shame at her loss of control. He sat back but didn't move away. They studied each other, two animals circling, looking for a weak spot. She'd shown him hers. Not just shame. He scared her spitless. He triggered such uncontrolled and uncharacteristic reactions in her. Ella had never taken a swing at anyone in her life, never lost her temper so completely.

The battle had become personal.

Hateful man.

And now he knew she was afraid.

The warmth of his body resting against her thigh, the steady regard, argued a comfort between them that would never be.

As if he recalled the battle lines separating them, he stood up and crossed to the mantelpiece. "Have you come straight from the centre?"

"What centre?"

"I'm not going to apologise for checking where you work." He straightened his tie and pushed the flap of his shirt into his trousers.

Ella's mouth dried as he tidied evidence of her attack. "I won't hold my breath waiting for any apology from you."

"Look, we got off on the wrong foot."

Was that his idea of an apology?

"An interesting way to explain your antagonism." She had no rational explanation for her own.

"Peter's vulnerable." He took a few steps back in her

direction.

"A man desperate for a grandchild?" Knowing that Peter, like Tessa, was an innocent made Ella's choices harder.

"You understand that?"

She'd surprised him. "I recognise the signs. My father adores Tessa. And you've made it crystal clear your mission in life is to protect Peter from my evil ways," Ella said. His mouth eased as if her answer confirmed something he'd already worked out. She swung her feet to the ground. "Surely he's not so desperate or naive he wouldn't insist on substantive proof?"

"I'd already prepared him for the possibility. The strong family resemblance was a game-changer." He spread his hands wide in appeal. "Tessa's eyes and colouring didn't come from your side of the family."

The russet-brown curls and clear grey eyes could have come from him. Ella quashed the unbidden fantasy. "Why did you prepare him for the possibility?"

"Drew and Chrissy were an item for a few months, an exclusive item by all accounts." He paused, as if choosing his words with care. "The separation was abrupt."

"Where was your open mind earlier this week, Counsellor?" She asked because he was talking to her, not cross-examining her.

"You walked into the room. It never occurred to me Chrissy could be dead."

If his surname hadn't been Taylor, she'd admit his sceptical reaction to her unannounced arrival was plausible. Tony's ringing endorsement of his friend made his caution reasonable.

"She was beautiful, effervescent." His gaze held hers. "I'm sorry she died so young. Sorry Tessa has lost her mother. And sorry for your loss. I should have said this the other day." His quiet sincerity undermined her resistance.

"What do you want now?" Two days ago Ella had received her own letter from Chrissy. Dropped off by the community nurse at Mrs. P's.

"You didn't know she sent the letter to me." A statement, not a question.

An image of Jacob Taylor's summons to a meeting flashed into Ella's mind, the vellum paper, the formal letterhead, the precisely typed sentences. The contrast between it and her sister's letter to her couldn't have been greater. Where Taylor's was unemotional, Chrissy's desperation splashed across the page as haphazardly as her handwriting. She'd been driven all her life. To escape the farm, to party, to live, and in the last days of her life, to ensure Tessa wasn't raised on the family farm.

"We've already had this conversation." She pressed her hands into the sofa on either side of her and straightened her spine.

"We had some of this conversation the other day. I want the rest. When did she tell you Drew is Tessa's father?"

He wanted everything. Ella was relieved at the familiar rebellion slowly trickling back through her veins. A rebellion urging her to fight when confronted by an autocrat. Taylor had reverted to being the mercenary issuing orders. She'd never bow to force. "I realised Drew was Tessa's father when you told me she'd written to you."

"Bloody hell!" Shock held him motionless, then his brain visibly started whirring into gear. "*She* didn't think Tessa's paternity might be a pertinent bit of information for you to have." He paced in front of the fireplace.

Ella bristled at his condemnation of her sister. "She was terrified. She knew she was dying." The desperation in Chrissy's letter to Ella was lodged like a hard knot in her gut. But she waited while he did the maths.

"She died ... when? In my office you said ten days ago. That's over two weeks now. Where was the funeral, Eleanor?"

"At home." If she'd stayed there even a day longer, she'd have missed the appointment with Jake. The coward in her wished she had, but the crusader for justice would have needed to find out the truth and defend Tessa's rights.

"When did you get back?" A frown formed between his eyes.

Ella wanted the interrogation to end. "The day before our meeting."

"I owe you another apology."

"What for?" She lifted an eyebrow.

"For jumping down your throat the second you walked in my office door."

"Taylor Law has a reputation." She deliberately needled him because he was getting too close to her secrets. "I assumed naked aggression was your default reaction to your opponents."

"Low blow," he murmured. "I've only been there the last six years. Are you thinking of a particular case?"

"Someone I know." Her hand tangled in the chintz spread. "Smithhouse. Taylor Law represented Smithhouse."

"I don't recognise the name," he said. "How long ago?"

"A lifetime." That betrayal had influenced her actions and decisions ever since. Jake Taylor had probably still been at university.

"Feels like I've been a lifetime in my cold car waiting for you." A disarming grin streaked across his face. "I hoped you might offer me a coffee while we discussed this."

"You've got to be kidding?" Ella didn't dare stand up yet because she wasn't sure her legs would hold her. "A minute ago you accused me of trying to up the price for access to Tessa."

"People often reveal more than they'd like when they're angry."

"You did it deliberately." *Another example of his sneakiness.*

"Let's say we're both guilty of provocation." He ran an assessing eye over her. "How about I make us both a coffee?" He shrugged in response to her suspicious look. "An apology for manhandling you."

"I don't think I can take any more apologies tonight."

"Are you sorry, Eleanor, for fighting me?"

"Maybe." She tried to stand and was swept by a wave of dizziness.

He leaned forward, placed a finger against her shoulder and gently pushed. She dropped back onto the sofa. "Truce?"

"You're not going, are you?"

* * *

"Not till we're finished. Taylor's law—I don't give up." Jake headed towards the tiny kitchenette, unsure why he needed to push when she was bone-tired. Why he wanted to stay when she'd made it clear he was unwelcome? Although "provocation" in all its senses was part of the puzzle. "And as the only man still standing, I get to make the coffee."

He assessed the setup. A fridge and pantry cupboards lined the left-hand side, while an L-shaped counter started under the window with the longer side abutting the dining area. The sink was below the window, overlooking the back lane. Appliances, like the kettle and toaster, were perched on the long counter. He guessed crockery was underneath and glanced over his shoulder. "Have you eaten?"

"I'm not hungry."

Jake digested her remark and matched it to his own grief as a nine-year-old when his parents had died. He'd found the answer to the too-big clothes. "I could eat a horse."

"I'm too tired for this, Jake." Her head rested back against the sofa and her eyes were shut.

"Why don't I rustle up something to eat? Raise your blood sugar level." He shrugged out of his jacket and hung it over the back of a chair, then opened the fridge. "Like cheese, do you?"

"My parents gave it to me to bring home."

"They want you to eat, too. What happened to the missing wedge?"

"I gave it to Mrs. P." She turned her head and opened

her expressive eyes, revealing she was slightly confused by his shift in manner. "She won't take any money for the babysitting."

"What are you planning to compensate her for Friday night's session?" Jake winced inwardly when she didn't challenge his knowledge of her working hours. Hiring Murphy gave him an unfair advantage. He'd confess before he left.

"Spaghetti Bolognese. Mr. P loves it."

Smithhouse, Jake turned the name over in his head while he worked. Not a name he recognised. Then again, he didn't remember all the names of people Rory Davies had swindled during his few years at Taylor Law.

Before Jake's time, but he'd heard whispers from the day he'd taken the reins. He'd investigated and found irrefutable evidence of malpractice. The discovery had brought anger, disgust and humiliation in equal parts, and an overriding compulsion to pay restitution. His parents' legacy and his aunt and uncle's investment in him all wasted unless he could rebuild the firm's reputation. He'd told his uncle some, not all of the story. He'd sacked Davies and begun the time-consuming task of tracking down victims. He thought he'd dealt with the last of them. Seems he'd been wrong.

Although "Smithhouse" provided another perspective on Eleanor's reluctance to talk to him. Taylor Law represented corruption and misuse of power to her. Back in Sydney a few hours, feeling her sister's absence, trying to be normal when life would never be normal again. Tired, grieving, unaware of the trap Chrissy had left for her. He glanced across to where she sat on the sofa. She hadn't hesitated to come to his office. A backbone of steel. Her gaze met his. His strategy puzzled her, but he saw the moment she braced for the next act.

She pushed herself upright. "I'll accept toasted sandwiches and tea. Coffee will keep me awake."

"Fair enough."

"I find it hard to believe High-rise Number Two Albert Street, Circular Quay belongs to a man who eats, much less makes, toasted sandwiches for dinner," she muttered. "For a start, you have to be dressed by Armani or Zegna or Lamborghini?"

Jake chuckled. "You know that last one's a car. And you're the one who looks like she doesn't eat." He was more aware of her soft curves than he wanted to be. The conversation about Tessa could wait. "Tell me about the farm."

"It's a dairy farm."

"I'm astonished." He plugged in the electric sandwich maker sitting on the benchtop, then assembled cheese and tomato sandwiches.

She ignored his sarcasm. "Between Lismore and the NSW coast, lots of rolling hills."

"You like the country?"

"Yes."

He sensed the hills were a refuge, maybe the only witness to her loss of control. Before tonight. "And?" he prompted.

"Sharing chores with my mother and sister Grace helped."

"How do they feel?"

"Stunned, struggling to understand why." She stopped, and he waited while she searched for words to explain a complicated cocktail of emotions. Given Chrissy's behaviour, the list had to include betrayal.

"And afraid? Like you?" He kept his voice steady.

"Yes, I'm afraid." She mimicked him and seemed to find her balance. "She's mine, ours. But she's also Drew's, his parents. So, I have to figure out how to make this work."

"If you're prepared to make it work, I can help." He turned and faced her. He'd come with a truce in mind—a negotiated, sensible set of steps based on Murphy's investigation and Jake's less-than-objective assessment of her. They shot sparks off each other. More worrying was his desire to ask her to confide in him. He constantly felt he was fighting a rear-guard action not to simply take her in his arms and tell her everything would work out fine. Pointless, and not in his power.

Hell! She had custody of Drew's child. Regardless of whether she had more, Drew's daughter would always be her first child. Drew hated Jake, and Jake's solution was to keep his distance from his cousin. Imagining a hug, much less a quick tumble with Eleanor was insane.

* * *

Ella wanted to believe him, but the price of a mistake was too high. And her conflicted feelings towards him made it sensible to keep her distance.

The odour of cooking cheese wafting through the kitchen stirred one kind of hunger, while watching him work stirred another. He fit into her small kitchen as easily as he'd fit into his plush office. Although there she hadn't fantasised about how he'd touch a woman, how he'd touch *her*.

Jake Taylor sharpened all Ella's senses. Like a sizzling hot day on the farm when the air shimmered with promise and colours were vivid and mesmerizing. He slid the sandwiches onto plates and cut them. The release of steam reflected the hiss of heat through her bloodstream, further weakening her defences.

"Would you like to eat at the table?" he asked.

"Thank you."

Placing the plates on the table, he took a seat opposite her. For a few minutes they ate in silence before she became aware his attention had shifted. He was looking around the room. Paintings and photographs covered most walls. French impressionism mixed with childhood photos, mostly of Tessa, but some of an older vintage.

"Are you one of the three little girls rolling in the grass?" He narrowed his eyes. "Of course you are. The one at the front, head thrown back, laughing."

"Like a loon." She flicked a look at the photo that had caught his attention, her heart aching a little for that carefree childhood.

"What happened to the pictures on this wall?" He gestured to the bare wall behind her, where small marks showed where pictures had hung.

"I gave them to my parents. They wanted some shots of Tessa and Chrissy. I've reordered them. They have to be framed, so it'll take a week or two." She lifted an eyebrow. "Are you thinking of adding a set of those to the list of 'evidence' you want me to provide?"

"I'm not bothering with a list you'll ignore. But I imagine Peter and his wife, Bronwyn, would like to see pictures of Tessa with her mother."

Her parents treasured them.

"Why haven't you been back to see me, EJ?" He bit into his sandwich.

"Who gave you permission to call me, EJ?" School friends had coined the nickname—a logical shortening of Eleanor Jane—although it had carried a barb, no-nonsense, useful in an emergency.

"Everyone calls you EJ."

"Not everyone." The name had followed her into her working life, although she never introduced herself that way.

"Everyone you work with, everyone you grew up with. It's in my report." He paused for a heartbeat. "I had an investigator run some checks on you."

"What did you say?" She lowered her partly eaten sandwich, shocked to her core.

"I had an investigator run some checks on you," he repeated without a scrap of shame.

"Typical!" Yet her heart sank, knowing Chrissy's actions were to blame for the violation, another humiliation she had to swallow. "That's the sort of outrageous behaviour I'd expect from Taylor Law."

He inclined his head and kept chewing, comfortable he'd

slipped under her guard. The pirate hadn't hesitated to slide the knife in when he got a chance.

"You had no right to invade my privacy." Although it explained his presence, digging for dirt to discover proof she was using Tessa as a meal ticket. There was none to find.

"Disappearing with Drew Browning's child rather forfeits your right to privacy."

"I live here. I've lived here for nearly three years. If you think that's a disappearing act you need to get out more." She slapped at his smug certainty. "And what about Tessa's rights? Don't they deserve respect? Even if you're prepared to ride roughshod over mine."

"That's the crux, isn't it?" He seemed untroubled by her verbal smack. "Given your line of work I should have guessed respect matters."

"I should have guessed using a snoop was how you'd operate." Ella picked up her sandwich, took another bite, chewing on it slowly, reviewing their earlier conversation for facts he shouldn't have known. "That's how you knew about the centre." She'd missed that earlier. "And Friday night."

"How else would I know?" When she didn't answer, he continued. "A legal firm funds your centre. A very flexible employer, prepared to timetable around childcare."

"They've been very generous to me." Those details could have been picked up from the centre's advertised hours and policy statements on the web. The childcare was a logical guess given her working hours. Was that as far as his private eye had gone?

"But you've had to compromise, hence the evening shifts. Not ideal with Tessa."

"Few single parents can boast of an ideal work-life balance," she said, but Chrissy had hated the late shifts.

"Is the night work necessary?" He sounded curious.

"It shares the load." She finished the last mouthful of her sandwich and pushed her plate away. Her blood sugar level had risen and with it her cool-headed approach to crises. Working the odd night didn't make her a bad parent. It did make her a good manager.

"Why didn't you answer any of my messages?"

"I expected Drew to be there." She was running out of plausible excuses.

"Old news, and don't pretend you didn't get them, because Mrs. P remembered hearing you replay a message on the phone."

Ella straightened the knife on her plate. The calls had been worse than the texts and emails. More compelling. Short messages in a voice unmistakably Jake Taylor's. Each starting with an unnecessary statement of who he was, his phone number and a request for her to call back. She knew who he was. The rough gravel of his tones on the phone had the power to bring his face into clear focus.

Short messages, but long enough to strengthen the conviction he wouldn't let her handle this her own way or pretend the visit to his office had never happened. Long enough to trip the switch in her head, which ran around in circles. By not answering immediately she was ignoring her sister's wishes and hurting an old man, Tessa's grandfather.

Even without his calls, she'd wrestled with her conscience. The morning after her visit to his office she'd told her family about Drew, about Peter. Had been relieved at the hundreds of kilometres between them so they couldn't see her face when she avoided their questions about *why now?* Hadn't told them about Chrissy's demand for money, that Chrissy might have offered custody if the price was high enough. Hoped she'd never have to tell them, hoped their last memories of Chrissy could remain untainted.

"You had no right to question Mrs. P." She knew focusing on Mrs. P was a red herring, but she hadn't found an answer to her quandary. Chrissy's letter two days ago to Ella had made it brutally clear her sister would hand Tessa to strangers in return for a promised life of luxury. She fisted her hands under the table. "I'm thinking of approaching

Drew directly."

"Have you tried?"

"Not yet." Her parents' instinct was to welcome the Brownings into their extended family, but they'd handed responsibility for the decision to her, trusted her to make the right decision for all of them.

"You became unavailable, Eleanor, after tempting an old man with the sight of Tessa."

Her nails bit into her palms as her mind returned to the merry-go-round of arguments and counterarguments for whatever step she took. "That's one of the reasons for my decision."

He pushed his plate away. "There's a twisted kind of logic in that. Let me think about it."

"You've already made it clear you're worried about Peter falling for Tessa, then discovering she's not their grandchild." Despite his role in Taylor Law, Ella hadn't been wrong about his concern for Peter.

"You insisted she is. The family resemblance is compelling. And the cute outfit."

"What are you talking about now?" She pressed her palms flat on her thighs.

"The perfect Madonna and child." He catalogued her sins. "A beautiful child to tempt a man longing to be a grandfather and your own beauty to distract everyone else."

Her heart trembled at the compliment. "Country town consensus is that Chrissy was the family beauty."

"The photo on the wall makes a lie of that."

Their gazes met and the heat in his made Ella's blood beat a frantic tattoo. "She blossomed as she grew up. Has your investigator been to Lismore too?" There were some in town who'd be happy to spread the tale that Ella had been dating a country lawyer, who'd run away to Sydney with her more beautiful sister.

"Not yet."

"Keep it that way." She watched his reaction to her demand. "My family's grieving. It's a small town. If someone starts asking questions about me, the gossip will get back to them."

"He doesn't need to ask questions if you'll answer mine." He was offering her a truce of sorts.

"That's where I got the nickname EJ. I'm the sensible sister, the capable one, the managing one." Ella's passion for justice had alienated a few of the local cops back home, just as Grace's passion for organics had alienated some local dairy farmers. Chrissy had been "pure silk" according to the bachelors around town.

"That's probably why EJ doesn't work for me, Eleanor. Being responsible is only part of the puzzle you represent. Murphy, that's my investigator, got as far as the integrity and good reputation of your parents and a general belief you take after them."

"Yet you've just accused me of dressing Tessa to … beguile an old man. Every second toddler in Sydney is wearing that outfit." She pushed to her feet. "You should go. Thank you for the sandwich. I'll tidy up. I need to get some sleep."

His intense scrutiny of her slashed at her composure. "What are your other reasons for disappearing?"

She narrowed her eyes on him and let fly. "Your animosity, your refusal to listen and the fact Drew wasn't there. I'm guessing his denial of paternity also includes a refusal to have a DNA test. You're offering a toxic conflict that could go on for years."

"All true but"—he lifted a hand and let it drop—"this doesn't feel right."

"What doesn't feel right is Taylor Law meddling in family law." She hadn't found a satisfactory answer to that conundrum.

"Chrissy wrote to me. I know the Brownings. This is a conversation, not a case."

"*Seriously?*" She had no idea what was driving him. "Bringing the full force of Taylor Law's resources to a conversation—your presence, your bloodhound—rather negates that statement."

"Something's happened." His insight rocked her. "You mentioned handwriting samples. I didn't mention her letter was handwritten."

"She was housebound. Of course her letter was handwritten," she argued. He had the investigative nose of a gumshoe.

"You said she left you no word." He searched her face, cutting through her rationalisations for her silence of the last few days. "Is that still the truth?"

Why, Chrissy, why? Withholding knowledge of Chrissy's second letter from him suddenly seemed counterproductive; a child refusing to give up the bat when they were clearly caught out. He and she each held half the secret to Chrissy's state of mind. Playing fair was a solemn oath in her family. Her rule, regardless of his.

* * *

The energy drained from her body as he watched. Jake's cross-examination of her in this state was arguably a violation of her rights under the Geneva Convention. He pushed because he had to know. Her sister was dead. Eleanor had shown up at his office. While all the evidence he'd collected in the last four days pointed to her being caught up in a desperate plan of Chrissy's devising, something had spooked her into hiding.

"She left a letter for me with the community nurse," she confessed. "The nurse left it when she called on Mr. P two days ago."

"Show me."

"This from the man who won't show me Chrissy's letter to him." She bristled, and her show of spirit was a relief he didn't want to question. "There's too much at stake to treat this casually."

"Tell me what's at stake." He leaned across the table.

She hesitated. Jake inhaled her scent. Its subtle

femininity enveloped him, inviting enough to make him want to lean forward and taste, to let her off the hook.

"If you're this offensive in all your dealings, I'm surprised you're still in business." She wrinkled her nose in what he could only guess was distaste.

"Doubting something until I have three kinds of proof is what keeps me in business." Jake waited while she hauled herself off the chair and crossed to the briefcase sitting by the front door. He cursed himself for needing to push.

She extracted a folder from her bag and handed him a sheet of paper. He scanned it, noting the clear, no-fuss, feminine handwriting and Eleanor's signature at the bottom.

"This isn't a letter from your sister. It's something you've written."

"Brilliant, Sherlock."

"I'll keep this so I can have the handwriting compared to the one we received." Jake shoved it into his coat pocket, knowing he didn't need an expert to tell him the two samples of handwriting were different.

"You will only surprise me, Counsellor, when you take something I say or do on trust." She was dead on her feet, and, still, she resisted him. He hadn't needed Murphy's report to tell him she was a fighter. And the most desirable woman he'd met in years.

Jake should go home now, especially since all he could think of was the soft feel of her when he'd held her on the sofa, the heady perfume of her skin. She made him want to bury himself in her, want to forget the vow he'd made when Julia walked out.

Sparring with her was a distraction from a conclusion he couldn't escape. The evidence supported the view she was an innocent in this bizarre game. Peter had raised the stakes—regular access to Tessa, without formal confirmation of paternity.

She crossed to the kitchenette and turned on the cold water tap, half-filling a glass then swallowing a few mouthfuls. Slowly she turned to face him. "Why are you still here?"

"The sofa looks comfortable. Why don't we move there?"

She returned to her straight-backed chair while Jake crossed to the sofa. Sinking into it, he leaned his head against the back so his eyes lifted to the ceiling. "The Southern Cross is the wrong size in proportion to the others."

"I like it like that," she protested.

Jake filed away that new piece of information. She liked the night sky. Not in his report, but it matched the yearning in her voice when she'd talked about the farm. Her parents had a reputation for helping, not scamming, their neighbours. He couldn't ignore the evidence she'd inherited those traits.

"'*They glitter like a swarm of fireflies*,'" she recited softly.

"Tennyson." He grinned—poetry wasn't his usual weapon. "Except for Merope, the only Pleiad to marry a mortal so her star burns less bright than her six sisters." He tilted his head until his gaze met hers. Maybe there was another reason for her wistful note. "Where did you buy it?"

"Chrissy bought it for my last birthday." A soft smile curved her mouth. She was stunning when she let her guard down. "It suited her madcap humour. 'The Southern Cross is allowed to be large.'"

"Are you quoting her?" If Jake hadn't already been convinced of Ella's integrity before he'd entered her flat, her quick giggle would have tipped him over the edge—honest, infectious delight.

She shook her head. "Not her, the packet. 'It's a stylised display, not the real thing.' But she knew it didn't matter."

"Tony Baldwin described you as a force of nature."

"Interrogating a senior partner in the legal firm that funds my work seems like overkill." Her shift to attack was swift, but she'd paled. "If I was a notorious fraudster, I wouldn't have the job."

"Didn't you ask him about me?" Jake was letting her know how close he'd come to the centre of her world. Tony wouldn't have betrayed her to Jake any more than he'd betray Jake to her.

"He said you were a friend." She refused to take the bait. "So, I didn't continue."

"You wouldn't, would you?" He nodded, tallying another point in her favour. Although it would become a weakness in any contest with Drew. "He told me about you months ago—his marvellous manager. I didn't have your name then. He has enormous respect for you."

"It's mutual."

"Something we can agree on then. We both trust Tony Baldwin."

"Using my faith in Tony is an interesting way to get my attention." She tilted her head to one side, considering him. "Are you looking for common ground?"

"Yes. Something we can build on, given we have to work together."

"Why didn't you start by saying you know Tony Baldwin?" She pushed herself to her feet.

"I gather evidence, but I like to make my own decisions."

"Well, bully for you. I'm tired of feeling like a cornered mouse with a malicious cat loose in my home. You prod then you procrastinate. Enough. Tell me what you came for, or go." She crossed to the front door, weary but determined.

"Peter Browning wants reasonable access to Tessa now." Jake accepted his dismissal, lifting his jacket off the back of the chair where he'd left it. "He understands a child of Tessa's age will take some time to get to know strangers, to feel safe with them."

Her hand twisted uselessly on the doorknob. "Tell me the rest."

"Peter wants you and Tessa to spend time with him and his wife. Starting with a weekend visit to their home." If he was wrong about her, Jake had just delivered her a royal flush.

* * *

"Am I crazy, or are you?" Ella counted off reasons on her fingers, while drums pounded in her head. "You're still questioning if she's Drew's child. Still haven't apologised for calling me a blackmailer. You don't want them to fall in love with a child who doesn't belong to them. And I think the fairest thing to do is to have the DNA test. I don't want Tessa to fall in love with them and then see them disappear like her mother if the results go awry."

"Probability says she's Drew's child. I'd prefer not to gamble even with good odds. But Peter's prepared to pay maintenance in exchange for access."

"Get out." Ella couldn't breathe, the tremble in her voice enraging her.

Her fury was directed at both of them. Him for his casual insult in offering money. Herself because the offer was like a trip switch, a reminder of the dark time when money bought power for Smithhouse, bought Taylor Law legal expertise, and used it to steal from her family. A reminder of her powerlessness.

"That came out the wrong way." He shrugged into his jacket.

"Get Drew Browning to come home and take a DNA test."

"We can do a test without him. But it's more complicated than that. Peter's wife is seriously ill. He wants her to meet Tessa." He strolled towards her, his deep-voiced concern shivering down her spine. "Thinks it will give her more to live for."

"Catch 22, Counsellor?" Heaven help her. Ella knew life was messy enough for his claim to be true.

"That's my dilemma. Will it do more harm for them to spend time with Tessa and then lose her? Or to know of her existence, but be forced to wait for irrevocable proof? Time

Bron can never get back."

"Damned if you do and damned if you don't. Welcome to my world. You're ready to condemn me whatever choice I make." Learning he was motivated by compassion shifted something inside her. "I'm prepared to make a deal." She closed her eyes at the surprise in his. Whatever Chrissy's state of mind or ultimate goal, she'd named Tessa's father. That was the gamechanger.

"Why?"

She let out a breath she hadn't known she was holding. "Because when Tessa explained that Tootles was a girl, Peter listened with rapt attention."

"Not sure I'm following."

"Good grandpas treat their granddaughters seriously." She'd have nowhere to hide once she took this step. "Can I see Chrissy's letter to you?" Reading Chrissy's words might help to understand what her sister really intended, to dissolve the ball of anger lodged alongside her grief. She was angry with herself for being angry at Chrissy, for being unable to forgive. The reality couldn't be worse than her imaginings.

"If you show me yours," he replied in a heartbeat.

Ella wrapped her arms around herself, suddenly cold. She blocked the wave of anger at his request, as dangerous and self-defeating as her distress when she'd first read Chrissy's desperate scribble. Her sister had dismissed Ella's attempts to provide a home and future for the three of them as worthless. Ella had hoped never to share the letter, never to have to justify its contents to a stranger.

"Better yet," he added. "Come and see Peter. We'll show him both letters. If yours reads like mine, I'll advise him strongly that nothing should be done without the DNA test. That we've discussed it, and we agree Chrissy was struggling to think straight at the end. It wouldn't be fair to Tessa to rush this. To let Tessa get too attached to them and then take her away would be cruel." His suggestion made sense. Chrissy's state of mind in the letters should make Peter think twice about making any hasty decision.

"Do you think it'll work?" she asked before she lost her nerve.

"We've got nothing else at the moment." The admission cost him and made her feel he was genuinely trying to find a workable solution.

"That's not reassuring." She exhaled. "I'm not going to agree to some quick and shonky DNA test."

"Australian Government DNA guidelines for immigration rulings," he replied. "A registered lab. They take about two weeks once they have the sample."

She cocked her head on one side. "You've thought about this."

"As have you."

Because it had niggled at her and spoke to his honour, and because he made her bold in ways she didn't understand, she asked, "Why did you admit to hiring Murphy?"

"As a rule, I play fair. I want to play fair with you." He didn't wait for her to answer. "Ten o'clock in my office. Just the three of us," he finished.

"I'll be there." She let out a long breath, afraid of how much she wanted to believe him.

He reached for his wallet and started to slide a few hundred-dollar bills from it.

"Don't even think of offering that to me. Or so help me ..."

"Someone told me child support is a child's right." He pushed the money back into his pocket and stopped in front of her. "That's twice in one night you've lost your temper, Eleanor. And I'm guessing that's out of character."

The roughness in his voice startled her, the sexual heat in his gaze burning through to the core of her. Ella gripped the handle as they faced one another, her heart rate wildly out of control.

He lifted a hand to her cheek, and with his thumb rubbed under one eye as if to smooth out the shadows there.

"I wanted to kiss you the first time I saw you. I didn't know who you were or what you wanted and resented you like hell. Now I know you better."

"And still resent me like hell." But she remembered his gentleness when she'd launched herself at him earlier. He excited her. Confessing he wanted to kiss her made her body tighten in anticipation, tempting her with a dangerous desire.

"Now." He unwrapped her fingers from the handle, lifted her fist to brush his lips across her knuckles. "I resent the situation. The way we met. It's a maze, Eleanor."

"We haven't time for an inconvenient attraction." But his words enticed her.

"So, you feel it too." He grinned ruefully. "I'm beginning to like you, as well as fancy you like hell. But you're right."

"Go," she whispered.

"Unfortunately, going won't stop the attraction between us, Eleanor Jane Anderson."

Slamming the door would have relieved her jumbled emotions, but would have also brought Mrs. P upstairs in seconds. Ella didn't have temper tantrums. Temper was a substitute for her real emotions. She reached a hand to trace the path of his thumb and marvelled anew at the tenderness to be found in the blunt, rough surface of a man's thumb pad. When his lips had dragged softly across the skin of her knuckles, the action had lit a wildfire inside her. A minute longer and she'd have stepped into his arms and taken the kiss he'd offered. He had fevered dreams too.

If Ella acted on impulse, she'd trust him to navigate this minefield with her. But Tessa's needs were her highest priority. She didn't know this man Tony Baldwin would trust with his life. His impassioned defence of family had shaken her. Was it possible for his interests to be so closely aligned with the Brownings', or was that for show? Was he the man who issued a convincing apology for his insensitive behaviour at their first meeting? Or the man who was plausible enough to make her consider Taylor Law's unscrupulous business practices were all in the past?

Whoever he was, his honeyed voice lingering over the syllables in Eleanor Jane Anderson started a slow blaze inside her.

She crossed to the window in time to catch him folding himself into an S-Type R Jaguar, sleek, barely-there silver and a wake-up call to her sluggish brain. A "rev head" client at the legal centre had pinched one. Without him she wouldn't have recognised this powerful beauty. Couldn't resist, he'd said, and the adjectives he'd mumbled flashed now as warning signals—supercharged, heavily fortified, smooth, refined. All true of her pirate.

His choice of this vehicle, his ease in possession were stark reminders of the balance of power in the contest between them. This was a necessary truce. Abiding by the rules of engagement was the minefield.

CHAPTER FOUR

Racing against the clock, Ella didn't glance at the Taylor Law building as she burst through the station's exit. Putting on a last spurt of speed, she caught the walk signal at the traffic lights. If she hurried she'd reach Jake before Peter Browning arrived. On the crowded train, she'd balanced Tessa and the stroller while she'd framed and dismissed multiple apologies. Jake would be pissed off. Justifiably. They had a deal.

"Me, push," Tessa demanded as they entered the elevator.

Lifting the lightweight stroller so the little girl could reach the buttons, Ella guided her hand to the number and kissed the top of her head. "Press for the tenth floor, honey."

Tessa then twisted in her seat, straining against the safety belt. "'Ootles?"

"You can have her when we arrive." Tootles, was tucked into her bag with Chrissy's letter. She hoped playing fair meant Jake would give her a chance to explain before jumping down her throat.

An older woman stood beside the receptionist's desk and turned as Ella stepped forward. "I'm Mr. Taylor's personal assistant, Merle. You must be Ms. Anderson. He's in a meeting, but should be here any minute." She smiled at the child. "He didn't mention Tessa was coming."

"I couldn't reach him," Ella apologised, hearing a noise behind her.

He possessed an austere beauty she'd barely registered at those first meetings, distracted by the unwelcome knowledge of Chrissy's request. Distracted also by the shocking sensuality of the ponytail and earring. She was on surer ground now. Tony Baldwin was working for her. But seeing Jake framed against the door to a conference room, she could imagine him commanding the floor at his meeting. The authority sparking off him was tangible. *Damn!* The combination made the pirate king an even more daunting opponent.

When his head swung towards her, the sense of déjà vu was hypnotic. Another demand to access her secrets. Another temptation to share. Then his compelling gaze dropped to the stroller.

"You've brought Tessa." He frowned. "We had a deal, Eleanor."

"Good morning to you too. Don't you answer your phone?"

He pulled it from his pocket, scanned the screen. "I missed your call."

"Calls," she corrected him. "Mr. P had a turn and Mrs. P needed to go with him in the ambulance. I assured her 'Jake' would understand if I showed up with Tessa." With her fingers crossed behind her back in case she was telling a lie.

"You planning on ruining my reputation with her?"

"You're safe." Ella rolled her eyes, the humour in his voice persuading her to share Mrs. P's compliment. "She's smitten. You're the first pirate she's seen in the flesh."

"I'll give you Merle's number for future emergencies." He hunkered down in front of the stroller.

He smiled. Mrs. P had fallen for his smile, whereas Ella

was reminded of the time she'd been crash-tackled at touch football. The star player had leaned over her and beamed, leaving her winded and unable to breathe. Jake's smile had a similar impact, leaving her breathless and starry-eyed. She knew better than to yearn for happily-ever-afters.

"Hello poppet." Jake glanced over his shoulder. "Couldn't you find another babysitter?"

"Maybe no one says no to you, but I don't have that kind of influence. So, no, I couldn't find another babysitter." Ella had wasted a frantic half-hour trying after handing Mrs. P over to the paramedic.

"The occasional person says no to me."

She opened her eyes wide, pretending shock. "How do they dare?"

"That's a question you should ask yourself." One eyebrow shot up, giving him a quizzical expression. "You've been saying 'no' since I met you." He switched his attention to Tessa. "Let's get you out of there."

He unbuckled the safety harness. Tessa, demonstrating that even little girls weren't immune to his charm, flashed her dimples and reached out her arms. With the child held against his chest, he stood up. "I don't want Peter to see her again. This'll be tricky enough without her in the room."

"I agree. I tried everyone I could this morning and drew a blank." She inched closer, and his warm scent settled her nerves. "Can you ring Peter and change the meeting?"

He checked his watch. "If you'd let me know earlier, maybe. But he'll be on his way."

"If you'd checked your phone in the last hour." Ella wasn't going to carry the can on her own.

"We'll call it a mutual stuff-up." He turned to his assistant. "What do you say, Merle? Could we get one of the girls up from downstairs?"

"You keep a harem in the basement?" Ella marvelled. "Girls waiting to be summoned?"

Merle snorted.

Jake unravelled another inch, a patrician in training. "We

have a company creche. Have you brought Tootles?"

"I'm sure we could fit her in for an hour." Merle was his peace-maker.

"'Ootles," cried Tessa, while Ella filed the knowledge he'd remembered the bear represented both playmate and security blanket for Tessa. He kept ambushing her with his perceptiveness.

"She's a little anxious with strangers at the moment—" Ella began, then stumbled to a halt as Tessa curled one hand around Jake's neck and started exploring his face with her other.

A noise at the elevators had their heads swinging in unison towards the sound.

"Merle make that call and hold on to Tessa for a minute." Jake patted Tessa's back before disengaging himself and handing her to his waiting assistant. He stepped towards the new arrivals. "Bron, I wasn't expecting you."

"You've brought Tessa."

The two voices merged and, for a moment, there was silence. Merle finished her soft-voiced conversation on the phone and nodded at Jake.

"Hello, Peter." Ella inserted herself into the charged atmosphere. "I didn't intend to bring Tessa. We're arranging a sitter for her now."

"There's no need for that." The woman in the wheelchair addressed Ella, but her eyes, like Peter's, stayed on Tessa.

Jake stepped directly into the older woman's line of sight to Tessa. "Bron, you shouldn't be here." Tenderness and exasperation blended in the look he gave the elegantly dressed matriarch. Another emotion Ella tried to identify was part of the mix. *Love?* Her pirate had admitted to knowing Drew, but his behaviour towards Drew's parents implied a far closer relationship.

"How could I stay away? When Peter told me ..."

"We don't have conclusive proof yet, Bron." Jake's gentle remonstrance feathered down Ella's spine.

She cursed herself for not camping in a nearby café or trying the general switchboard to reach Jake. The naked yearning on the older woman's face justified Jake's insistence on excluding Bronwyn Browning and Tessa from this meeting.

"Stop behaving like a stuffy lawyer and take something on trust," Bronwyn Browning chastised him.

"Jake's speaking the truth, Mrs Browning. Today's meeting is to work out the next steps to protect everyone," Ella said.

"Caution is for the young. I don't have time to go slowly. My illness is progressing too fast. I don't know how long I have left to play with my grandchild," Bronwyn Browning's matter-of-fact statement hid the personal agony of such a diagnosis. Her plea had its own heartbeat, loud and insistent.

The same fierce determination had driven Ella's mother to grab life with both hands after her tractor accident. Ella didn't envy Jake's job. The elevator doors opened to eject a vigorous young woman in a uniform with the logo, Taylor Law Child Care. Merle moved towards her.

"Excuse me." Ella joined Merle, digging in her bag for the faithful Tootles.

"Hi, I'm Ruby." The woman nodded at Ella but spoke to Tessa. "Do you want to come and play with me and my friends for a little while?"

"'Ootles play too," said Tessa, reaching out a hand to take the bear.

"If she gets panicky, ring me immediately." Ella kept her voice low. "No more than an hour."

"We have internal CCTV for the centre, so parents can check if they're concerned," Ruby explained.

"I'll keep an eye on the screen," said Merle. "And pull you out of the meeting if she seems over-anxious."

The no-nonsense answer reassured Ella. "Where can I collect her?"

"Second floor at the rear of the building." The young woman opened her arms. "Hey, Tess, are you and Tootles ready?"

"Bye, Ellie. Kiss." Her niece presented her cheek for Ella's kiss.

"See you soon, honey pie." Ella kissed the child and the bear. "Look after Tootles."

"Me push." Tessa's demand floated back to Ella as the elevator doors closed.

She turned, ready to help Jake convince the Brownings that proceeding with caution was her decision, as much as his, and saw them disappearing into Jake's office.

"You may be my favourite nephew, but I've made up my mind," the woman grumbled from her wheelchair.

"Nephew!" Ella's head spun with the information. They weren't clients. *They were his family.* His promise of fair dealing had been a lie!

He nodded to Merle. "Hold all calls."

"Already got that message, boss." His efficient assistant nodded before turning to leave.

"Coming, Eleanor?" *The sneak!*

Ella preceded him into the room, channelling her disgust into a look that in a *fair* world would have stripped paint off metal.

"Peter, Bron." Jake closed the door. "Eleanor and I need a few minutes alone. I know you'll excuse us."

He gestured to a side door inside his office and ushered her into a tiny space. Ella followed slowly, scrambling to fit this new piece of information into a coherent picture. The snick of the door closing sounded like the clang of a prison gate.

"You lied to me."

"It didn't come up." He held up a hand to stop her from interrupting. "Not a lie. It just didn't come up."

"That's a sneaky lawyer's excuse. Maybe it didn't come up in our first meeting, but it was pertinent to our second." She gripped her elbows across her chest. "You held all the cards. An investigator tracking me and your own little secret about who you are. Hardly fair play."

"They're important to me." His eyes blazed with conviction. "And nothing else I've told you is a lie."

"You expect me to believe you!" she sniffed. But he'd never hidden his concern for Peter from her. He'd told her about Murphy when it would never have occurred to her to ask. "It changes things."

"How?" He flung a hand in the air—a toreador's flourish. "I still don't want them to care too much and then lose her. I don't want a cash-for-access exchange. That would permanently taint their relationship." His blunt summation of her misgivings hammered at her heart.

"You should have told me." But she couldn't dispute his conclusion. Cash-for-access was vile, an insult to her family and a crime against Tessa. Her niece was not a commodity to be traded on a whim, or her sister's irrational death-bed fears.

"I should have. And you're a nicer person than me, Eleanor. If you'd hired your own Murphy or even asked Tony, you'd have found out."

That he was Tessa's uncle, or that he wasn't a nice person? "You mean a naïve idiot." Her instinct to trust first then pick up the pieces was bred in the bone, a legacy from her father, and despite Smithhouse, hard to shake.

"A decent human being who cares about right and wrong." His mellow voice soothed, and he'd found her Achilles heel.

"Your loyalty is to them and Drew." And loyalty mattered. It was the bedrock of love that enabled you to soar. She'd given up expecting to win that kind of loyalty from a lover.

"That hasn't changed since our first meeting."

"You're not objective." But discovering he was emotionally rather than financially invested in the case gave her hope in the tentative trust they were forging.

"Who is? That doesn't mean I won't look after Tessa's interests." He was as soothing as a hypnotist.

"You have no idea what she needs." She raised a hand,

then let it fall.

"My parents died when I was nine. I probably have a better idea of what it means to be orphaned than you do." His smoky-grey gaze rested on her face, his body still while he described shocking loss.

"Peter and Bronwyn raised you." Her guess made perfect sense ... *now.*

"Yes."

As Ella absorbed his explanation, it crowded out anger, giving her a new set of questions to grapple with. "Did Chrissy know?"

"Possibly. Probably," he said impatiently. "We didn't discuss it. Drew would have given her his version of family history."

The relationship explained the love in his voice when he spoke to Bronwyn. *Orphaned at nine.* He'd been bereft, confused, and living in a state of suspended animation. After a fortnight, Chrissy's death still didn't seem real. Ella turned around in the apartment expecting to find her sister, her breath catching in her throat when she remembered she'd never see Chrissy again.

Loss and loyalty were familiar companions to her too, making it harder to maintain her guard against Jake. She'd offer sympathy, except she ached to comfort him in the most basic way. Not the child he'd been, but the man he'd become.

"I don't want them exploited. *By anyone.*" The suppressed violence of his frustration underlined his determination to protect. "They're getting older. Peter's watching the slow deterioration of the woman he loves. They're vulnerable. It's my turn to look out for them. I *owe* them."

His words triggered an old memory. "Chrissy said you owed her. It was all your fault. She didn't tell me your name. Didn't tell me Drew's name. Her boyfriend's *cousin.*" Ella searched his face. "That's you, *isn't it?* Drew caught you and Chrissy coming out of a hotel bedroom together and said he wouldn't take her back because she'd cheated on him.

You'd cheated on him."

"Is that in your letter, Eleanor?" The light in his eyes died.

She shook her head. "Chrissy was incoherent. I arrived in Sydney because someone told my parents they'd seen her. That she was pregnant. She wasn't looking after herself. She was desperate and depressed. Chrissy said nothing happened between you, but you wouldn't help her fix things. She said everything went wrong after that."

"Fixing things meant making Drew go back to her." He turned to the window, stared out for endless seconds, then swung back to her, arms crossed. His body screamed at her to back off. "I couldn't make that happen."

She pushed for the bigger story. "Couldn't clear up a misunderstanding, or wouldn't?"

"Drew had a new girlfriend with him that night." His voice was clipped, drained of all emotion. "They left a few days later for England."

"That's why she wrote to you." Another piece of the puzzle fell into place for Ella. "She thinks you owe her."

"You've worked out most of what's in my letter, Eleanor. Show me yours."

Ella tried to remember the rest of the story, but it was gone. Chrissy had become hysterical. Coaxing her into a taxi to the doctor's was a Herculean feat. When the doctor made his diagnosis, Ella had been too devastated to care about pursuing Chrissy's old boyfriend, about who was right or wrong. Chrissy had made some wild remarks about the woman who'd seduced Drew, about how Jake had introduced them, but the memory was elusive.

The knock on the door startled them, before Peter put his head around it. "We want to be part of this conversation."

"We'll be right out," Jake unfolded his arms.

Peter closed the door and withdrew.

"We should finish this," Jake said.

Ella stretched out a hand to stop him from leaving.

"How bad is Bronwyn's condition?"

"She doesn't use the wheelchair very much at home, but, yes, she's losing mobility. I don't want them hurt." His eyes were the colour of storm-tossed clouds. "I don't want her hurt."

"I've got that message, Counsellor." Loss and loyalty—maybe she had more in common with him than she realised. "It may be too late to protect them."

Two letters from Chrissy had started a chain reaction, each discovery a booby trap waiting to blow up in her face. And the number of people who could be hurt by Ella's decisions kept growing. Her legal training and experience counted for little when custody of Tessa was at stake. A maze she needed to navigate. Alone. Except Jake had planted himself firmly in her path. She wasn't sure which was the greatest risk, going around him, through him or accepting his help.

* * *

"Ready?" Jake inhaled, letting her perfume fill his nostrils, reminding him of having her pressed against his thigh on the sofa last night. An alluring scent, fresh and fragrant as a bunch of sweet peas. He'd wanted to bury his face in it and her. "I planned to tell you. In another place, at another time, when we'd worked out which role each of us is taking."

Sometime between meeting her and leaving her apartment last night he'd decided he wanted honesty between them. Although, he hadn't quite worked out what to say about his relationship with Peter and Bronwyn, his relationship with Chrissy. He never spoke of his relationship with Drew.

"They'd be defenceless in the face of this claim without you. I didn't expect sensitivity from a Taylor Law operative." She scrunched up her face as if she'd swallowed some foul-tasting medicine. "You forced me to see another side of you."

"When I realised the significance of the timing, I intended to tell you about the night Chrissy and I were together." Jake wasn't prepared for this yearning to have Ella believe him. Chrissy had demanded Jake fix things. She'd been uncontrollable, insisting he stop Drew from cheating on Chrissy with Julia. He hadn't known himself until that night, until Jake had opened the door of his hotel room to find Drew in bed with his fiancée. He'd been battling his own demons, but Chrissy had been too distraught for him to abandon her that night.

"A hard confession to make?" She was listening, rare in his experience.

"Most people draw the same conclusion as Drew." The scandal had run like wildfire through Sydney's social and business circles, while Jake had remained silent, avoiding questions from his aunt and uncle. Unwilling to make them choose sides, afraid to test their loyalty to him. Drew was their only child. And Jake's self-imposed vow of silence on the whole messy affair had become an ingrained habit.

"The obvious answer isn't always the truth." Her openness was a balm.

Tony Baldwin had been waxing lyrical for months, and Jake hadn't believed her advance press. Tony's EJ sounded like a personable, efficient, no-nonsense administrator. When Jake looked at her, he saw a beautiful, compassionate woman.

"Unlike me, you do play fair. I figured today would be the day. And I understand why you wouldn't believe that." He reached forward to push her hair off her forehead and was comforted when she didn't step away. "But today hasn't panned out as either of us planned. I hoped Chrissy's letter to you might answer questions raised by her letter to me. Two halves of a whole. I'm sorry you found out about my relationship with Peter and Bron this way."

"And Tessa," she said. "You're her first cousin."

"Technically, I'm her first cousin once removed." He'd

tried not to let the possibility cloud his decisions. An innocent child was not responsible for her father's transgressions. Although, she'd always be Drew's child.

She pushed through the door to his office. Jake cursed his growing need to simply help her. Each time he spoke to her, his respect grew—for her humanity, for her tolerance and for her generosity.

"About time," said Bronwyn. "Thirty more seconds and I was coming after you."

"We had a few things to sort out, Bron." Jake prepared for the inquisition.

"Has he been browbeating you?" Bronwyn studied Ella.

"No." Ella sat on one end of the sofa, her legs tucked gracefully to one side.

"You don't look like you'd be easily browbeaten," his aunt said.

Jake winced, silently apologising for the times he'd tried to do just that.

"I make my own decisions, Mrs Browning." Eleanor was looking at him when she spoke, and showing remarkable patience given the snare she'd toppled into.

"Call me Bronwyn. You call my husband Peter." She flashed her most charming smile, making Jake uneasy.

"Bronwyn. Tessa has lost her mother. Her moods fluctuate from sunny to anxious. Neither my family nor I want to deny her or you a part in her future, but for all our sakes, we need to be sure. I've asked Jake to wait for the results of the DNA test."

"Peter said you believe your sister?" His aunt persisted.

"I'm not objective." She folded her hands on her lap.

Bronwyn sniffed. "No one ever is."

Okay, none of them was objective. Jake's major concern was Drew's reaction to reports he'd fathered a child. Because the news would get out if they proceeded with the DNA test. Bron and Peter would introduce Tessa as their grandchild to anyone who cared to listen. It wasn't his role to warn Eleanor that Drew could be a dangerous enemy.

"But," Bronwyn added, "that doesn't mean they can't make balanced decisions or compromise where it's important."

"That's what Jake and I are trying to do, Bronwyn." Ella sounded so damned sincere. With Murphy's report ringing in his ears and the evidence of his own eyes, Jake knew she was. And too appealing for his peace of mind. He admired her integrity while her sexy smile stirred cravings he'd be better off ignoring. He'd seen her expression when he'd admitted he was family. For her, family came first. She'd nearly walked when he'd admitted the connection.

He'd learned silence as an adolescent, when he didn't want to repay his aunt and uncle's generosity by carrying takes about their son. Keeping his relationship to Tessa secret would leave questions in Ella's mind.

"At least you're talking to me, Ella." Bronwyn swung her chair in Jake's direction. "Stop pretending I'm not here."

"You shouldn't be here," Jake muttered. Bron and Eleanor were kindred spirits. Idiotic to think keeping Tessa away from his aunt was the safest way to keep a lid on this until they had the DNA results. An asinine mistake. He should have kept her away from Eleanor.

"Ella, we'd like you and Tessa to come and visit us, perhaps stay with us for a weekend," Peter said, taking his wife's hand. "We want to get to know you both."

"Did you listen to what Eleanor was saying, Peter?" Exasperation tugged at Jake's composure.

Bronwyn interrupted. "She's the image of you as a baby, Jake."

Eleanor's head swung accusingly towards him, and Jake raised his hands in another apology.

"My sister, Jake's mother, and I were twins. Drew's the genetic throwback, but the dominant genes have asserted themselves in Tessa." The longing in Bron's voice hit Jake squarely in the solar plexus. She'd already accepted Tessa as family. Damn the resemblance. Damn the circumstances that had thrust them together this way. *Damn bloody Drew for his irresponsibility.*

The insidious progress of the crippling disease robbing Bron of her energy and ultimately her life terrified him. Unable to slow her illness, he'd do anything in his power to make her happy.

He could curse Eleanor for bringing Tessa, but Peter had broken their bargain too. Jake sensed Ella's tension before she searched his face in mute appeal. Eleanor Jane Anderson finally understood the trouble they were in. Knowing she shared his quandary brought some satisfaction.

"We don't have sufficient proof, Bron." Jake rested a hand on his aunt's shoulder.

"I'd like to add my invitation to my husband's, Ella. We'd love to have you both in our home. Even for a short visit," she pleaded.

"Let's wait for the DNA test." Jake signalled Eleanor with his eyes. *Your turn.*

* * *

Ella closed her eyes against the assault on her conscience. To her mind, Bronwyn's claim was fair and just. The normal musings of grandparents tracing tiny resemblances. Her parents could spend hours in similar idle speculation. A simple but profound pleasure. The gift of a child. The next generation. The Brownings needed the pirate king to protect them from themselves.

"I agree with Jake," Ella said.

"Not in your heart, you don't." Bronwyn included her in a conspiratorial smile. "And I've made up my mind."

Bronwyn's words brought Jake's frown back. He glared at Ella. She shook her head in apology. Circumstances had conspired against them both. Mr. P hadn't had such a violent episode in months. Jake hadn't been on hand to take her call. Peter and Bronwyn had arrived early. Minor mischances leading to this current impasse.

"We'll let you talk about it some more and let us know your decision. Don't take too long," Bronwyn said. Peter moved behind his wife's wheelchair. She stretched out a hand to shake Ella's. "Don't let him talk you out of doing what you think is right, my dear," Bronwyn finished.

"Eleanor works in the justice system, too, Bron. She knows what the law requires in situations like this," Jake muttered.

"I manage a community justice centre." Ella answered the question in Bron's eyes.

"How wonderful. Then you'll have a heightened appreciation that small j, justice is very different from big J, justice." Bronwyn winked at her nephew.

"She's right," Ella agreed, recalling a recent case. She could still picture the despair in the eyes of a couple sitting in her office, holding hands and leaning against each other as she tried to explain their daughter-in-law's decision.

The case was nothing like this one. That mother had been devastated by the discovery of her husband's infidelity. Repeated infidelities, often at sports fixtures, while their older son was on field. She was sustained by her drive to prove her husband was unfit to have access to his children. By focusing on her anger, she didn't have to deal with her pain. But she'd included her husband's parents in her vendetta. They hadn't warned her. Not that they'd even known.

Nothing Ella had said had changed that mother's mind. She'd talked of her own childhood, casually dropped memories into conversations. Story time on her grandmother's knee or trailing her grandfather around the paddock learning the names of the herd's prize cows. Daisy, Maisy and her favourite, Gertrude. She'd described being perched on a stool beside her mother's mother, learning the rituals of baking. Her grandpa would come into the kitchen, topple her off that stool and swing her high into the air, throwing and catching her until she giggled helplessly and begged him to stop. Memories that had shaped her. Had reassured her she was loved. She couldn't dismiss Tessa's grandparents' genuine claim.

Bronwyn's wheelchair rolled past.

Jake stopped beside her. "Don't go yet," he murmured. The pressure of his fingers closing around her wrist burned like a brand, compelling her agreement. The contrast between his light hold and the force, which held her motionless, stole her breath. "We haven't finished."

"We've finished for now," she said.

"She's going to keep pushing to see Tessa." He sounded battle-weary.

"It's not her decision." Ella accepted the justice of Bronwyn's plea.

"It's yours, Eleanor. And you're wavering. They're prepared to make a financial contribution."

"When will you get it through your thick head that I don't want your damn money!" she snapped. He was deliberately pulling her chain.

"You'd rather be evicted," he said bitingly.

"Murphy has been a busy boy." Ella pulled free of his light hold. "Are all our conversations going to be punctuated with snippets your bloodhound scratched out of the mud?"

"I'm sorry. That was frustration talking." He paced to the window, then swivelled to face her. "But when it comes to thick heads, I'd say we're even. Look, the balance of probability is that Tessa is Drew's child. He, or his family, should have been making a contribution to her living expenses since her birth. It's too late to make up for that, but it's not too late to stop you from being evicted."

"Does possessing all this dirt increase your sense of control? Do you know how much I've got in my bank account?" For some, the pursuit of money, the theft of money, were the weft and warp of life, their only lover. She despised how the super-rich could use money to seduce or bludgeon others to their will. He'd sunk to playing the same game. Her sympathy for his dilemma over Bronwyn evaporated.

He strolled towards her.

"You do, don't you?"" Her hand curled into a fist. "You bastard."

"Down to the last cent, Eleanor. And I'm not going to apologise for that. This is my family." He dragged a hand through his hair, dislodging the tie restraining it. Thick, wavy locks spilled around his ears in sinful abandon. "Now Bron's seen Tessa; it just got harder."

Ella's breath quickened, her heart pumping in her chest as she pushed her hands behind her back to stop herself from reaching forward. An overwhelming urge to slide her fingers into his tumbled mane washed through her. To test the luxurious thickness of it and, with her fingers entangled, tug his mouth closer.

"Is there anything that will get Drew here sooner?" she asked.

"I'll give it some thought." His gaze was fixed on her mouth with spellbinding concentration.

"What are you going to tell them?"

"I may have to sacrifice you." He was half-serious, circling, trying to punch through her barricades. A shiver of anticipation slid down her spine. "Tell them you're the author of the letter. That their generosity has shamed you into withdrawing the plea for money," he growled. "You can't face them."

"What about the paternity claim?" The tension, which shimmered between them so often when they were alone, returned now. Ella stood her ground. "Am I withdrawing that?"

"Ah! The flaw in my plan." He took a step closer. "I could say Drew believes I had a fling with Chrissy, and Tessa is mine."

"That's not what Chrissy said," Ella enunciated each word with care.

His eyebrows shot up, challenging her certainty. "We spent a night in a hotel bedroom and left together in the morning."

"Drew was in the same hotel?"

He nodded.

"With his new girlfriend?"

His full-bodied laugh squashed Ella's doubts, easing the constriction around her heart. Jake Taylor had never been her sister's lover.

"Why didn't you finish your law degree, Eleanor? Your forensic skills would be an asset to any law firm."

"I was needed on the farm." She'd make the same choice again.

"I imagine a lot of people need you." He tucked a curl behind her ear. "I find I want you. Very much." He rested his hands on her hips, drawing her closer.

"This isn't a good idea, Jake." She linked her fingers behind his neck.

He gathered her closer still. "Feels like the best idea I've had all day." He raised one hand to catch her chin and tilt it upwards. Holding her gaze with his, he searched her eyes and waited. "Kiss me, Eleanor, please."

"Not a good idea." She liked that he made no assumptions, and rose onto her toes. His scent was its own lure, and she stepped willingly into the trap.

Satisfied, he bent until his mouth was a mere whisper from her own. "Bet it is."

CHAPTER FIVE

Warm breath brushed Ella's lips, which she opened on an involuntary sigh, both confession and admission she yearned for this. His tongue slid across her lower lip, the rough tip sparking tiny explosions in her belly. Ella moaned, and he captured her soft exhalation and returned it as another kiss. His mouth was an instant addiction. Her toes curled inside their sensible shoes.

Ella's arms slid under his jacket to hold him closer. Her mouth sought his, wanting the heat, the excitement, the roar of blood in her head. For this moment there was only him. The world dropped away. When his head lifted, she groaned her loss aloud.

"Don't you agree, Eleanor?" he insisted with a husky growl.

Before Ella could challenge his certainty, he was kissing her again, this time without restraint, his arms drawing her against him so they were pressed length to length. She breathed when he breathed; she gave when he gave. Her hands were as greedy, fisting against his shirt. Her mouth as demanding, nipping at his bottom lip. Her senses as urgent and untamed.

She gave up thinking, buffeted by a swirling tempest

where his scent, his touch and his taste were all that drove her, all that satisfied her, a craving that was boundless.

"Eleanor?"

As her eyes opened, she became aware of her surroundings. One leg was wrapped around his thigh, locking her intimately to him. His hand held her against him, burning like a brand through the fine wool of her skirt. She remembered she'd rocked against the hard ridge of his arousal like a woman who had the right to make uninhibited love to him. Her boldness stunned her. Nothing else had mattered to her except meeting him as an equal. She'd never lost herself so totally in a man's kisses before. With care, he set her back on her feet, holding her at arm's length while her breathing steadied.

Two buttons on her blouse had slipped their lugs. Her nipples, pressed against the lace of her bra, throbbed from his caress. Heat rose up Ella's throat. She turned her back, her fingers clumsy as she tried to pull her shirt into place.

"Here, let me." He tugged her back to face him and smiled grimly before covering her hands with his.

"I can do it."

"It's not about whether you can do it. It's about whether you know when to accept help." He was talking about more than straightening her clothes. He rested his forehead against hers, his heavy locks falling forward to shield their faces. "Let me," he murmured.

Drawing the edges of her shirt together, he redid the two buttons then did up two more. The backs of his fingers brushed against sensitised skin from her midriff to the base of her throat as he closed each loop. Ella's breathing was unsteady, and her mind in chaos, when she raised her head and stepped back.

A knock on the door startled her. "Come in," Jake called.

Merle opened the door, and Tessa burst through. "When the Brownings left I collected her for you, Ms. Anderson. She seems relaxed and happy."

"Thank you." Ella had bent to catch Tessa, and now

swung her high into the air. Merle backed out of the room. "Hello, Tess. How's my girl?"

Tessa made some satisfying noises, and Ella listened intently, blotting out Jake, using this moment to calm herself. Grounded by having Tessa in her arms, she turned to him. "If you can convince them, I'd prefer to wait for the DNA test. However, my parents said having a granddaughter was a wonderful gift. They'd never deny that joy to Peter and Bronwyn."

"Bron read you right. You'll give them access before the results come in."

"You've been offering me money before the results are in."

"You need money!" His grin was lopsided in an effort to tease.

"So does a sizeable proportion of the world's population. Why make me your charity?" Chrissy's demand for money made Ella determined to take none.

"Money pays the bills and puts food on the table." He shrugged.

She'd rather starve. Having him dole out a wad of bills wouldn't change her distaste. "I've got food."

"Cheese is not a balanced diet." Frustration bounced off him at her resistance. "Maintenance, not charity, is because all the circumstantial evidence supports the claim. And, yes, I've checked birthdates, hospitalisation and everything else."

"Still no trust?" The idea hurt.

"There's a chance you're wrong." He sucked in a breath. "That I'm wrong. About the paternity."

"I'm often wrong, Counsellor. But not on this. Tessa is their grandchild." Ella had heard Chrissy's confessions before.

"They're captivated by the idea of a grandchild." He was restating old ground.

"What's worrying you?" Because his worry was starting to infect her.

"There's a lot to lose if this goes wrong. On both sides."

"It's our job to make sure nothing goes wrong."

"We're not the only players here, Eleanor." His tone and sudden frown sent a shiver down her spine.

The knock interrupted Tessa's bedtime routine. Ella rose from her sofa, the sleepy child propped on her hip with her head resting against Ella's shoulder. Two storybooks tonight and a make-believe tale about the man in the moon before Tessa's eyes had drifted closed. Ella squinted through the peephole, her heart doing a slow somersault in surprise, followed by a whip of pleasure. She opened the door.

"Why are you here, Jake?" She leaned against the doorjamb, blocking his entry.

"I like the teddy bear pyjamas, Tess." He ran a hand over the child's head, then met Ella's eyes. "Can I come in?"

"Not if you plan to rehash today's conversation." But the sparks rocketing along her veins and capillaries were a sensory reminder of their explosive kisses, not their conversation. She'd yet to work out how to manage her attraction to him.

"I wanted to check that Tessa survived our childcare centre." Even now Tessa was reaching out to him.

"She's fine."

"I brought a bottle of wine."

She'd given him licence to rummage through her cupboards the other night. A few bottles of wine, but she didn't have the spare cash to spend on the label he brandished. "Another attempt at bribery?"

"An apology."

She hoisted Tessa higher on her hip.

"I'm flattered by the blush, Eleanor. But I'm not apologising for kissing you."

His words re-ignited the awareness between them. An added energy in the room to cloud common sense. Ella barely knew him. Still, an invisible thread connected them, making it unnecessary for them to touch because the electrified air snapped and crackled between them. The taste of him lingered on her lips, a rich dessert wine where she'd survived on plain fare for an eon. Ella caught her lower lip between her teeth, and his eyes followed the movement as if drawn by a magnet.

"What are you apologising for?" She concentrated on pulling Tessa's pyjama top down over her midriff.

"Smithhouse."

"You've remembered?" Her gaze snapped back to his.

"I've researched." With a wry smile, he stroked Tessa's cheek. "That's why you didn't want me to talk to your family."

"They didn't need to be reminded of Taylor Law when they'd just buried Chrissy." She turned back into the room, leaving him to follow. "I'll be a few minutes. Tessa and I have a bit of a routine going."

"Have you eaten?" he asked with the ease of a regular visitor.

"Not yet."

"Let me guess." He scratched his ear as if giving it serious consideration. "Toasted cheese sandwiches?"

Ella smiled in spite of herself. "I was thinking of a cheese omelette."

"Italian or Chinese?" He shrugged. "They're the two take-away restaurants I passed a few blocks back."

"I'm not sure." Because she didn't have regular visitors who made her wish she was the girl most likely to be prom queen.

"Not sure about which you'd prefer to eat, or not sure about having a meal with me that could be construed as a date?" He studied her with the concentration of a cat who'd found a treat. Unblinking, focused, working up to a purr— or a pounce.

"You don't date like this." Her heart skipped a beat. She didn't know if he had a partner or a lover, but she wanted to believe he wouldn't be here with her now if he did.

"At the moment, I'm not dating." He gave the answer she needed. "And I'm open to new experiences."

"Italian. Pasta. Arrabiata," she replied.

"Decisive. And a tomato chilli sauce means you like spicy food. So do I."

"Would you have preferred me to dither?" She stroked her hand down Tessa's back.

"Life hasn't left you much time for procrastination, Eleanor."

"Your own idea or a Murphy insight?" She didn't like the idea their conversations might be dictated by scrapes of information uncovered by a private investigator trawling through her life.

"Murphy's off your case," he said softly. "And Tess is falling asleep on your shoulder."

Ella headed for the bedroom, emerging fifteen minutes later.

He rose from the sofa and swung to face her, holding aloft two crystal goblets. "I found a corkscrew and these. Heirlooms?"

"Jumble sale."

"I like them."

Ella settled into the armchair, avoiding the implied intimacy of joining him on the sofa. The memory of her loss of control this morning prickled along her skin.

He passed her a glass and sat down. "I've ordered dinner. Won't be long. *Salute.*"

"Cheers, we always say on the farm."

"The farm Smithhouse tried to steal from you."

"He got a few prime acres with the help of Taylor Law." She raised her glass to toast him.

"There are a few of the old hands who remember a young woman, a law student, confronting a senior partner walking into court." He sounded admiring. "She slammed his morals, his ethics and even questioned his understanding of torts."

"I didn't win," Ella murmured, watching the rich red liquid swirl in her glass when she tilted it to the light. Her family had made sacrifices for her to study law. A year of classes hadn't given her sufficient skills to help her family when they'd needed it. "I didn't even put a dent in his smirk."

"Because the deal was done on a handshake and the only independent witness was you." He *had* done his homework.

"They argued I wasn't independent, that I'd say anything to support my father, that I was too emotional." She sniffed the wine: luscious, full-bodied, plum with a hint of spice she couldn't identify.

"Insulting on so many fronts to someone who believes in justice as passionately as you do." His mouth curved in sympathy.

"I was bloody emotional." Ella recalled her rage at her helplessness. Her vow never to be helpless again. Never to let a lack of power deny her family, anyone, access to justice. Her experience as a nineteen-year-old had led to her current job. "I still get emotional about justice."

"I'm sorry."

"For something that happened when you weren't there?" She studied him—the calmness in his posture and the sincerity in his voice. She could get lost in the steadiness in his grey gaze, if she let herself.

"It's taken me six years to rebuild the firm's reputation. I still come across cases like yours," he said, resignation tinged with bitterness. "It explains a lot of your initial hostility."

"Do you get much?" She imagined the burden if he accepted the weight of wrong-doing attached to his name. "Hostility, I mean?"

"Hostility I can deal with. It's the people who've vowed never to deal with Taylor Law again, who stare and whisper and badmouth us to would-be clients."

"Ouch." Ella threw up a hand in acknowledgement of the hit.

"You had cause."

"I accept it had nothing to do with you." The certainty settled around her, like the silence at the end of a thunderstorm on the farm. And she realised the name Taylor Law no longer held any fear for her. Ella sighed and took a sip of the wine. "Why is it so important to you?"

"Can't you guess?"

"The Taylor in the company name is a relative." She'd figured that out, hadn't guessed he wanted her curiosity.

"Founded by my grandfather. Enlarged by my father. My mother worked there. That's how they met." He shook his head. "That thieving bastard had the job less than two years and trashed a reputation built on decades of hard work."

"You don't want their legacy to you tainted. I understand that."

He lifted an eyebrow.

"My parents are fourth generation farmers. Continuity is important. Having a reputation for honesty and fair-dealing is important."

"I've paid restitution for other cases." He left the question hanging.

"Talk to my parents and my sister." Ella respected his need for justice. "The farm belongs to them."

"What about what he took from you?" he asked with a perception she was coming to expect.

"He refocused my interest in the law." She held the glass loosely between her hands. Trust was as fragile as glass. She and her pirate were dancing towards it even though they each worried about where it would lead. "I'm happy where I've landed."

"As an administrator, as a handmaiden to others, doing the hack work for cases." He was playing devil's advocate, but she'd long since made peace with her career choice.

"That would be the forensic research and investigation, Counsellor. My job makes a difference. Community is important. Individual lives and small problems are important. Solving a dispute between neighbours is a very big deal. And I count every victory my team scores against some Goliath as payback against the Smithhouses of this world."

His phone rang. "That's Bron." He slid it from his pocket, scanned the message, turned it off and placed it on the table between them. "Third time since they left the office."

"If you answer her, she might stop." But Ella's stomach had flip-flopped at the sound.

"I answered the first call. Peter has contacted Drew. Told him he believes Tessa is his granddaughter. That they've asked for immediate access and are prepared to pay."

"Money's an irrelevant distraction." She waved her glass at him. "Offering it to me all the time pisses me off."

"I'd never have guessed," he said ironically. "The offer's from the Brownings, not me. Peter asked me if I'd made it."

"He thinks I can be bought?" The idea a man Ella had liked on sight had tagged her as a gold-digger left a sour taste.

"He feels helpless and is offering what he has." Jake was an eloquent champion for his uncle.

"Bronwyn's made up her mind." Ella took another sip, savouring the flavour as it slid down her throat. His explanation took some of the sting out of the offer.

"So have you." He placed his glass on the table and stood. "You're going to take Tessa to see them, aren't you?"

"My mother saw Tessa as a newborn. She held her in her arms and cried with joy. We have pictures of them. And pictures of major milestones in the last two years. Birthdays, standing on her own, learning to walk, even riding a cow. Moments Bronwyn didn't share, can't share. It seems almost bloody-minded to deny her more."

"Why did Chrissy keep Tessa's parentage a secret until now?" He crossed to the fireplace, then swung to face her. "It makes no sense to me that she talked about us but didn't use our names."

"When I arrived in Sydney, she was close to collapse. It took a few weeks until we reached equilibrium, until she was coherent for more time than she was confused. Her letter explains a bit. She didn't want to believe she was going to die." Ella wanted him to see another side of Chrissy, to see beyond her sister's demand for money. "But from the beginning, the illness changed her. She lost weight. Her hair fell out because of the treatment. Her movements were laboured. Cancer killed her. But it was a monstrous bedfellow, daily demanding sacrifice. One day her beauty, the next her grace of movement, the one after that her vivacity. Before the end, it robbed her of all her self-confidence.

"The sicker she got, the more frightened she became. She didn't want people, particularly her lover, to see her like that. She feared rejection." Ella took a deep breath. "That memory does stick. I offered to contact her friends, let them know what was happening, ask if they wanted to visit. She said he wouldn't visit. What kind of man wouldn't visit an old girlfriend who was dying?"

"Drew and Chrissy lived in the limelight. Their world together was about gala events and parties and being seen looking beautiful," he said without inflection.

"I get the superficial lifestyle." But Ella was impatient with it. "Is Drew cruel as well?"

He didn't answer.

"Chrissy was flawed, impetuous, but never consciously cruel. She held him up as a hero." Ella still marvelled at that. "She'd tell Tessa stories. Your daddy is handsome and smart and rich."

"Can I see Chrissy's letter?"

Ella crossed to where she'd dumped her bag earlier. "I brought it to the meeting." She set it down on the coffee table.

"My idea of using the letters to stop Peter was never going to fly." His jacket hung on the back of a kitchen chair.

He slipped a hand into the inside pocket and took out a crushed envelope, placing it on the table beside hers. "I'm sorry, Eleanor."

She stared at him across the table.

"That she died, that she suffered. That you don't have her anymore."

Ella swallowed a sob. His simple empathy caught at the knot of angry grief deep in her belly, unravelling a corner. His compassion filled some of the empty places in her heart and soul, left by Chrissy's death.

In this mood he was hell to fight. She returned to her chair. "I worked out every detail months before she died, you know. The need to establish new routines for Tessa. I changed her program to include a few hours at a childcare centre two days a week, rearranged the flat and negotiated new working hours." Ella closed her eyes on the memory.

"In those final weeks, I slept in her bedroom. She needed me, to tend to her and to comfort her. Intellectually I prepared for her death." She turned to face him. "Intellectually I managed it well."

"When you lose someone you love, intellectual solutions don't cut it, do they?" he said gently.

He understood, which allowed her to ask. "Is that how it was with your parents?"

"One day they were here, the next they weren't. They'd taken a second honeymoon. On an impulse joined a helicopter joy flight above Lake Eyre. One of its rare occasions in flood. From what the inquiry could work out, they delayed their return until after dark. Spatial disorientation was the official finding. The chopper went into a spiral and everyone on board was killed."

"That must be worse," she said. Nine was old enough to know what he'd lost; too young to be able to control what was happening to him. "Not to be able to say goodbye."

"There's no worse. Just different."

Ella stared at the two letters on the table, then him. She'd memorised Chrissy's letter to her, or rather, it was etched into her brain. She doubted she'd ever be able to forget her sister's last words to her.

Dear Ella,

Drew Browning is Tessa's father. He told me from the start he wanted fun, not permanence or children, but so did I. I hated the farm even before mum's accident. Wanted to escape. To be rich and famous. It would have happened too. I was on my way. Before Tessa. Before the cancer.

I wouldn't believe it for such a long time. Hoped something would happen to make it all go away. But it won't. I know you're thinking of taking Tessa back to the farm. But I won't have it. Just because you don't have the money for any other choice. Drew's family is mega rich. I've been following Drew. Tessa's the only grandchild. She deserves her place in the family, to live with beautiful things, not make do with hand-me-downs.

I should have told you what I did, but you might have stopped me. I love you, Ella, but I don't understand you. Any more than you understand me. Even after Robert, you gave up more than two years of your life for me. I don't think I could have done that. But I'm grateful. If you hadn't, I don't know what would have happened to me.

I'm afraid of dying, Ella. More afraid of Tessa being buried alive as I was. The Brownings will give her everything I dreamed of for myself. Life's nothing without money.

I want the best for my beautiful baby.

Love,

Chrissy

P.S. Forgive me. I chickened out at the end, like always, and am leaving this letter for the community nurse to deliver.

She exhaled a long slow breath and reached for her sister's letter to Jake. "Let's do this." For a few seconds, she couldn't make out the words on the page. Her vision blurred. Not tears. She blinked furiously. Chrissy's wobbly penmanship splattered across this page in the same way it had with her letter. There were no soft words to end this letter, no expressions of love or gratitude. *"I want what Tessa's owed."*

Tension uncoiled in her belly, while Jake, sitting stiffly

beside her, communicated disgust without saying a word.

* * *

Jake read Chrissy's last words to her sister, aware of the emotional strain in the woman opposite him. Then scanned it a second time with mounting annoyance. The letter was indifferent to the sacrifices Eleanor had made. Sacrifices he knew about thanks to Murphy. Uncaring of the love with which Eleanor had fashioned a home. He'd call the letter and Chrissy's actions monumentally selfish. His initial suspicion would have been another blow. His jaw clenched at the memory of her face in his office at their first meeting. What he'd interpreted in his arrogance as guilt had been shock. She blamed herself for Chrissy's discontent.

"Say what you're thinking, Jake." She folded Chrissy's letter to him in half.

He waved the letter he held. "Her letter to you isn't as cold-blooded as the one to me, but it's egocentric and heedless."

"She was dying," she insisted.

"We still have to ask if it's possible she lied." He liked Chrissy even less than he had before tonight.

"Lied, no."

"There's a but in your voice."

Reluctantly she met Jake's eyes, but she wasn't with him. She was caught in Chrissy's world of insecurities and blame. Jake waited while she searched for words she was prepared to share. "She didn't lie, but she kept secrets."

"Secrets and lies keep tripping us up, Eleanor." And sometimes they're the same thing. Jake couldn't be certain his silence on Drew wasn't a lie or his own secret.

"This is the biggest secret she ever kept," she whispered.

"Didn't you push for his name?"

"I said it's important for children to know where they came from. More than once." She wrinkled her nose. "I stopped pushing, but I know Mum pushed and Grace continued to ask questions. Chrissy was good at distractions and subterfuge. As she got sicker, she'd just say she was tired, and none of us would push. When you know you have a finite time with someone, you don't waste it. We love Tessa. We want her. We'll let her know she's loved and wanted always."

"A lot of children start seeking answers about their parents when they grow up." He leaned forward. "Even children who are loved by their adoptive or foster parents."

"Chrissy loved him." She gripped her hands tightly in her lap. Was she trying to convince him or herself?

Jake remembered Chrissy as shallow, as shallow as Drew, but he respected Eleanor's loyalty. "I'm not disputing that. In the hotel, she told me again and again she loved him." Jake had remained silent knowing Chrissy wouldn't listen to the truth. "She was devastated by his desertion. And not just because of the baby."

"She didn't give me his name. But she couldn't help but let things fall about what they'd done or her feelings for him. Especially after Tessa was born." Eleanor raised her head, bewildered by her memories. "She said Tessa was a love child. Conceived in love, carried with love and welcomed into the world with love. If Chrissy hadn't named him, we'd have told Tessa that."

"Except her story's bullshit, given the evidence in front of us." Impatience pushed him to his feet.

"Chrissy was dying." She used the fact as a justification. "She wanted the best for Tessa."

"Damn it, Eleanor, stop making excuses for her." Unable to settle, Jake strode to the mantelpiece and picked up a photo of Eleanor with Tessa in a backpack. Both with sunhats and wide grins. A frail woman he recognised as Chrissy leaned on her arm, too weak even then to carry Tessa. Eleanor took responsibility, allowed herself no mistakes, but granted Chrissy endless licence to mess with other people's lives.

"If I don't find excuses for her, I might go crazy." The

despair in her voice clawed at him. "Did you notice your letter is undated too?"

"Is that important?" he asked.

"Yes. No. It means she wrote them a while ago before she got too sick to write." Her chin wobbled. "And held on to them."

"Somehow that makes it worse." He hadn't known Chrissy had it in her to keep secrets with such far-reaching consequences. *It was a hellavu deathbed confession.*

"Yes."

Jake ran through her reactions in his office, at her apartment, and understood what her sister had done. He turned to face her, his gut clenching as he pinpointed her fear. "She hung you out to dry. You don't have legal custody, do you?" He hated challenging her, but he needed to know.

She stilled as if caught in the beam of a powerful spotlight. Suddenly exposed. "My parenting rights have been established over two years." Her face was white.

"So you've got a strong case, but it hasn't been tested. You know grandparents, as well as parents, can apply for parenting rights if the circumstances are suitable?"

"Is that a threat?" She sat up straighter.

Her courage made him want to tumble her into his arms. "That's what you're really afraid of. You'll grant access, you'll share, but you want custody." He walked towards her.

"She's my child," she said fiercely. A lioness defending her cub. Bron had defended him with equal passion when Jake had lost his mother.

"Unfortunately, if push comes to shove, a court will consider financial security, emotional security, relationship to Tessa, capacity to nurture and support a child as young as Tessa and Chrissy's stated wishes, however crudely worded."

"I can provide all of that. And there are witnesses to her pleas over months that I take care of Tessa."

"I'm not disagreeing with you, Eleanor." He gripped the

arms of her chair, crouching in front of her. "Have you started proceedings?"

* * *

"Tony's preparing the brief." Ella forced herself to exhale slowly, forced herself to let go of the fear in short puffs until her lungs were empty. She was fighting the fear the best way she knew how. "I've commenced formal proceedings for legal custody—parenting rights."

Seeking formal custody of Tessa before her sister's death had never been on the table. A brutal slap in the face to her sister, who'd concentrated all her love and what little energy she'd had on Tessa. But the conversations they'd had and the life Ella and Chrissy had built with Tessa were designed for Ella to step into the role of surrogate mother. Until Taylor's letter, she'd have sworn Chrissy had no other intention.

One paragraph from Chrissy's letter to Jake made Ella's blood run cold.

If you'd done the right thing, everything would have been different. It's your fault. You owe me. You can fix it by making sure Tessa takes her rightful place as a Browning, lives with the Brownings and gets her share of the money.

"This hurts you, but it has to be faced." He rose to his feet, his expression grim. "She put Tessa up for sale."

"Not for sale." Ella stumbled on the words, but she needed him to understand. "She panicked. She didn't want me to take Tessa back to live on the farm. The apartment lease was in both our names. We both got the email announcing the rent rise. I floated the idea of the farm as a short-term measure, until I got some money behind me."

Ella stopped, knowing she was babbling, remembering he knew she had no money, Chrissy had no money. "Chrissy's letter is not relevant to what happens now." She spoke with absolute conviction.

"You're not that bloody naïve. It's admissible evidence.

It testifies to the wishes of the mother."

With a queasy feeling in her stomach, Ella's eyes dropped to her hands. She still held Chrissy's letter. She wanted to shred it into tiny pieces, then it wouldn't exist. Except it did. "Have you shown this to anyone?"

"No. Just as I imagine you haven't shown your letter to your parents. Am I right?"

Ella nodded. She'd believed she knew grief, but this was something entirely new. She didn't want to remember Chrissy this way. Wanted to hate Jake for revealing this side of her sister to her. Except if she was honest with herself, Chrissy had always taken the easiest option, wanted what she couldn't have.

"Drew knows there's a letter. It can be subpoenaed." His phone vibrated on the table beside them. He flicked it open and shook his head at the question in her eyes. "Not Bron. Dinner. I'll get it."

* * *

Jake handed the courier a few notes, then carried the bags to the bench. *Hell.* His mind raced as he considered implications. Eleanor was terrified at the prospect of losing Tessa; still, she was considering giving Peter and Bron access. Without bothering to check the order, he organised plates, cutlery and served the food. He crossed back to stand in front of her. "Dinner's on the table, Eleanor."

She lifted her head, her eyes clouded with distress. Sympathy wouldn't help her with this. Taking the letter from her, he dropped it on the table, then handed her the glass of wine. "Drink."

She obeyed, then choked as it hit her throat in a rush.

"A sip, not the whole glass."

"Bully," she said without heat.

He ached to hold her, but she might cry. She'd hate that. "Dinner," he repeated.

"I'm not hungry."

"I don't care if you're hungry. You want to convince a court you can look after Tessa properly, you'll need to demonstrate you can look after yourself first. Starving is not a convincing demonstration of responsibility." A strong breeze would blow her over.

"You're a cold bastard."

"Remember that." He liked it better when she fought him, and if annoyance at him made her eat, that was better yet.

"Except we both know you're not,'" she murmured.

Jake crossed to the table and sat down. She followed to sit opposite and seized her fork, eating half of her pasta before stopping.

"Any good?" he asked.

Her face lifted, and their eyes met before she dropped hers to the food. "I didn't notice."

"I'm glad I didn't take you to a hatted restaurant like Quay." He tried to tease.

"You knew what your letter said."

"But I had no idea what she said to you." He held up a hand when she started to protest. "I didn't need Murphy to tell me she was thoughtless. Although he filled in some gaps. She was nineteen when she came to town, looking for fun, a party girl, irresponsible and carefree."

"Murphy never knew her. She didn't want to miss out on anything. She just wanted to live."

"Did she ever consider an abortion?" The Chrissy he'd known ran from responsibility, so he risked the brutal questions. "Because she was alone? Because she was dying?"

"Chrissy said she wanted the baby." Eleanor's voice was a whisper. "But thinking back, she also wanted the link to Drew—the possibility of reconnecting in some way."

"You didn't let her down," Jake wanted to banish the regret shimmering in her glorious green eyes. Failure was a demon he'd battled over the years in his relationship with Drew. His cousin and he might have come from different planets, their values were so incompatible even though they'd been raised in the same house. A bit like Eleanor and Chrissy.

"Are you trying to make me feel better, Counsellor?"

"I met her. She was pretty and immature, like a butterfly landing in one place for mere seconds. She never deliberately intended to hurt anyone. What I'm trying to say is that in some twisted, impulsive way, maybe she convinced herself she was being unselfish. Providing for Tessa and making your life easier."

"Do you really believe that?" She was desperate for reassurance.

"I remember the last time I saw Chrissy. She was stunned by Drew's desertion. Inconsolable. If she knew she was pregnant, it goes a long way towards explaining her behaviour."

"You're tougher to fight when you're being understanding." She sighed.

"An enemy should never be predictable."

"Are you my enemy?" She wound some pasta on her fork.

"I'll fight you if I have to." His aunt and uncle came first, but increasingly Jake's desire was to make love not war with her. Her prickliness hid a brave and loyal heart. "Are you going to eat any more?"

"I don't think so." She flopped back in her chair.

"Then let's sit more comfortably while we sort this out."

"I'll put this away first."

"Let me help?" He waited for her reaction. Would she remember his earlier accusation that she didn't accept help often enough, and let him help with this insignificant task?

"Thanks." She pushed lids on containers and passed them to him, while he stood in front of the open fridge. "That's the last."

He picked up the bottle, his glass and settled in the armchair she'd taken earlier.

* * *

Ella met his innocent look as she stepped past him to sit on the sofa. She placed her drink on the table, certain he'd engineered this arrangement for a reason. "What's the next step?"

He moved from the armchair to sit beside her.

"You did that deliberately."

"Uh-huh. A necessary ruse if I want to sit beside you. And that's necessary, if we're to consider this fairly." He set the two letters out side by side on the table in front of them. "How about we pay some child support. You've already decided to grant Bron's wish and go and stay with them."

"I understand Peter's need to offer, but linking access to Tessa to money makes me physically ill." Her hands curled into fists, and he covered one with his own.

"Tessa's entitled to child support," he repeated.

She forced her hands to unclench, knowing her reaction wasn't logical. "I tell that to non-paying fathers all the time." Instead of releasing Ella's hand, he linked his fingers with hers. "I've decided to go and stay with them. But I won't accept child support just yet."

"'Just yet'?"

"Let's discuss it after we get the DNA results."

"Would that be before or after you get evicted?" he asked conversationally. "Your bank account is running on empty because you've had a lot of bills over recent months. Tessa at childcare, Chrissy's medical expenses and then the funeral. Now you've got a rent increase, a single income without even the small pension Chrissy would have attracted."

"I can manage." She wasn't stupid or irresponsible, and she would manage. Tessa would not go without.

"I'm beginning to think you may be the closest person to Superwoman I've met, Eleanor Jane, but failure isn't your biggest challenge. Learning to accept help as well as offer it seems to stick in your craw." He released her hand to sit back against the sofa.

"Like you."

He grinned, acknowledging the point. "I accept help when I need it."

"Is that often?" She wondered if he'd ever let himself be vulnerable enough to admit he needed help.

"Often enough. Remember our common ground, Tony Baldwin?"

"He said he'd trust you with his life." That assurance had given Ella pause, but it had also been one of the reasons she'd continued negotiating with him in the absence of Drew and a DNA result.

"It's mutual. We have a history, and I've accepted help from him."

"I'm accepting help from Tony." That was truthful, although she'd refused to let him provide his services for free. Like her, he had a young family to support.

"Have you told him everything?"

"Everything he needs to know," she said.

"He's the best judge of what he needs to know." He inclined his head when she remained silent. "Trust takes time?"

Ella picked up her wine glass, ridiculously bereft now that he'd released her hand, and took a steadying sip. "I trust Tony. I'm inclined to accept people as honest until they shaft me. You're the one who needs time and lots of proof." She studied him for a moment. "Do you take anyone on trust at first sight, go with an impulse, an instinct?"

"Not anymore."

"That explains Murphy and keeping your relationship with the Brownings secret. Apart from the unscrupulous former partner, is there another reason you're not prepared to trust?" she asked. He didn't answer, and his reluctance to confide in her settled like a weight on her heart. "Not telling?"

"You're saying you make impulsive decisions to trust?" He stared into his wine glass.

"After the debacle with Smithhouse, debates about trust,

gullibility and the impact of the choices we made dominated family meals." Loud, messy arguments and Chrissy had hated them.

"Yet you didn't tell your parents my name?" His question was tentative, but for her trust was like thread woven into the fabric of shared lives.

"My father and I decided we'd rather make another mistake in judgement on a business deal than confront everyone we meet with suspicion. Grace is our next-generation farmer, so she's more cautious, especially if anyone starts sniffing around the farm. But it's more a case of feeding my family manageable chunks of information at a time." She was far less trusting with her heart, but that wasn't relevant to this conversation.

He toasted her again with the wine. "So you trust me."

She could offer reassurance, if that's what he needed before he'd take a risk. "Despite our rocky start, I do. After several meetings, we have some history, we have Tony as common ground, and small children and animals like you." She chuckled. "You can't be all bad."

"Animals?"

"Tootles gave you quite a rap."

"Tessa's bear." He didn't disappoint her by asking who Tootles was. He paid attention to the details that mattered, to a two-year-old, to the two-year-old's surrogate mother. "Everyone likes you."

Something in his tone alerted her. "Snooping again, Counsellor?"

He shrugged. "A lot of people speak highly of you. Why should that upset you?"

"It doesn't."

"Robert Hall says you're one in a million."

A sip of wine hit the back of her throat, and she coughed. Ella knew where he was heading now. "Will I ever be able to go home again? Or will everyone know a private investigator is dissecting my life as if I'm a rat on a lab bench?"

CHAPTER SIX

"Not Murphy. I called Hall. Your reaction to my description of my first meeting with Chrissy prompted me to follow up."

"You said she had a boyfriend in tow." Ella remembered his tone more than his words. "I don't recall reacting." He'd implied Chrissy and Robert were convenient partners. Robert forgot to tell Ella she was an inconvenience. "How did you find out his name?"

"I checked with Chrissy's modelling agency from the time. He's the Robert mentioned in her letter to you."

She nodded. "He rang Mum and Dad to say Chrissy was in trouble."

"Not you?"

"I moved to Melbourne for a few years when Chrissy moved to Sydney. Lost contact with most of the old crowd." Ella had needed to hide for a while, find her balance again. Her mother had recovered enough from the tractor accident to resume some of the farm work, but they'd needed money. Money Ella sent from the multiple part-time jobs she'd worked, in law offices, courts, community justice centres and pubs.

"Tell me about him," he coaxed.

"He moved back home." She shrugged. "There's no point not resolving differences in a small town. It just creates more talk."

"And there was enough talk when your boyfriend ran away with your youngest sister?"

She put down the wine and turned to face him.

"Did they talk, Eleanor?" he asked softly.

"For weeks." Going into town to shop had been like running the gauntlet. Whispers and titters from people who should have known better.

"That must have hurt."

"Not as much as discovering I'd been living a lie." She'd been numb until rage had given her the energy to take control of her life.

"Don't you blame Chrissy at all?" he asked curiously.

"Chrissy left me a letter. He didn't." Ella shook her head. "If it hadn't been her, it would have been someone else. We started as friends, moved to being friends with benefits. He was doing me a favour taking me to bed."

"A favour!" It was Jake's turn to choke on his wine.

"An act of kindness." By the time he'd blurted this out, Ella had developed a rhinoceros hide where men were concerned. "After all, EJ's a good mate."

"Is that what he said?" His horror was making her feel better. So, too, was the discovery that when Jake touched her it was like entering another world bounded by the two of them.

"Not at the time, but it was the gist of his let's-let-bygones-be-bygones speech. I was useful in a crisis, but a bit like taking your sister to bed."

"And he lives?" He placed his wine on the table. The clink of glass hitting wood a bass note to his scorn.

"I take my vow of non-violence seriously."

"Not that I noticed."

"Stop grinning. It's ungentlemanly to remind me of losing my temper so badly."

"You didn't lose it. I pushed." As apologies went, his

was perfect.

"Ah, gee, Taylor." She waggled her eyebrows.

"Nobody could be so cack-handed as to utter such drivel after running away with your sister."

"He didn't see Chrissy as a sister," she deadpanned.

"He's a blind idiot." He dismissed the absent country lawyer. "Just to be clear, I don't see you as a sister, a mate or in need of sex as an act of kindness."

Instantly the room was filled with tension. Ella's images of Jake had become more explicit each night, until her dreams had taken on a restless quality. Their explosive kiss in his office this morning had made her fantasies real. Easy to imagine making love with him. Of bringing his body to the point where sinking into her offered exquisite release, the only release. Her feverish imaginings astounded her.

"I'd stop there if I were you, Jake." Her voice sounded scratchy to her own ears. "You're sailing perilously close to a conflict of interest."

"You're not my client." He toppled her into his lap. "And there's no conflict of interest between my clients' interest and my own."

Ella's heart slammed against her ribcage, beating so fast he must have been able to feel it through their clothes. She inhaled his woodsy scent, and settled. "Ah, but I don't think you're supposed to have someone you distrust in your lap." She pushed a hand against his chest to give herself some space. His face was close, his eyes laughing. Concentrating on her as if at this moment she were the only other person in the world.

The only person who mattered.

"Perhaps I'm thinking of trusting you, Eleanor." He had such long lashes. They dropped over his eyes, momentarily hiding the twinkle sparkling there, making her catch her breath.

"Don't break the habits of a lifetime on my account."

His mouth covered hers, warm, smiling—Ella could feel him smiling—before his tongue teased hers. His kiss moved from friendly to passionate, while she raced to catch up.

Her arms crept around his neck, slid up to release the thong restraining his hair. With her hands full of that dark mass, Ella tugged him closer. His arms wrapped around her, binding her to him. Leaning back on the sofa, he cradled her against his chest, kissing her with a thoroughness that left her dizzy.

Finally, her breathing ragged, Ella rested her cheek against his shoulder. "What are we doing?"

"We're consenting adults acting on a mutual attraction. We don't know where it's going, but we're interested to find out." His fingers tangled in her hair.

"That's a complicated parsing of a kiss." She smiled against his throat.

"It was a special kiss." He laughed, and the rumble trembled through her, carrying uncomplicated affection. "I'll drive you to the mountains to see Bron and Peter next weekend?"

"What's changed your mind?"

"Taylor's law—I always try to lose gracefully."

"I need a better reason than that." Slipping off his lap onto the sofa beside him, Ella reached for her glass to give her something to do with her hands. If she touched him again, she doubted she'd have the fortitude to turn him loose.

"You offered access, no strings attached." In six little words he offered her the trust he guarded so tightly.

"I'm not going to get evicted." She hesitated. One confidence deserved another. "My parents are lending me some money for a few months."

"You would have offered access anyway. And if you accept money from your parents, why won't you accept a small, regular contribution from the Brownings? Think about that."

"I am." Her response was irrational, but with so much unresolved and the bitter taste of Chrissy's demands for money still in her mouth, she didn't want money clouding these first meetings between Tessa and the Brownings.

"Your father's deal with Smithhouse was based on a handshake. A written contract with the Brownings will give you a greater sense of control." He swallowed his last mouthful of wine and set the glass carefully on the table.

"Where property and assets are concerned, I'd never act again without a contract. This is about family and love. My family doesn't see relationships as financial transactions," she stressed.

"I'll pick you and Tessa up on Saturday morning."

"That's not necessary." *But lovely on so many levels.*

He touched a finger to her lips. "I'm going up anyway. Think of the planet. We don't need two cars on the road."

"No, we don't," she whispered, closing the door behind him.

Crazy to dream. He was Jacob Taylor, CEO of one of the biggest law firms in Sydney, devoted nephew and incredibly sexy man. He accepted responsibility for his company's past record and had offered to pay restitution to her family. He also kept secrets, made beautiful apologies and wasn't looking for a relationship with his first cousin's once removed aunt.

Whereas she, Eleanor Jane Anderson, was a single mother by choice, practical and responsible. Tessa's needs came first. And she had a monumental problem. His touch ignited a flashfire within her. His kisses made her heart tremble, and she liked him too much for comfort.

"Damn the man!" Ella swallowed the curse while waiting for Jake to arrive on Friday morning. She hadn't seen him since the night they'd read Chrissy's letters together, but that didn't mean his face didn't swim into clear focus whenever she shut her eyes. They'd moved from animosity to an unarmed truce spiced with simmering attraction with a speed that had her on tenterhooks.

She'd started to look forward to his daily calls.

Innocuous calls where he checked on how she and Tessa were doing, renegotiated pick-up times, and talked her into extending a two-day visit into a three-day long weekend leaving on Friday. Innocent yet intimate.

His name at the top of the daily news bulletin explained why he didn't drop by. A major case involving a public-private transport contract, where taxpayer funds needed to be salvaged. Given the intensity of negotiations and the non-stop media coverage, Ella was half expecting a call to postpone the weekend. She jumped like a startled bird at the knock on the door.

"Car!" Tessa clapped her hands. Lifting her from her playpen, Ella placed her on her feet and let her walk to the door.

A casually dressed Jake Taylor made her mouth water. Worn black jeans moulded to long legs, an open-necked teal shirt, and a lived-in leather jacket. He still oozed charisma, but it reeked of get-down-and-dirty charm rather than the remoteness of the boardroom. A little burst of lust exploded in her lower belly. The stubble from a day's growth of beard combined with his unconventional ponytail were a sexy provocation. Meeting his crooked grin, Ella discovered she'd missed his smile. In some indefinable way, it reassured her, as if the world had been tipped off its axis and now had righted itself.

"Hello, Eleanor."

"Hello, Jake."

He squatted on his haunches to bring him closer to Tessa's height and reached out his arms. "Hello, Tessa."

"Car." Tessa stepped into his arms to be raised to shoulder height.

His fluid movement brought him close enough for Ella to see the tiny laugh lines at the corner of his eyes. His irises were gold-flecked. This close his eyes were the colour of a midsummer storm cloud, requiring a new shade on the colour palette—tempestuous passion.

He leaned forward to meet Ella's mouth. A swift,

delicious statement of intent. Then nuzzled Tessa's neck, making her giggle. One action following the other, as if they were the most natural in the world. "Miss me?"

"Have you been away?" she asked, not ready to confess to something she'd just discovered and wasn't sure how to handle. "Did you have a tough week?"

"Satisfying," he admitted. "A big contract. A government client. A mutually successful outcome."

"Congratulations. Taylor Law must do good work to pick up government contracts." Her version of an apology, and recognition he'd sweated blood to rebuild his company's good name.

"A compliment from an Anderson! A prize beyond price," he teased. "We're not where I want to be yet. But, yeah, Taylor Law is regaining its reputation for ethical practice."

The contract hadn't featured in any of their phone calls. Professional confidentiality, or, as she was beginning to suspect, an innate discretion, practised in his private as well as his professional life. He was as circumspect about family business as he was about his work. An enigma. Dignified, serious, discreet, but his pirate's grin fascinated her, and his ponytail incited a recklessness alien to her character. His contradictions were dangerously addictive to someone who'd accepted respectable responsibility as her allotted role in life.

"Why the ponytail and earring?" She hadn't intended to ask.

"Why do you ask?" His words emerged as a husky caress.

Ella wanted to stroke back, aware all the time of the air crackling between them, of the unspoken passion drawing them closer to each other, as if they were in the grip of some powerful force field. "The unorthodox style threw me that first day," she admitted. "I instantly dismissed you as the corporate lawyer."

"There's your answer. Or part of it." He set Tessa on her feet. "Family tradition. My father had both. A reminder not to judge people on their appearance."

"Does it work?"

"I try to look past the superficial to get to the truth." He shrugged. "But, like most people, I'm a work in progress. Are you ready?"

Ella gestured to two bags and the collapsed stroller in the corner. "I've packed on the assumption this is an informal family gathering."

He took her explanation as permission to run his eyes over her in open appraisal. Old blue jeans, white at the seams, black R. M. Williams boots that she'd had forever, topped by the emerald sweater Ella had worn the other night. Her wardrobe contained few choices, fewer since she'd lost weight. She'd pushed her shoulder-length bob back with combs and applied light makeup. Her usual outfit for a visit to her local country town, so she figured it would suit a visit to Leura, in the mountains west of Sydney.

"My legs won't give you much more than superficial information, Counsellor." His lingering study made her itchy.

"It's the boots. Sturdy, no-nonsense, but perfectly fit for purpose. They tell me I don't have to ask if you've packed coats, hats and gloves for both of you."

"I'm the sensible sister. Remember," she said. His matter-of-fact assessment didn't sound like a compliment. "Your average plain Jane, not very exciting, but reliable in a crisis."

He ran a finger down her nose, his intriguing eyes twinkling at her. "We agreed the other night Robert Hall is an idiot."

"Did we?" Knowing her family and colleagues depended on her good sense and ability to navigate difficult situations was a source of pride. That didn't mean Ella didn't hanker for a man, just once, to lose his head over her.

"Fishing for compliments?" His smile was a compliment all by itself.

"Not at all." But she'd treasure his.

"Sensible is sublime. And an underrated quality. I'll grab the gear while you bring Tessa." He hoisted the bags and stroller as if they were weightless and headed out.

After locking the apartment, she hurried after him, slowing as she neared his vehicle. The Jaguar was an unqualified statement of sophisticated power. *Why did that elicit a tickle of anticipation?* Her usual caution with powerful men went AWOL around him. But she hadn't wasted the hour Tony Baldwin had given her to go over her case. He'd contact Drew formally within a fortnight. Pending the outcome of the DNA testing—with or without Drew— Ella's next step was offering generous access rights to Drew and his parents, and she'd adopt Tessa.

"Jake, wait, we'll need Tessa's car seat from my car." She turned towards the car park at the side of the building.

He straightened from the open boot. "No need. I borrowed one from Tony."

He'd done it again. A random act of kindness? Or practical evidence he did consider the needs of others? He scared her to her bootstraps, because she found it impossible to think around his spontaneous acts of thoughtfulness—toasted sandwiches, takeaway dinners, sending flowers and chocolates to Mr. and Mrs. P as a welcome home from the hospital. Defensive actions like flight or fight refused to kick into gear.

"Thank you. Most people without children don't think of them." Ella walked towards him, knowing she smiled like a loon, but she couldn't help it. He disarmed her, stroked all her defensive plumage into place.

* * *

Jake's world shifted when she smiled, when she reversed direction and came towards him. He hadn't known he'd been waiting all week to see her face light up with joy, to see her. The tension from the long workdays slipped from his shoulders. "Tony Baldwin's the kind of mate who insists his friends share some of the joys of parenthood."

"His twins have changed his outlook on life," she said.

Attraction had been immediate. Unwelcome and inconvenient, making Jake want to abandon his suspicions within minutes of meeting her. Discovering she was grounded, balanced, and unselfish drew him closer, simple qualities he'd found to be rare. The situation had dictated their encounters so far. They didn't have the luxury of exploring each other slowly, getting to know each other gradually. Dining, dating, the slow dance that would end in making love.

His desire to touch her all the time made a nonsense of going slowly.

His mother had been his first love. He'd adored her. Bron had been his second, glamourous and generous. Peter's career as CEO of Ritzzauto, a German-made automotive paint supplier, had required extensive travel and entertaining. Bron and Drew had often accompanied him. With Jake's arrival, Bron stayed home more. On trips where she was needed to organise partner events, he and Drew remained behind.

Jake had been a bit of a knight errant in his twenties, thinking he could rescue women from Drew's lack of commitment. He'd discovered most women preferred the high-living, loose-with-the-truth rake Drew to Jake's serious plans to make something of the family law firm. When Drew seduced Julia with lies that could easily be checked, Jake recalled a conversation he'd overheard before his parents had taken their fatal flight. A whisper of infidelity, a threat of separation. The confusion he'd buried resurfaced at his own betrayal, making him withdraw further. He dated occasionally these days, ended up in a friendly bed even less frequently, and worked his butt off to re-establish Taylor Law's reputation.

Jake opened his arms automatically as Tessa threw herself at him. "I'll strap her in."

When he slid into the driver's seat, Eleanor was buckled

in beside him. He started the engine, adjusted temperature controls, then selected a playlist.

"That's one of Tessa's favourites." She beamed.

"I spotted it in your collection and guessed it wasn't for you." Jake checked the rear mirror to reassure himself Tessa was secure before pulling into the stream of traffic.

"That's thoughtful."

"I can be, but hopefully this comforts her, and we can talk," he said.

Eleanor threatened his hard-learned caution. When she frowned, as if she was thinking hard about something or someone else, he found himself wanting to draw her attention back to him. Getting close enough to catch her scent made him itch to possess her. At full wattage, without the defensiveness or wariness that had clouded their early meetings, her smile could make him beg. For a split second, on this chilly Friday morning parked on a suburban street, he basked in the generous warmth of her pleasure.

"Thoughtful just took a nosedive to ominous." She twisted in her seat to face him.

"What's worrying you?"

"What makes you think I'm worried?" she asked carefully.

"The tiny frown between your eyes, the hint of trouble on your face when you opened the door, which you tried to hide with a smile." He reached out to cover her tightly clasped hands with one of his. "And this. Have you changed your mind?"

"Not about giving Peter and Bronwyn the chance to spend time with Tessa."

"Then what?" When had easing her worries become important to him?

"We can't go on indefinitely like this." She hesitated. "We need to reach a settlement with Drew. Sooner rather than later."

"I agree. So does Peter. He's grateful for your generosity to Bron. He said he'd call Drew again. I'm not sure what he planned to say, but he implied it included an ultimatum of sorts."

Peter rarely commented on his son's relationships, but discovering Tessa's existence and learning about Chrissy's struggles had Peter seeking answers. He hadn't yet asked Jake outright when Drew had ended his relationship with Chrissy and started dating Julia, but it couldn't be far off.

"Are Drew and his parents close?" She'd moved past her initial shock to asking difficult questions.

"What makes you ask?" Jake took the entry ramp to the expressway, keeping his voice non-committal. Answering a question with a question was the sort of cheap gameplaying she didn't deserve, but he didn't feel qualified to comment on the Browning family dynamics.

"I'm not sure. Something doesn't feel right." She was asking for answers he'd never given anyone.

"They miss him, and his career has kept him in London for the last two and a half years." Jake gave her the barest outline.

"When did Bronwyn get her diagnosis?"

"Does your brain ever stop working?" Jake glanced sideways. Her instincts were razor-sharp, especially when it came to protecting Tessa. Chrissy and Murphy had both put in writing that she'd given up two years of her life to nurse her sister. Drew's callousness towards Bron would puzzle her.

"About as often as yours, I imagine."

He could tell she wasn't buying his evasiveness. "She was diagnosed about six years ago, but she's had some serious setbacks since he's been away. She hasn't pushed, and he hasn't offered to visit. He's as self-centred as Chrissy was, but his actions are more premeditated than hers were." It was the closest Jake had come to warning a woman about Drew in years. Eleanor roused protective instincts grown rusty from misuse.

"Is he still with the woman he left Chrissy for?" She tucked one leg under the other, getting comfortable.

"They broke up within six months." He kept his voice emotionless. Drew hadn't wanted Julia. Seducing her hadn't been Drew's only attempt to punish Jake for taking some of his parents' attention away from him, but it had been the last.

"Did she return to Australia?"

"What's going on in that brain of yours now?" Julia was back in Australia. Jake had crossed her path at parties and work functions. Julia's brother remained a friend, so contact was inevitable, but he'd limited it to meaningless social chitchat—enough contact not to raise uncomfortable questions for either of them or to come to Bron's ears.

"She might know if Chrissy contacted Drew, if she told him she was pregnant." She was turning her attention to what Drew was doing when Chrissy fell pregnant, and her caution was a good thing. "Do you know her?"

"She's not in my circle." Not a lie. Not the truth either. Eleanor was right. He was slow to trust, and demanded proof of loyalty. Although he hadn't fully understood he feared being rejected again until confronted by Eleanor's openness. Her bad experience with Taylor Law hadn't shaken her essential trust in people. Years of Drew baiting him, undermining him had bred a hard cynicism into him. "Drew's denied knowing about the pregnancy."

"I can't help wondering how much he knew." She wrinkled her nose. "I can believe Chrissy didn't tell him after the cancer diagnosis. But I can't see why she'd keep quiet before then."

"I'll keep contacting the woman Drew dated after Chrissy in reserve." *Would he ever be able to have a conversation with Eleanor without Drew intruding?* "What did your parents say about this visit?" Jake commenced the climb out of the Sydney basin to the mountains.

"They supported it, but like me, they think we need more certainty, and soon." She unwound her leg and faced the front.

"You still haven't shown them the letter?" he asked.

"They don't need to see it. They weren't blind where she was concerned, but they're still reeling from her death." She led with her chin.

"And you're not?"

Her profile was grim. "A good reason to keep it from them. I know how it feels."

"You stagger me, Eleanor." Her alarm when she'd read Chrissy's letter to him had been unmistakable, yet she hadn't backed away from this visit. "Your capacity to absorb hurt and not use it to lash out or blame others."

"I'm no saint. I am so angry with her it hurts, but blaming others for what's happening doesn't solve problems." She placed her hands flat on her thighs before she spoke. "Blaming Chrissy is pointless; a) she's not here, and b) the quantity of meds she was on in those last weeks compromised her ability to think clearly. Before that, she regularly begged me to look after Tessa when she died."

"Do you have witnesses to any of those conversations?" He'd stayed away from her custody case until now.

"Yes. And Tony's already collecting affidavits. But I need to find a solution that works for all of us." She scrunched up her face considering the ticklish issue; a lot of people were depending on her problem-solving skills.

"A just outcome." Her essential honesty tripped Jake up. Lust was tangled with admiration.

"There's no need to mock. Tony wants to contact Drew and get a written statement from him."

"I'm not mocking you. Justice is more than a word to you. You're willing to include Tessa's paternal family in her upbringing, even though you'd never heard of us until a few weeks ago. That's more than generous. Whereas Drew's procrastination is bloody unfair." He let his anger show through.

Recognising Peter's number on his phone, Jake answered through the car system. "We're less than an hour away, Peter."

"Drew's here. He arrived about thirty minutes ago."

"I've got you on speakerphone, Peter. Did you know Drew was coming?" Jake already knew the answer: a typical Drew ambush. Peter was letting him know as soon as he could, but Eleanor had stiffened beside him, her body hunched forward.

"I spoke to him Tuesday night, told him what we'd agreed, what we were doing. Told him I expected him to take the DNA test. There or here, it didn't matter. He said he'd get back to me." Peter hesitated. "His arrival is his way of getting back to me." Peter didn't sound thrilled with the development.

"Thanks for letting us know." Jake ended the call. Peter wouldn't tell him what inducements or threats he'd offered his son. But Drew was here because he'd somehow worked out how to use this new arrangement to his benefit. Jake pulled into a layby. He swivelled to face her. "Your choice. Do we continue or turn back?"

She steepled her hands over her mouth, her eyes on the blue distant hills. The silence in the car allowed him to hear her short, shallow breaths. His family and Chrissy were making a habit of springing nasty surprises on her.

"Tony was prepared to give Drew another fortnight," she said.

"What if he still refuses to have the test?" Although his return convinced Jake he'd accepted he was Tessa's father.

"I'm banking on having the test is the reason he came home." She was judging Drew by her rules.

"Next question—what about his custody rights?" Jake had contingency plans to minimise his interaction with his cousin. Drew's presence in the mountains sabotaged one of those plans: Jake's claim to barely knowing Eleanor.

"Custody of a two-year-old is full-on. He wasn't in love with Chrissy when Tessa was born. He doesn't know Tessa." Her voice trembled. "I'm hoping he'll want to get to know her, but also hoping he'll agree to her living with me. After Chrissy's cancer diagnosis, she didn't try to contact Drew. Then she wrote two off-the-wall letters contradicting everything we planned. That's my lived experience." She paused, and when she continued, her voice rang with conviction. "I don't want to deny Drew or your family access to Tessa or a major role in her life and upbringing, but I believe I'm the best primary caregiver. She knows me; she's happy with me."

Jake couldn't envisage a scenario where Drew would seek full responsibility for a two-year-old, but his cousin was unpredictable. There was no point in taking unnecessary risks. "Call Tony. Tell him Drew's here."

She stared at him blankly. Her slow reaction worried him. "Eleanor?"

"Why?"

"To get his advice on whether you should go ahead with the visit." He covered one of her hands with his. It was icy. "To tell him to keep preparing your case."

"He's preparing the case." She huffed out a breath and summoned a small smile. "Drew's the missing piece of the puzzle. I'm assuming I'm not entering hostile territory."

He couldn't answer that. Yet.

"Turning back now would break Bronwyn and Peter's hearts," she added.

Jake wanted to howl at the moon. Eleanor needed protecting from herself. The children's music tape ended. He checked the rear-view, and saw Tessa was asleep, Tootles locked to her chest with a small arm. He selected a different piece for the final leg of the journey. A symphony by Mozart, something to soothe the savage beast. Drew's unexpected move made him feel savage.

He doubted Drew had come home to resolve Tessa's parentage. He'd spoken to his cousin more often than Peter in recent weeks, and Drew's mood hadn't been cooperative. He'd moved from dismissive to truculent, ending with his old accusation that Jake had shared a bedroom with Chrissy, and why didn't he have a DNA test.

Drew's arrival signified game on, and Drew planned to be a player.

Under the influence of the purr of the motor and the soothing music, Eleanor's eyelids drifted shut. He slowed his speed and exited the expressway, taking the long way to his uncle's mountain home.

* * *

"We're here." His soft whisper matched her dream.

Ella blinked sleepily to find Jake leaning across her to undo her seat belt. Unconsciously her hand reached up to encircle his neck and draw him closer.

"Careful, Ellie. We're about to have witnesses," he growled.

"What?" His use of Tessa's name for her ensnared her.

"You've been asleep. I wish I could have joined you." His lips brushed behind her ear too briefly to feel real. "Too many sleepless nights lately with you as the cause."

Struggling into an upright position, she pulled her jumper back across her midriff. With him so close, his tangy scent surrounded her, the leather thong restraining his hair was within reach. She closed her eyes on temptation, groaning with the effort of keeping her hands off him.

"Dreaming?" He slipped his hand under her knee, massaging gently, exciting rather than reassuring her. "Or is fantasising a better word?"

Hearing Peter's voice, her eyes snapped open. Jake's face was mere inches from her breasts. If he leaned any further forward, he could nuzzle at her cleavage. Then he was gone.

Peter started down the steps as Jake opened the driver's door. Ella steadied herself, before pushing open her door and moving to the back one, astonished she'd fallen asleep. Her head had been filled with questions about Drew and his motives, about the need to confirm her custody of Tessa yet Mozart, the warmth, the smooth motion of the car and the fugitive conviction Jake had her safe had lulled her to sleep.

"Tessa, we're here." She lifted a drowsy toddler into her arms and turned to face the house. Stone, broad-beamed timber and slate were her first impressions. Well-kept, nestled amongst trees. Welcoming.

"Hello, Ella. Tessa." Peter brushed a hand over Tessa's cheek. "Sorry we couldn't give you more warning about the surprise guest."

"Hi, Peter. It will be good to meet Drew." She said the words to remove the frown from his forehead. A white lie to cover the butterflies residing in her stomach.

The front windows were leadlight, and when she followed Peter up the steps, the front door carried the same old-fashioned glass. The foyer was broad, with polished timber floors and stairs rising to a second level. More wood, cream tones and paintings everywhere.

Peter didn't pause but turned to the left—a comfortable living area. Sofas and armchairs arranged around a fireplace lit in welcome, with one wall lined with books. Bronwyn was seated on a sofa near the fireplace, her eyes fixed on the doorway. Her face lit up as they entered.

"You've arrived at last." Bronwyn patted the seat beside her.

"Hello, Bronwyn, there was a bit of traffic," Ella apologised, although she had no idea if there'd been traffic. She crossed to sit beside the older woman, settling Tessa between them and automatically reaching into her shoulder bag for Tootles.

A movement at the side of the room drew her attention. A man stood to one side of the French windows. He'd been hidden by the fall of the heavy drapes, watching her before she'd been aware of his presence.

"I'm Drew Browning, Ella. May I call you Ella?" The tall, slender man stretched out a hand.

"Of course. Hello, Drew." She stood to shake his hand, wary when he kept hold of it.

"I've been keen to meet you." His smile was bashful, as if feeling his way, but his eyes were watchful, assessing her, and flicking over Jake before settling on Tessa. She reflected on his choice of words. Not keen enough to come home in response to Jake's first request.

"The family resemblance is amazing. She could be you, coz, at the same age." Drew's glance towards Jake, who'd halted with the bags in the doorway, was mocking. "But Chrissy said she's mine."

"Welcome home, Drew.'" Jake nodded at his cousin and abandoned the bags, crossing to kiss his aunt on the cheek. "Hi, Bron. Sorry we're late."

"You're not late. I'm impatient." She smiled. "Would you like a drink before lunch?"

"Maybe a chance to freshen up first. Eleanor said Tessa needed the bathroom before we pulled up." More thoughtfulness on Jake's part, or a ruse to get her out of the room?

"If it's not too much trouble. Tessa." Ella scooped the child into one arm, hauling her bag onto her other shoulder. "We'll leave Tootles to keep you company until we come back."

"I've given Ella and Tessa the cream room, Jake," Bronwyn issued instructions. "There's a cot already there."

Jake led the way upstairs. The worn jeans and soft leather hugged his masculine form, broad shoulders, narrow waist, flaring out to tight gluteus maximus muscles, which right this minute were at Ella's eye level. Reach-out-and-pat level.

He could distract her, even when her mind was filing images of Drew for later consideration. Lost in daydreams, she cannoned into his back when he stopped outside a door.

"Are you able to get that, please?" He nodded at the door handle. "My hands are full."

"Sorry." Ella's palm burned where she'd accidentally touched him. Stepping around him, she turned the handle and preceded him into the room. Large bay windows took up most of the opposite wall, while dull-gold damask drapes were drawn back to reveal extensive gardens stretching to a wide rock wall and beyond that, the great Australian bush. Warm cream walls with fittings and furnishings to harmonize. Money, class and care. The care soothed her unease at Drew's presence. Unease, and if she was honest, a little resentment at his gate-crashing the weekend.

"The bathroom's through here." Jake dumped the bags on a stand and headed towards the ensuite.

Scampering after him, Ella protested, "Wait a minute. I want to talk to you."

He took Tessa from her, set her on her feet, pulled down her trousers and lifted her onto the toilet to hold her in position. "First things first."

She hunkered down beside him and waited for Tessa to finish. "Aren't you a clever girl?" She kissed the top of Tessa's head. "Another skill you picked up from the Baldwins?"

"A few of my friends have kids."

"Apart from that. Why did you give me the bum's rush to get up here?" Although sharing the intimate chore made her heart ache.

"Five minutes ago you were asleep, Tessa was asleep. You're suddenly introduced to Drew. This gives you a few minutes to adjust." He hauled up Tessa's pants, sat her on the edge of the sink and washed her hands before carrying her into the bedroom and setting her down on the floor beside the bed.

"That's considerate of you." Ella studied the squared shoulders, the hint of tension in his upright frame.

He crossed to the window and looked across the valley. "Are you okay?"

"Is there any reason I shouldn't be?" He remained silent so long she gave up on getting an answer. "Look at it from his perspective. A few weeks ago he had no knowledge of Tessa's existence. Chrissy wrote to you, not him. He's come home. If he's a bit prickly, he's entitled."

Another long silence, then he turned to face her, his expression shuttered. "You're right. And without him, we can't resolve this. If you need my help with anything, ask." He crossed to stand in front of her. "As I'm representing Peter and Bron's interests, I'd like to be present for any conversation about Tessa's future." His retreat into lawyerly mode struck a discordant note.

"That's not going to work." Her skin prickled. "And I don't like the implication, Counsellor. That their interests and Drew's might be different."

"Drew hasn't confided in me." His voice dripped ice.

"Now you're scaring me." Her kissing companion was gone. "I don't play games, especially with people's lives."

"I believe you, Eleanor Jane Anderson." He leaned forward until his forehead rested against hers. "And it's messing with my head."

"He's shown up," she reasoned with him. "That means he's considering the possibility he's Tessa's father. The Pandora's box Chrissy handed us is well and truly open."

"In mythology when the box was opened, all the evils flew out." He stepped back. "I'm not being pessimistic, just agreeing we can't foresee all the consequences."

"His wishes are central to a negotiated settlement." Until now she'd thought Jake had agreed with her. "Stop looming over me."

"Looming?"

The mood shifted, the static around discussing Drew replaced by the electricity constantly bouncing between them. He stepped forward. She stepped back. The mattress caught the back of her knees, and Ella tumbled onto the bed.

"Get out of my way."

He stretched full length beside her, not touching her except with his gaze. "I'm not in your way, Eleanor."

But he was. He filled her mind even when he wasn't present.

Placing a finger on her lips, he silenced her. "You demand the right to defend Tessa. It's only fair I have equal rights to defend my own."

He undermined Ella's resistance at every turn. She considered what she'd learned about him, from his interactions with Tony, Mrs. P, his aunt and uncle, Merle, even Tessa. He was a gentle man. Envy that she didn't fall into the circle of people deserving his protection was unexpected and unwelcome.

Cupping her jaw, he looked into her eyes, and Ella was lost in the promise lurking in his. He lavished love on his second parents but walked alone. Why?

When he kissed her, her vision blurred. She floated untethered and reached for him to ground her. In response, he deepened the kiss, his tongue teasing at the edge of her mouth until she opened it and her arms to him. He tasted of restrained desire, and she moaned, inviting more. His hands danced down her arms, before he slid one under her jumper to trace the softer skin of her midriff. She trembled, her skin heating beneath his splayed fingers. Time simply stopped when his hand inched higher, covering her cotton-covered breast. He squeezed gently, his touch sure yet reverent, and her nipple peaked.

"More," she begged, before he gathered her closer, rolling over until she lay beneath him, stretched against the lean strength of him, straining to get closer.

"Ellie." A small hand pulled her hair, bringing her back to reality with a thud.

He lifted his head.

"You make me forget where we are," she murmured.

"In bed, where we want to be."

She respected his honesty, but the events of the last half-hour made her hesitate to admit she wanted the same thing. "They're holding lunch for us."

"We'd better eat, then." He rolled away from her.

Ella sat up, her hands tugging her jumper down, then finger-combing her hair.

"No one will guess I pounced on you."

"We pounced on each other." She demanded equal billing.

"You're irresistible, you know." His carefree grin boosted her confidence. "The way you take responsibility for your own actions."

"If I don't, no one else will."

He'd been tickling Tessa, and at these words, plopped the child on his shoulders and headed for the door. Ella made to pass him. "Be careful."

Her pulse spiked, sensing the words were dragged from him. A warning? She hadn't warmed to Drew in the few minutes she'd spent with him. Maybe because she'd expected him to be like Jake. He hadn't been interested in Tessa, not really. His eyes had darted everywhere as he spoke, gauging the reactions of his parents, of Jake. Observing, rather than being part of the action. Emotionally detached, yet deeply interested.

To be aroused by Jake, then have him withdraw left a vague disquiet. He'd won her initial cooperation through their common link to Tony Baldwin. A link based on their trust of and respect for her absent lawyer. Tony would warn her if there were pitfalls to watch out for with Drew. The few comments Jake had made about his cousin were like pulling teeth, "*Self-centred, like Chrissy… actions more pre-meditated.*" Nothing especially ominous.

His reticence about family, his training in the law explained his insistence on need-to-know information, compartmentalising facts so they didn't taint a newcomer's perspective. All part of ensuring justice was not only done, but seen to be done. But this wasn't some abstract case. Drew's arrival meant he'd be spending time with her niece.

She expected Jake to take sides. Her side.

CHAPTER SEVEN

Walking back into the living room ahead of Jake was like walking into a spider's web. The sudden silence wrapped around Ella with sticky discomfort. Her stomach knotted. A different dread to the morning she'd entered Jake's office. Drew represented a dark shadow where she couldn't find the contours or angles to the threat. Jake didn't break stride, swinging Tessa from his shoulders and plopping her on the sofa beside Bronwyn.

"'Ootles." Tessa giggled, gathering the bear into her arms.

"Is 'Ootles a friend?" asked Bronwyn, laying a hand on the bear's leg.

"'Ootles," repeated Tessa. "Me car." Tessa pointed towards the door.

"Does the room suit you, Ella?" An old-fashioned gentleman, Peter had stood when she'd entered and, when Ella sat beside Tessa, resumed his seat on the other side of the fireplace.

"It's lovely. I could have looked out the windows for hours." Ella passed the cloth bag she'd collected from her suitcase to Bronwyn. "Tessa and I brought you a gift from the farm." Tessa's head swung from her aunt to Bronwyn.

"You didn't need to." Bronwyn peered into the bag. "Cheese."

"Farmhouse cheddar." Ella met Jake's gaze across the room. His raised brow asked the question, *Are you sure you could spare it?* His unspoken communication cut through the tension swirling in the room, making her feel less like she was facing a firing squad. *A firing squad of one*, she reminded herself.

"Chrissy said you liked the country. She hated it." Drew wandered to the sideboard. "Can I get anyone a drink before lunch?"

"White wine would be great." Ella guessed she and Tessa had been the topic of conversation before they'd arrived. She hadn't expected the farm to rate a mention. "You're right. I can't remember a time when Chrissy didn't want to leave the farm."

"Not for me," Jake said, leaving the room. *And abandoning her.*

Drew took centre stage, pouring wine into long-stemmed glasses before handing one to each of his parents and her. Collecting his own, he quickly swallowed a mouthful. Not as elegant as his earlier moves.

"Hearing of Chrissy's death shocked me. I hadn't heard of her on the scene for a while. Assumed she'd stopped working. But dead?" Drew shook his head as if struggling to come to terms with old news.

"It was an aggressive cancer, detected during her pregnancy." Ella's hand tightened on her glass.

Drew waved towards Tessa with his glass. "The child. Is she mine?"

The bluntness of the question coupled with his offhand gesture enraged Ella. She glanced towards Tessa to check she was absorbed introducing Tootles to her grandmother. "Chrissy said so."

Drew downed the rest of his wine and returned to the sideboard to refill his glass, leaning back against the graceful walnut antique to survey them. His eyes narrowed to slits as he focused on Bronwyn, then Peter, who smiled benevolently at the picture of his wife and grandchild. The hairs on the back of Ella's neck rose, like tiny antennae, an early warning system. Before Drew, she'd been in no doubt about where the Brownings' or Jake's loyalties lay.

Jake reappeared, carrying a two-handled cup. "Some juice for Tess." He passed the cup to Bronwyn and turned to Ella. "Hannah, Bron's housekeeper, has made macaroni cheese for Tessa's lunch, but is happy to discuss food options if that doesn't suit."

"Macaroni cheese is fine. I'll talk to Hannah after lunch."

"If everyone's ready, she asked if we could move to the dining room." Jake was acting like hired help rather than a member of the family.

"I've been thinking about it." Drew pushed himself off the sideboard. "Chrissy and I broke up in July three years ago. I was moving to London, and she wasn't interested in tagging along."

Making it on the London scene had been one of Chrissy's biggest dreams. She'd never have refused an offer to go there. When Peter frowned at his son, Ella worked out he knew about the new girlfriend who'd gone to the UK with Drew. Now he'd added a pregnant Chrissy to the equation, and holes were appearing in Drew's story.

"I don't know why she didn't tell me. But, hell. I've seen Tessa now. It's true. I'm a father." Drew raised his glass in a toast to himself.

"As simple as that?" Jake asked.

Drew shrugged, his eyes glittering with satisfaction. "Ella believes her sister, so do Mum and Dad."

"You'll have the DNA test?" Jake's demand for a public declaration before witnesses corded tension across Ella's neck and shoulders.

"Is that necessary? The timing's right. You can confirm Chrissy and I were together at the time, can't you, coz?" Drew's dismissal held a barbed undercurrent, not quite disguised by his open smile and friendly manner. And Jake, who was giving her no hint of his thoughts and telling her to be careful, was the recipient of most of the barbs.

Before anyone could answer, a light tap sounded on the door and Hannah entered. "Lunch is served." The sizzle and pop of unspoken antagonisms swirled in the room.

Ella observed the intricacies of the pecking order. Bronwyn took the head of the table with Peter on her right. The highchair was placed on Bronwyn's left. Drew commandeered the other end of the table. Jake accepted the seat next to his uncle, while Ella took the obvious option beside the highchair.

"Asparagus soup." Hannah ladled an aromatic liquid into bowls. "I've cooled a little for Tessa." The housekeeper lifted her chin towards the Royal Doulton Bunnykins bowl she'd placed near the highchair. "Found that at the back of the cupboard."

"I'd forgotten any survived Drew's childhood." Bronwyn laughed in delight. "He was a bit hard on crockery."

Ella buckled Tessa into the highchair, using attending to Tessa to cover her roiling thoughts. Claiming paternity but refusing a DNA test was bizarre, akin to a scab you kept picking at, which gave the wound no chance to heal. Drew could change his mind at any moment, and Tessa would grow up surrounded by unanswered questions. She waited for Jake to tell Drew the test wasn't negotiable. His silence added to the anxiety crawling up her spine.

Hannah finished serving and left.

Drew scratched his head. Then topped up his glass from the bottle he'd brought to the table. "She told Jake and you about the baby, but not me. Why didn't you contact me sooner, Ella? Let me know she was sick?"

"Chrissy didn't tell me you were Tessa's father until too late." Meeting Drew upended Ella's assumptions about Chrissy's motivations in contacting Jake. Saying Jake owed her wasn't a good enough reason anymore.

"She kept it to herself! Doesn't make sense." Drew

leaned back in his chair.

"Any ideas why, Drew?" Jake finally asked Ella's burning question.

"None at all. I would have helped if I'd known. But you were closer to her, after I left the country." Drew swirled the liquid in his glass.

His answer catapulted Ella back to her initial rage and confusion. "Thank you for coming home, Drew." She fed Tessa the last spoonful of her soup. "It's important to my family to resolve this."

"I guess that's what it means. Coming home." Drew scanned the faces at the table, a smile, which didn't reach his eyes, spreading as he watched her. "Hope I can bunk down here, Dad, until I get digs in town?"

"Of course you can," Bronwyn answered swiftly.

"Drink." Tessa tugged on Ella's sleeve.

Ella lifted Tessa's cup. Undercurrents swirled like the steam above a witch's cauldron—portents of misfortune in a dark fairy tale. Peter was uneasy, while Jake had retreated to a patrician distance, giving nothing away. The easy affection she'd seen between the three of them in Jake's office had gone missing in this strange pantomime.

"However," Ella continued, tired of Drew side-stepping responsibility, "my family wants the DNA test. To provide certainty for us, but also for Tessa. She won't be a child forever. As an adult, she'll want to know we took every care."

"If you put it like that." Drew flashed his cocky smile, but to Ella, he was all flash and no substance. "I'll place myself in your hands. Name your medico."

You couldn't manage a busy community justice practice and not meet men like Drew. Cold, calculating, selfish. Drew was interested in furthering Drew's interests. He took his cues from the moment. He'd been testing her, was testing her, to see what she wanted. Ella was every bit as interested in what was motivating him.

"There's a certified clinic attached to Royal Prince Alfred

Hospital at Newtown. You can ring this afternoon, register with them and organise for a mouth swab or blood test." She hadn't expected to meet Drew, but she'd done her homework.

"Don't you need samples from the mother?" Drew tones were dulcet soft, but he prodded at her grief. "Does it work if the mother's dead?"

"Drew!" Bronwyn protested.

"Fair question," Ella answered, the memory of her earlier call to the lab shuddering through her.

She hadn't been able to escape the sensation of being a ghoul cross-examining the technician. In the paternity cases she'd dealt with at work the main parties had all been alive. Ella sat on her hands to prevent angry fists from forming. She knew the stages of grief, just as she knew she'd stalled at anger. No matter how many times she told herself Chrissy hadn't been completely sane in those last few weeks, acceptance was a long way away.

"Maternity's not in doubt," Jake's voice cut through the miasma of distrust with the precision of a scalpel.

"I thought you might want proof from us as well." Ella had known it wasn't necessary but had prepared herself for suspicion to stretch that far.

Drew shrugged. "I'll make the call. No point in delaying the inevitable."

A shiver of foreboding slithered down Ella's spine with Drew's cool unconcern. Tessa's biological father was an unknown quantity, while Jake's inexplicable detachment made her feel more alone than when she'd first arrived at Taylor Law.

Hannah returned, cutting across another awkward moment. Deftly, she replaced their soup bowls with lunch plates. Jake helped her transfer large platters of food from a trolley to the centre of the table, frenched lamb cutlets, baked potatoes with a selection of salads.

"Thank you." Ella smiled when the housekeeper set the plate of macaroni cheese in front of Tessa. "It looks delicious."

"Me eat." Tessa reached for the spoon.

"You can eat it yourself, honey. Like this." Ella placed some on a spoon and helped Tessa guide it to her mouth.

"Me," Tessa insisted.

Ella exchanged a look with Bronwyn. "What's the bet half of it ends in her hair."

"Just half?" Bronwyn queried.

"Where are you living, Ella?" Drew offered her the meat platter.

"An old apartment block in Glebe." She dished two cutlets onto her plate and passed the platter to Bronwyn.

"Not quite where the action is, but better than the farm. Chrissy never stopped talking about your mother's accident." Drew handed her the potatoes. "It scared her."

"I think she was born wanting to leave, but the truck accident made her hate the place." Ella checked Tessa was concentrating on her food and not a conversation about Gran being hurt, and was grateful when Jake distracted the child with a question about Tootles. *So he hadn't completely abandoned her.*

"Overturned tractor, wasn't it?" Drew shuddered.

"That sounds horrific." Peter's sympathy was a welcome contrast to his son's morbid interest.

"Trapped for a few hours before anyone found her," Drew added. "Pretty grisly. She was hanging upside down and unconscious."

Two hours and ten minutes, to be precise, but, hey, Ella had tried to forget that. If Drew was going to rehash every major tragedy of her life over lamb chops, she'd scream. "Things were tricky until she recovered."

Aware of Jake's steady regard, she guessed no one at Taylor Law had remembered the incident that triggered the Smithhouse case.

"Chrissy hated big machinery." Drew accepted the meat platter back from Jake and served himself four plump, perfectly cooked lamb chops, which Ella hoped would choke him. "Loved my BMW because it was the opposite of anything you had on the farm."

Eleanor chuckled, taking the chance to steer the conversation to less revealing topics. "We've got some precision German-engineered equipment now, but nothing that looks like a Beemer."

"What's the precision equipment for?" Jake caught the cup Tessa pushed to the edge of the table.

"Something your bloodhound didn't discover?" Ella mouthed, as Drew rose to fetch a second bottle of wine.

"Murphy's not much for rural life." Jake's murmur was almost inaudible.

"I'm confused," said Bronwyn. "Is it a farm or a cheese factory? You said the cheese you brought us was from your farm."

"We now have both the farm and a cheese factory. The cheese is my sister Grace's brainchild. She's a passionate producer, determined to make the farm profitable." Ella boasted. "She'll succeed too."

"How exciting." Drew's expression signalled the exact opposite.

"If you listen to Grace, it's endlessly fascinating. The equipment's her pride and joy. She makes unique, farmyard cheeses, and has started to make a name for herself in recent years." Ella channelled Grace's enthusiasm.

"And, er, is there a fortune to be made in cheese?" Drew yawned.

"Grace plans to buy out Mum and Dad."

Peter guided the conversation away from Ella, asking Drew questions about his work and life in London. Ella was content to use supervising Tessa as an excuse to watch the interactions between the other adults, filing impressions, answering only when asked a direct question. Hannah returned with coffee, tea and petit fours.

"Peter, if you have a few minutes, I've got some papers for you to sign in the library." Jake poured himself a coffee. "Family business."

Jacob Taylor could make *"family business"* sound like a mafia contract. Ella suspected maintenance was the hot topic, but meeting Drew had cemented her reservations about accepting any money from the Browning family without absolute confirmation of paternity.

"Tessa and I will leave you and Drew to catch up." Ella stood when the two men had withdrawn. "It's time for her afternoon nap." A feeble excuse, given Tessa had slept for most of the trip to the mountains, but Ella needed space to think.

After settling Tessa, she slipped out of a side door into the extensive gardens. Wandering randomly, she found a hidden nook protected from the wind. She released a slow breath and let her shoulders relax—the perfect escape. In spring, she imagined this garden of azaleas, rhododendrons and fruit trees would be full of blazing colour. With winter approaching, leaves had started to fall, creating a peaceful sanctuary. Closing her eyes briefly, she opened them to absorb the timeless serenity of the bush valley stretching to the mountains.

Drew's leading-man good looks and disreputable air hadn't appealed to Ella. Ridiculously unfair and unprofessional of her. His quick acceptance of Tessa as his child should have reassured her. The perfect story to tell Tessa as she grew up. Daddy took one look at you and said you belonged to him. Except Ella didn't believe it. His change of heart was unexplained. His words echoed with insincerity.

Unreasonable to expect him to love Tessa at first sight. But he'd barely glanced at his child, hadn't touched her or spoken to her. His focus had been on his family and their reactions to Tessa. Peter and Bronwyn were hopeless at pretence. Their captivation with their granddaughter was writ large in their faces and actions. Jake's indifference to Ella had been the more interesting development. To her and to Drew.

While Ella might wish she could read Jake's mind to find

out what he thought about her, indifference wasn't in the volatile mix. Drew's arrival had changed the family dynamic. The wind rose, and with it, a whirlwind of fallen leaves. They swirled and tumbled around her with no control of their destiny. She refused to be helpless.

"*Be careful,*" Jake had said.

* * *

At six o'clock, Ella slipped into the country-style kitchen to organise Tessa's dinner. A large Aga dominated the space, although the cherry laminated benchtops provided their own warmth. The cosy kitchen had every time-saving appliance her mother had ever fantasised about, and then some. Hannah set her up at the table in the centre of the room to feed Tessa, and chatted with the ease of one parent to another about menu options and meal times.

"Anything you need, just help yourself," Hannah offered the generous invitation.

"Thank you." With a chocolate cookie clutched in Tessa's hand, Ella made her escape upstairs.

As dusk faded to darkness, she sat in the rocking chair in front of the bedroom window with Tessa snuggled against her. She'd risen once to open a window to let the solid black of night mix with the subdued light provided by the bedside lamp, watching as the Milky Way appeared star by star, trailing a magic that had always comforted her.

"Once upon a time there was the Milky Way ..." Ella began the favourite bedtime routine. Tonight she had the real galaxy as a prop.

"Milky," Tessa repeated.

"In the galaxy are planets and millions of stars."

"Gazillions of stars."

"Venus, the Southern Cross, the Dog Star, Pleiades—the seven sisters, the Jewel Box," Ella recited as she pointed to each in turn. Tessa wrapped her fingers around Ella's pointing one, following her movement across the sky.

"You can wish on stars." Softly, Ella started to sing and rock. "*When you wish upon a star, makes no difference who you are, anything your heart desires will come to you.*"

Ella hadn't had much time for dreams in recent years. In the last few weeks, they'd been filled with a pirate king, who moonlighted as Prince Charming, and who made her want things she hadn't sought in a long time. The combination of too many people needing her and the leftover bruises from men she'd trusted had kept her single. Men like Robert Hall, who'd described her as too managing to be sexy. Her eyes strayed to the bed she'd rolled on with Jake before lunch.

Her skin sang where his hand had moved, his thumb gently and with erotic intent grazing the line of her jaw until she couldn't find the will to resist. He'd lowered his head with infinite slowness, his smoky gaze transfixing her with blazing heat.

His kiss in this room, with Tessa on the floor beside her, had been a devastatingly passionate assault on her senses. Wave upon wave of sensation had swept through her body until she went under, locked in his embrace. Madness.

She'd forgotten good intentions, responsibilities, even where she was, spinning in a maelstrom of unfamiliar longings. His tongue had pushed past her teeth, a mini invasion, mimicking the real invasion she craved. Her body had betrayed her, a traitorous languor making her mould herself more closely to his hard contours. She'd inhaled him, and breathing became more than an act of survival. Her hands had curled into the warm softness of his shirt. With new-found boldness, she'd traced a path in cotton she wanted to trace on bare skin.

Her sense of loss, when Tessa had called her name, had been immediate. She'd hated feeling his hands loosen, feeling him withdraw. She'd wanted to taste him again, to explore the planes and angles of his face with her lips and fingers.

She was falling for him and didn't want to be careful. His actions matched his words, and when his eyes found hers across a room, she'd swear they'd shared a secret.

Until today. Until Drew.

"Eleanor, are you there? I'm coming in." Jake pushed the door open so light from the hall spilled in. "Is everything all right? Why are you sitting in the dark?"

"We were counting stars." The half-light hid the heat creeping up Ella's neck. "She's asleep."

"Did Drew give you a date for his test?"

Did he have to talk about Drew now? "He mentioned Monday morning."

"How do you feel about that?" He crossed to crouch in front of the rocking chair, and she admitted she'd wanted Jake to find her this afternoon in her hidden garden.

"It's like I've been living in a parallel universe since I got back from the farm. Each time I think I'm getting a grip on what's happening, the goalposts shift," she confessed.

"Speed isn't the main objective here, Eleanor. You can delay, choose another day."

The laugh caught in her throat. "We've been sweating on this test since we met, and now you're talking about delaying it."

"You have the right to control the pace."

"Doesn't feel like it anymore." Ella shared her misgivings.

"Give her to me." He slipped his hands around Tessa, brushing heart-achingly against Ella's breasts as he transferred Tessa to his arms. "Bron said you were getting Tessa ready for bed."

"I told you I had a routine."

"Stargazing for real instead of sparkles on the ceiling?" he teased.

"You work with what you have." But his swift understanding reminded her of why she'd accepted his company for this weekend trip. "But I meant singing."

"An Anderson family tradition?"

"Uh-huh." She inhaled, savouring his scent. Tonight it held a hint of mountain air and open spaces—maybe a dash of eucalyptus and honey. "Another bit of information Murphy missed?"

"Did you find your mother, Eleanor, after the accident?" He rose to his feet. Tessa was safe in his arms.

She nodded. "It was one of those hazy summer days, when the heat in the air shimmers and sweat covers your body in a fine slick. We'd had some rain, but the fields could still be ploughed. Mum had put the pasta sauce on simmer—dinner was her chore. When my parents went out alone on the tractor, they gave us estimates of when they'd return. A precaution." She exhaled on a long breath, easing the constriction around her chest.

"I checked the old railway clock we had in the kitchen. I was checking minutes, then seconds, aware Mum was later than she should be, later than she'd promised. Nearly an hour overdue. Chrissy and Grace followed me. I climbed the rise to the back paddock. I remember so clearly—the blue sky and silence were dragging me onwards. Then I ran. The tractor hung upside down, half in the mud. At first, I couldn't see my mother." She brushed tears from her cheek. "The angle of the vehicle was all wrong. Mum was inside, unconscious. Blood everywhere. Chrissy was screaming. Grace ran for the house and phone. I kept counting the minutes, afraid I'd waited too long to go look for her."

"How old were you?" he asked quietly.

"Does that matter?" She crossed to the cot and pulled back the bedclothes and waited for him to pass Tessa to her.

Tessa stirred. "Kiss."

Ella kissed Tessa's cheek. "Goodnight, darling."

"Kiss," cried Tessa, pointing to Jake.

He curled his hand around Tessa's head, leaned forward and bussed her tummy, coaxing a giggle out of her, while Ella's heart thundered at the simple care of his action. She tucked Tessa into the cot.

"You were needed on the farm," he said slowly, stepping back. "That's what you said. End of first-year law. You found her, you got help, you cared for your younger sisters.

Just like you became Chrissy's carer. Why do you excuse Chrissy when you and Grace got on with what had to be done?"

"She was fourteen, the baby. I should have sent her back to the house with Grace. Kept her away. She had nightmares for months about what she'd seen."

"I imagine you didn't have much choice. Helping her would have meant not helping your mother." He drew her towards the door.

"I should have handled it better. Chrissy was depending on me."

"Life's a bitch. You can only really rely on yourself." Losing both parents at nine had scarred him in ways Ella would never understand, unless he shared.

"Did you and Drew ever get on?" The silence stretched until it pressed against Ella, like a great weight, so she could only suck in shallow breaths. She respected his loyalty to his family but would fight it and him if it threatened Tessa.

"When we were kids. I followed him around. I wanted to be where he was, play his games. For a few years he let me. Seemed to get a kick out of the hero-worship."

"What changed it?"

"I came to live with them." He rolled his shoulders as if releasing a great tension. "I became competition. Not that I ever was, but he saw it that way. Gradually, I learned he always had to win. At any price. If there are no boundaries, no rules to any game, it becomes more like warfare."

"How did Bronwyn and Peter deal with that?" *Please don't tell me they took his side without question.*

"He and I shared a conspiracy of silence. As he grew older, he spent more and more time away from home. At twenty he inherited some money from his grandfather. It allowed him to create his own profession, he said—a blog of the Sydney social scene. He could shoot people into the stratosphere with a few well-chosen words."

"Or bury them?" Her sister had read Ella some of Drew's posts. When she'd described them as spiteful or malicious gossip, Chrissy had claimed Ella didn't understand the game. She understood. She just didn't want to play those games. "Do you protect him from the consequences of his actions because of what happened?"

"Not anymore. But I understand life would have been different for him if I hadn't arrived." His voice was sombre.

"Your life would have been different if your parents had lived." Ella reached for him. He caught her hand and turned it over to press a kiss into her palm.

"I'm getting a clearer picture of you. Responsible as well as beautiful. Have you always been the linchpin for your family?"

"I was the oldest." She was whispering secrets to him in the intimate half-dark. Not just because he'd said she was beautiful. "When Grace was born, I was big enough to help, wanted to help. Mum had some complications after Chrissy."

"And you were expected to help again." He was objecting on her behalf.

"It wasn't a problem. After the accident, I needed to do more, wanted to do more." She stood with her back to the door, almost touching him.

"You didn't fail Chrissy."

She caught a whiff of wood smoke mixed with his familiar scent. His solidity comforted her more than his words.

"While her letter said a lot of things that hurt you, she loved you. She didn't understand you, but you were friends." He sounded envious.

"And you and Drew aren't."

"You're hearing my side here, Eleanor. You need to hear his."

Her magic moment shattered by reality. Ella expected Drew to tell her his side of the story. He'd already made it clear he had stories to tell. In her work, you learned to watch as well as listen. Changing your normal actions and reactions was harder than saying the words your audience wanted to hear. It was proving harder than she'd imagined to use those skills and be objective when it was your life, your dreams being threatened. When the stakes were so high. When Tessa's future hung in the balance.

Drew and Jake weren't friends. That shouldn't impact on Tessa's relationship with the Brownings. But Jake's tension was infecting her, and she shivered in reaction.

"Are you cold?"

"A goose walked over my grave." She preceded him out of the room. "We'd better go down."

Ella readied herself for what waited on the other side of the dining room door, her heart beating a little faster. Sitting down to breakfast with the Browning family was way more complicated than when she'd left Sydney yesterday morning. At dinner, Drew had been charm personified. Ready smiles, amusing stories of his experiences in London, people he'd met—easy to see how he'd charmed Chrissy. But listening to him, he had no plans to stay in Australia, regardless of the DNA test outcome. His description of his world left no space for the twenty-four-seven demands of children or disease or ugliness.

Chrissy had known he'd be repulsed by the hollowed-out, bald stick figure she'd become. Understanding the reason she'd kept his identity a secret, Ella had wept and let go of some of her anger at her sister. Hitching the toddler higher on her hip, she pushed open the door.

"Good morning Ella, Tessa." Bronwyn and Peter spoke in unison.

"I've put the high chair beside me," Bronwyn said. "To give you a break this morning, if that's okay?"

"Tessa's been telling me she's hungry since she woke up, so I can't guarantee her table manners." Ella smiled, settling Tessa in the high chair, before crossing to the sideboard where breakfast was laid out. She chose slices of fresh fruit for Tessa. "Finger-food might be simplest to start." Ella passed the plate to Bronwyn before returning to the sideboard to make fresh toast for herself and pour a coffee.

"Jake's out working somewhere," Peter said. "And Drew hasn't surfaced yet."

"I imagine he's still in another time zone," Ella offered the excuse to soothe Peter's embarrassment at his son's absence and to hide her relief.

"You're more tolerant than I am."

"I was tempted to stay in bed myself." Ella nodded in Tessa's direction. "I had more encouragement to get up."

Peter laughed, a quick guffaw that brought Tessa's head around in wide-eyed surprise. Ella locked her doubts away. This was why she'd come. To give Peter and Bronwyn time to establish a relationship with their grandchild. The room lacked the cosy homeliness of the farm kitchen, but Peter and Bronwyn had fallen for Tessa just as her parents had.

Bronwyn pointed to an envelope beside Ella's plate. "We keep talking about the family resemblance, so I went looking for some photos. That's a sample. I have whole albums, but I'll save them for another time."

"When have I heard that before?" Peter teased his wife.

"You said she looks like Jake." Ella upended the envelope and about a dozen photos slid onto the table.

"I've included that photo and a few more," said Bronwyn. "Maybe you'd like to show your parents?"

"They'd love that." The photo of Jake about Tessa's age was on top. A gorgeous baby, all big eyes, dark curls and mischief. The resemblance jolted Ella, making her imagine Jake as a father. She'd buried her own dreams of love and babies when she'd taken on the care of Chrissy and Tessa.

The pile included other photos from the same period. A few of Drew as a baby as well. He'd inherited his father's ears, nose and chin, and she silently acknowledged her prejudice. Even as a child he'd lacked Jake's charm. She smiled as she sifted through the shots, but the last photo held her attention. Jake, about nine years old, in oversize jeans and a T-shirt saying *"Save our rivers,"* alone and forlorn.

She traced a finger over the words.

"It was taken not long after his parents died. The shirt belonged to his mother. I can't look at that photo and not remember what it's like to lose a sister." Bronwyn smiled through tears.

Ella's throat burned. "And you have her child."

"I have Jake," she answered simply. "He's very like her. Independent, with a finely-honed sense of justice. But his arrival changed the family dynamics."

Ella didn't want a breakfast confession about conflict between Jake and Drew. She wanted Jake to trust her enough to tell her if old conflict jeopardised Tessa's future, not have Bronwyn try to explain it away. She stared blindly at the photo in her hand; she'd already given Jake her loyalty.

CHAPTER EIGHT

"It's different for you." Bron surprised her by moving in a different direction. "You had time to prepare. Not that that's any easier, but Tessa's so young I imagine there's been less disruption to her life."

"I made lots of changes to her routine over the last six months." Trying to balance Chrissy's needs with Tessa's was a juggling act she wasn't sure she'd always got right. "Increased the amount of time she was away from the house."

"I imagine Chrissy's illness meant you had to do more than that."

Ella met the sympathy in Bronwyn's eyes. "Chrissy wasn't physically strong enough to care for a baby most of the time, but she loved Tessa."

"We appreciate you taking the risk of bringing Tessa to stay with us." Bronwyn watched the toddler.

"You have a right to know your granddaughter." She'd already made the decision. Whatever else happened, granting access to Peter and Bronwyn Browning stood. She'd prefer to mimic the pattern she had with her own close family. Invitations made and accepted, casual, easy, frequent exchanges, extended and adjusted as Tessa got older. "When everything settles, my parents would love to meet you and share grandparent stories. My sister Grace and I are a big disappointment in that area."

"I'd love to meet them." Fresh tears slid down Bronwyn's cheeks, and she hastily brushed them away. "They must be very proud of you."

Ella grinned. "I hope so, but I also exasperate and frustrate the hell out of them as well."

"Normal parenting," Bronwyn replied. "You'll have it all with Tessa one day."

Peter reached out a hand to grip his wife's. "Is there anything you'd like to do today, Ella?"

A strong gust of wind rattled the windows. Ella wrinkled her nose at the rain slashing sideways at the house. "Looks like the perfect day for lounging around in a warm room. A little reading, a few games, and maybe, if we're extra good"—she winked at Tessa—"a Wiggles show."

"Wiggles." Tessa clapped her hands, bobbing her head from side to side to a song only she could hear.

"But first we might read Tootles a book and make her a car to drive in," Ella said, both activities Peter and Bronwyn could share.

"'Ootles." Tessa banged her spoon enthusiastically on the tabletop.

"Good morning, all." Drew breezed into the room and aimed a vague smile in the direction of the table. "Practising to be a drummer, is she?"

"A normal reaction if your best mate's a brown bear." Ella didn't explain.

Confusion clouded Drew's face. "You'll have to excuse me. Jetlag. Plus, I'm never at my best before coffee." He crossed to the buffet and poured himself a cup. "I thought I'd go into town after breakfast. It's years since I've been to Katoomba, but there must be something happening in town."

"It's still the retreat of bushwalkers and people who want to curl up in front of fires when winter arrives early, rather than celebrity types," Peter said drily.

"Come with me, Ella. It'll give us a chance to get to know each other. I'm sure we'll find something to do." Drew sauntered to the table, coffee cup in hand. "Go out for lunch."

"Thanks for the offer, Drew, but we've just made plans for the day," Ella said. Drew hadn't included Tessa in the invitation. Ella couldn't help unfavourably comparing his treatment of Tessa with Jake's.

"What sort of plans?"

"Peter Rabbit, racing cars if we can find a cardboard box the right size and ..." Ella glanced at Tessa. "W-I-G-G-L-E-S."

"Are they still alive?" He blanched.

She chuckled. "A few cast changes, but they're still going."

"I might pass. Where's Jake?" Drew almost sounded interested.

"He's in the office at the moment, but he said he'd check the wood supply and, if the rain clears, trim the side hedges later." Peter set his knife and fork on his empty plate.

"All work and no play. Can I borrow the car, Dad?"

"The keys are on the sideboard in the hall." Peter looked like he wanted to say more.

"If you've finished, Ella, maybe we can make a move," Bronwyn suggested.

"I'll talk to Jake first and join you when I can." Peter moved to assist his wife from her chair.

With the help of a walking stick, Bronwyn slowly led the way across the hall to a small room on the north-eastern side of the house. Ella registered the subtle design features. An elegant writing desk with enough room to fit a wheelchair underneath. Low bookcases, more comfortable chairs and a sofa angled to catch the warmth from a fireplace. But these chairs had remotes tucked into discreet pockets at the sides. Bronwyn would be able to get out of them by herself. There were other features to support someone with mobility issues, but all were cleverly incorporated so the room looked like a conventional study.

"It's been designed to accommodate my condition." Bronwyn lowered herself onto the sofa. "But you saw that for yourself, didn't you?"

"We didn't have the money to modify our house after Mum's accident, but we repurposed rooms. We converted a living area close to the bathroom into a bedroom for Mum and Dad." Her mother had hated any suggestion of pity.

"We've built a small bathroom into that corner." Bronwyn gestured to a huge tapestry screen.

"I could spend all day here." Ella turned a slow circle, taking in the peace and the garden and bush views from the windows.

Bronwyn laughed. "To sit quietly and read a book."

"Heaven." She sighed.

"Can you turn on the fire, please, Ella?"

"Heaven just became nirvana." Ella sat Tessa beside Bronwyn while she bent to start the fire. It flared into life.

"I hope my son's questions didn't upset you last night." Bronwyn should know she wasn't responsible for an adult son's crassness.

"He has every right to ask questions." Although he'd asked very few about Tessa, her likes and dislikes. His lack of interest scraped against Ella's pride in her little girl. "This must have come as a shock to him. I'd be asking questions if I were in his position."

"That's probably why he's going into town," said Bronwyn apologetically. "To give himself time to think about things."

"Mmm," Ella replied. Drew gave her the impression he was bored witless in a country house. He demanded more "lights, colour, action" in his life than could be found entertaining a toddler.

"The box in the corner has some books and toys in it." Bronwyn pointed to a large red plastic playpen. "Old ones from when the boys were smaller, a few recent additions.

Tony and his family come here with Jake sometimes. So there's playdough, colouring pencils, crayons. Oh, a whole load of stuff."

"Sounds like everything we need." Ella lifted the box and started back towards the sofa, feeling relieved and a little guilty Drew wasn't with them. "What would you like Tessa to call you?"

Bronwyn's mouth opened and shut several times, and her jaw wobbled. "I called my grandmother Nana. Is that okay?" She hesitated. "Or does she call your mother that?"

"Mum likes Gran, and Dad's Poppa. Do you think Peter will be okay with Grandpa?"

Peter walked into the room. "Peter will be delighted," he said. "But are you sure you want to do that before we have the DNA results?"

"I've spoken to my parents. We want you to feel part of Tessa's life." Ella sank to sit cross-legged on the floor.

Upending the box, she examined its contents. Tessa slid off the sofa into the middle of the pile and started exploring. Ella manoeuvred herself so Tessa played near Bronwyn's feet, encouraging the toddler to use the sofa to lean against or as a lever to pull herself up, and making it natural to include Bronwyn in the games of make-believe. Peter was in and out of the room over the morning, acting as a runner to fetch and carry glue and extra scissors and string. His design for Tootles's cardboard car was a huge success. When he pushed Tessa and Tootles around the room, Tessa screamed with delight.

"Show Nana or show Grandpa what you've done," Ella repeated the names until Tessa became familiar with the words and with them, climbing onto the sofa and nestling into Nana's side when Bronwyn offered to read a book to Tootles.

Hannah delivered a picnic basket for lunch. Ella laid out a tablecloth on the floor and unpacked sandwiches and lemonade. Tessa passed serviettes to the adults, while Ella served sandwiches on paper plates. As afternoon shadows closed around the house, Peter withdrew, leaving Ella, Tessa and Bronwyn alone. Drew hadn't returned from town, and Hannah reported that Jake had grabbed some sandwiches and gone back to his gardening. The contrast between the cousins was sharp. Drew searching out entertainment, Jake doing heavy labouring to spare his uncle. She'd also learned Peter and Bronwyn had endless patience and love to give a granddaughter.

"Would the window seat work for Tessa's nap today?" Bronwyn asked. Her hands were clasped in front of her, her head on one side. Part plea, part insistence on making the most of every minute Tessa was here.

"That's a great idea." Ella arranged cushions to hold Tessa in place in the low, wide window seat and tucked a soft angora blanket around her. With Tootles under her arm, Tessa settled without any fuss.

"I hope you aren't offended by Jake's absence." It was Bronwyn's first mention of her nephew since breakfast.

Ella disguised her feeling of desertion with a grin. "Tessa and I came to see you and Peter. He said he was coming anyway." But she hadn't expected him to treat her as if she had a contagious disease.

"We have a regular gardener, but Jake claims to like chopping wood and mucking about in the chook pen." Bronwyn pleated the cashmere throw she'd drawn over her knees.

"Is that what he's been doing?" As a country girl she knew the value of fresh eggs, but she suspected his cousin's arrival, rather than clearing cobwebs, might have more to do with Jake's sudden preference for unnecessary gardening.

"As well as talking business with Peter."

Ella shot her a quick look.

"Drew's arrival was unexpected. They have more to talk about than Tessa, my dear."

"Am I that obvious?" Ella had been disappointed every time the door opened to reveal Peter or the housekeeper.

"Jake explained you don't want to talk about maintenance until you have certainty. That's understandable. We didn't mean to steamroller you."

"You didn't. I …" Maintenance was Tessa's right, although Chrissy's demands made it stick in Ella's craw. Realistically, extra money would provide more opportunities for Tessa. But Drew's appearance had made the voice inside her head louder. *Not yet.* Not until paternity and custody were officially confirmed. Until her custody of Tessa was a fact of law. Until this rollercoaster ride was over and she could relax knowing her sister's child was safe.

"You don't have to apologise. It must be an anxious time for you. Your sister died so recently, and now you're having to deal with complete strangers who want a share in Tessa."

"I can share, Bronwyn"—Ella gentled her voice—"when it means Tessa has more people to love her." With paternity confirmed, Tony could finalise her case. She didn't anticipate opposition, yet the fear of losing Tessa shadowed her. "Is it okay if I go for a walk in the garden?"

"Go ahead, my dear." Bronwyn smiled, her eyes on Tessa. "I'd love to have some alone time with my granddaughter."

"She normally sleeps for about two hours. I'll be back before she wakes."

Ella collected her coat and woollen cap and stepped through the side door into the silence of the garden, grateful for the understanding of the older woman, who recognised she needed time on her own. She'd come willingly into their home, not anticipating any traps. Ella thrust her hands into her coat pockets and strode across the garden, chastising herself for looking for threats where none existed.

She wanted to talk to Jake. About Drew, about her initial impressions and her misgivings. Drew wasn't used to being a father, to being around children, but to disappear for the day argued a complete disinterest in Tessa. She huffed out a breath, the air in front of her mouth condensing. She wasn't giving Drew enough time. One day he'd been a bachelor protesting he didn't have a child, the next he was being shoehorned into a DNA test.

But she also wanted to tell Jake about Bronwyn and Peter, about the day they'd spent with Tessa, and how well it had gone. *Damn it.* She just wanted to talk to him. *Insanity.* If she relied on his presence, she'd want to keep relying on it. If she confided in him, she could see her independence slipping away.

Despite the sensual, seductive magic when they touched, he was a loner. He'd given no hint he was looking for a relationship. Or to be a father to Tessa.

His cousin's child.

A cousin who didn't like him.

Ella leaned against a stone wall at the bottom of the garden and stared into the distance, letting the reality of the relationship between Tessa and Jake seep into her bones. Wind buffeted her, the cold sneaked under the edges of her jacket, and she pulled her woollen cap lower around her ears. Last night, Drew had essentially accused Jake of having an affair with Chrissy, claiming Tessa resembled Jake more than Drew. Drew hadn't told her of the shared night in a hotel room, hadn't directly attacked Jake in her hearing, but there'd been some indirect digs in almost every story he'd told. Some reference to make Jake seem less and him more. She wasn't imagining it.

A vague disquiet invaded her, as menacing as the storm clouds swirling overhead.

* * *

Jake finished raking up the hedge clippings. A mindless task he enjoyed because it left his brain free to wander. Usually he solved complex legal problems. Today it had been a way of releasing the ropey frustration entangling him. He didn't like the way Drew looked at Eleanor, the fact that he didn't look at Tessa.

Jake was convinced Drew didn't give a damn about

Tessa. Drew's idea of sport was finding an opponent's weak spot and applying pressure. He'd twigged in seconds that Tessa was the most important person in Eleanor's life, and his parents were besotted. Early days yet, but Jake could see his cousin assessing the players, considering how to use the knowledge he'd gained.

Custody wasn't on his radar. Or any action requiring a personal commitment. Wrong-footing Jake, casting him as the villain was Drew's go-to modus operandi. Jake had stayed away from Eleanor all day, so he'd have an alibi if asked. *Alibi!* What a bloody stupid idea. All so Drew wouldn't guess he was beginning to care more than he wanted for this argumentative and practical woman. Her preparedness to shoulder burdens others would walk away from earned his respect. Her generosity to Peter and Bron earned his admiration. And the curve of her mouth when she flashed her ready smile made him want to kiss her senseless.

He'd avoided Eleanor because he didn't want Drew speculating about their relationship, and Drew had stayed in town.

Shaking off his despondency, Jake rounded the side of the house and found her there, silhouetted against the skyline, as if he'd conjured her. He remembered the feel of her against his body, the humbling sense of power at having someone so fragile and yet so strong locked in his arms. Striding towards her, he called out her name so she wouldn't be startled. "You weren't tempted to go to town with Drew?"

She turned to face him. "The purpose of this weekend is for Bronwyn and Peter to get to know Tessa."

"Don't a father's rights take precedence?" He shoved his hands in his pockets to keep from hugging her.

"You don't reject one invitation because you've seen something shinier and newer." She sounded like she was reading from a catechism.

"No one's described Drew as shiny and new to me

before." Jake liked the quick character assassination. "And that's a strong moral compass you've got."

"I keep saying I believe Chrissy. I do. I plan to spend time with Drew because I want Tessa to know her father. But I'm more conflicted than I was before I met him. I want incontrovertible proof of paternity before demanding Drew play Daddy." She wrapped her arms defensively around her torso. "Grandparents don't pose the same threat. Their usual role is to give children back."

"Has Drew threatened you?" Jake's earlier concern crowded back.

"I haven't seen him since breakfast." Her head tilted to one side. "Will he? Threaten me?"

"I can't see how." Yet Jake had gone on guard the minute Peter said his son was home. Drew was weighing up how to turn Tessa's existence to his advantage. His cousin would eliminate anyone who stood in his way, including Eleanor.

"Neither can I." She searched his face. "But it seems neither of us is prepared to rule it out."

"You won't let fear dictate your actions. I admire that in you." Wind whistled up the valley, and he turned his back on it. "You forced me to confront my prejudices about you. In my experience, guilty parties don't choose irrefutable scientific evidence as their defence of preference, much less their weapon of choice."

"So we wait for the DNA results." She leaned against the wall with him, close but not touching. "The law is supposed to be based on facts."

"You're confusing justice and the law again, Eleanor." His cousin was claiming he'd hadn't known about the pregnancy until recently. The law might accept his argument, but it was hardly just.

"My father called. You've offered him money. More money than he lost in the original transaction with Smithhouse."

"Inflation has been shocking." Jake had been waiting for

her to bring it up.

She looked at him from under her lashes. "Careful, Counsellor, you might convince me you believe in my brand of justice."

She was a honey. "Consider the possibility," he answered.

"Dad offered me the money. Said they didn't need it at the moment, but I did." Having her share confidences made up for every betrayal Jake had ever known.

"Haven't you given them money in the past?" Before he'd pulled Murphy off the case, his hound dog had picked up a few facts. On her move to Melbourne, she'd been alone and worked sixteen-hour days to send money home.

"You aren't just trying to bypass me on maintenance, are you?" She scrunched up her nose.

"Not my money, Eleanor. Your father can do what he likes with any just reimbursements he may have received."

"Mmm."

Jake enjoyed the way her mind worked. She was smart enough to work out his intention with the money, and direct enough to challenge him on it. He'd planned on offering her parents restitution but had upped the amount after she'd told him her parents were helping her out. "What do you think of this place?"

"It's special." She inhaled deeply, her smile blissful as she savoured the sweet, sharp mountain air.

"High enough for the clouds to roll in below you, which they do on autumn and winter mornings. An amazing sensation, sitting in a sea of clouds. Tends to dwarf everyday irritations." In his gut he'd known Drew wouldn't pursue him to the garden. "Is it like that on your farm?"

"More gently rolling hills and contented, fat cows, but it's as if you're holding your breath in the city and when you get to the farm, you let it go."

"If I'd seen it first, I might have bought it." Jake scanned the valley. A stupid fantasy really. Julia would never have wanted to live here. Like Drew, her last sight of sunrise would have been by accident at the end of a long night.

Absurdly this exchange lifted Jake's mood.

"Bronwyn said they'd been here more than two years. A lot of things happened about that time." Her words held a question.

"I've got nothing to add." The wind had dropped, the rain was taking one of the short breaks it had taken throughout the day and, for a moment, there was peace.

"I'm surprised you're speaking to me at all." She swivelled her head back from the valley to face him. "You were monosyllabic at dinner last night and you've avoided me all day."

"As you explained. This visit is to give Peter and Bron time with Tessa." He angled his body towards hers, his spirits lifting when she scowled. "You're beautiful, you know," Jake said. "Even when you're annoyed with me."

Wisps of hair escaped and flew across her face, a few strands catching in her mouth. She untangled it and pushed it under her cap. She was gorgeous. Smart, brave, and whenever Jake was within reach of her, he remembered the feel of her in his embrace and wanted her back there. Backed by clouds in a palette of greys, her hair trapped by a dark knitted cap, hunched into her coat, she was without defences. Her mix of vulnerability and Amazon warrior attracted him more than he'd ever expected. Getting to know her was playing havoc with his vow of non-involvement. He could spend hours looking at her.

* * *

Ella breathed him in, holding close the enchantment of him finding her beautiful. He carried the healthy smell of honest labour intermingled with the lingering scent of wood smoke in his clothes. She lifted a hand to his cheek. "'*Beautiful*—especially *when I'm angry*.' That's what they say in all the classics."

"Uh-uh. You get deep frown lines when you're annoyed"—he stroked a finger across her forehead—

"here." He was laughing at her.

"Under your hand-made business suits and pirate's ponytail and earring lurks a sensitive and compassionate man." She ratcheted up the tension sparking between them.

"Not a rebel? I'm crushed." But the laughter in his eyes dimmed, replaced by an intensity encouraging her to boldness.

"A rebel can be a traitor or a renegade. You're too honourable." She brushed her lips across his. His actions betrayed him. "And you taste of heaven."

His arms wrapped around her, pulling her close, and Ella waited for him to kiss her again, to sweep her into the magical world where she forgot everything except him. But his head lifted, and an engine died in the distance. He stepped back.

"It's still a maze, Eleanor. You need to be careful."

She fought disappointment he hadn't followed through on his kiss. "Are you warning me against yourself, now, Jake?"

"What do you want at the end of the day?"

He was frightening her again, but she knew the answer to that question. "Legal custody of Tessa."

"The child of your heart." His understanding made his warning more ominous. He'd been as appalled as she had by the implication custody of Tessa could be bought. He'd given her a list of critical questions to ask Tony. He understood the insecurities of a small child and that Tessa went nowhere without Tootles.

"We should go back," she said. "Tessa will be awake now."

Turning back towards the house, she allowed herself to brush against him. She wouldn't allow him to frighten her. Life had taught her to distinguish good from bad, right from wrong. His actions hadn't just made her revise her opinion of Taylor Law, they'd shown her wealth and power could be used for good. She didn't understand all the powerplays going on, but she knew she trusted him.

It was after seven on Sunday when the Jaguar glided to a halt outside Ella's apartment block. An accident in the lower mountains had created havoc on the drive home. An accident to compound the traffic jam caused by the continuing storms. Their journey time doubled. The music selection Jake had loaded for Tessa had been on reruns for the last hour. If Ella met the Wiggles now, she might be forced to throttle them to remain sane.

"Thank you for an—" Ella paused, selecting her words carefully—"interesting weekend."

"Not the word I would have chosen. And I'm coming up." He wasn't offering her a choice.

"There's no need." *And I mean, really no need.*

"Tessa's asleep. I'll carry her up." He handed her his keys, then unbuckled Tessa and scooped her into his arms.

With their bags slung over her shoulder, Ella locked the car, before hurrying past him to unlock her apartment and open the door. Turning on lights, she faced him, uncertain what to say now that they were alone. Their arrival in Leura on Friday had signalled his disappearance. Aside from those few heady moments in the bedroom on Friday afternoon and a few more in the garden on Saturday, he'd been the invisible man.

"I'll take her." She stepped towards him.

"Do you want me to put her to bed?" he asked at the same time.

"She's waking up. I'll give her something to eat first."

"I'm not going, Eleanor." He buckled Tessa securely into her high chair and met Ella's gaze. "Not until we've talked this through further."

"Talked *what* through?" Tired of trying to be strong, of being scared witless about what the morning would bring, Ella wanted the Jake she'd learned to trust to stay. For simple comfort. For the reassurance of being held safe in his arms. "Do you even remember what talking is?" She threw a hand in the air, letting him see her exasperation.

"I had work to do." His jaw set.

"I know! Gardening when it wasn't wet and legal briefs when it was. But I recognise bullshit when I hear it."

"It wasn't bullshit," he said with exaggerated patience.

Tessa roared, and Ella hurried across. "I'm sorry, honey," she soothed. "We've been ignoring you. I'll get some dinner."

She opened the freezer, pulled out a container of pre-prepared food for emergencies and popped it in the microwave before turning back to Jake.

"You're expecting Drew to go ahead tomorrow?"

"Why wouldn't I?" she demanded. Jake's objection made no sense to her. "He agreed to accept the first appointment for a DNA test."

"It's possible to test grandparents," he explained. The microwave pinged off in the strange silence left by his off-key remark. "I checked when Drew refused, and we thought he wouldn't come home."

"We don't need to do that now." She tested the temperature of the food and carried it across to Tessa, uneasy at this new sign of Jake's resistance to Drew's role. "Can you let yourself out?"

"You're in a hurry to get rid of me."

"You're the one who bolted every time I entered a room over the weekend. Clearing your head for work, you said. Well, don't let me keep you." She offered Tessa a mouthful, her body braced for the slam of the door.

"Sarcasm doesn't suit you," he chided gently.

She spared him a glance. "You don't know what suits me."

* * *

"I can hazard a guess." Jake watched the colour heat her skin. All that beautiful bravado when she was the most vulnerable woman he'd ever met. And the sexiest. Tousled, distracted by Tessa, determined to be independent, holding him at bay when the hunger in her gaze matched his own. "For a few hours tonight, I'm at your disposal."

Her confusion at his last remark was adorable. He edged past her into the kitchen, and she whisked herself to the other side of the high chair to spoon more food into Tessa's open mouth. "Do you need something from my fridge?"

"On the available evidence, I'd say cheese sandwiches are on the menu for dinner again."

"I don't need dinner."

So, she didn't eat when she was troubled. Jake was responsible for tonight's troubles. "At the risk of getting my head snapped off. I disagree. You need to eat. You can't afford to lose any more weight." He was being deliberately provocative.

"Too scrawny for you, am I?" Her mocking question didn't hide the hurt in her eyes.

"Don't go there, Eleanor. Not unless you're prepared for the consequences." Knowing she wanted him as much as Jake wanted her flashed like fire through his blood. He'd stay the night, but his hunger for her wouldn't be satisfied with one night.

She dropped her head to focus on feeding Tessa.

"Cheese sandwiches again. But after our *'interesting'* weekend, I need a drink." He patted his pockets, then remembered she'd locked his car. "Where did you put my keys?"

"In the bowl beside the door." She tipped her chin in the direction of an old-fashioned plant stand with a pottery bowl on top.

"Did you want me to stay?" Relief warmed him. They might scratch, but it was frustration at the circumstances, because they'd both prefer to stroke and soothe. Not tonight.

"Habit. That's where I automatically put keys." Her denial was without bite.

"I'll be back."

"Somehow I guessed that from the moment we met," she muttered.

The cluster of shops two blocks away included a bottle shop as well as the two restaurants Jake had spotted on earlier visits. The hamburger joint smelled as if the cooking oil hadn't been changed since it opened; a florist offered two spindly philodendrons in the front window; a hair and beauty salon advertised full-body waxes. Two Harley motorbikes parked on the footpath outside a tattoo parlour completed the set. Taking one of the many vacant spaces, Jake headed into the empty shop. Not a night to attract much custom.

"I'll take this, thanks." He picked up a bottle of Merlot, a label he was familiar with and good enough for a private feast with toasted sandwiches.

Back in the car, Jake rested his hands on the steering wheel, the cold darkness surrounding him matching his mood. His actions confused Eleanor, but, *hell,* she'd sat sedately at dinner last night when Drew had cross-examined her. Okay, *questioned* her about how Jake had come to drive her to the mountains, how she and Jake had spent their Saturday. His cousin's special brand of selfishness made him perceptive to the relationships between others, a skill that allowed him to take maximum advantage of them. Had Jake been the only one who'd noticed the trend of the questions? Planting a fist in his cousin's face, especially at his aunt's dinner table, was another temptation he'd had to resist.

Slowly he started the car.

Drew had always taken what he wanted.

His cousin hadn't wanted Jake's fiancée, Julia, but he couldn't resist the temptation. A few weeks before Jake's marriage, Drew had shown up at a family gathering after yet another unexplained absence. With brooding, Byronesque looks and Italian suits he'd cultivated an image of romantic decadence. And he was at permanent leisure. Leisure he devoted to seducing Julia.

Jake had asked about Chrissy when Drew arrived alone,

and his cousin claimed their relationship was long over. Jake had discovered the truth the night of the legal society function he was scheduled to co-host with Julia.

There was no sign of Eleanor when he let himself into the flat, but he could hear her voice, slightly off-key, singing a lullaby.

"Do you want the moon to play with or the stars to run away with? They'll come if you don't cry."

She wasn't perfect then, he grinned at another flat note, his eyes drawn to the out-of-proportion star chart covering the ceiling. Lullabies and night skies. All those people who called her EJ missed the essence of her. The aptly named Eleanor Jane—a shining light, sparkling and sensuous, with a deep vein of responsibility through her core. She couldn't see the combination was the knockout.

The full truth about Drew would be her best protection against his cousin. Jake hadn't told her, wouldn't tell her. He knew he was being bloody unreasonable. But he'd be damned if he'd rehash petty stories from his childhood and teens now. They reflected well on no one. At the time, he hadn't known how to stop Drew's bullying. He'd believed he'd somehow deserved it. Being three years younger than Drew, Jake had convinced himself he bore responsibility for Drew's dissatisfaction with how life had turned out. He had, as Drew endlessly reminded him, gate-crashed their family and been a terrible cry-baby in those first few months, demanding a lot of Bron's attention.

Jake wasn't a helpless adolescent any more, but Drew hadn't changed. Jake admitted some of his silence was fear, that if Drew switched to charm, Eleanor would believe him not Jake.

CHAPTER NINE

When she emerged from the bedroom, Jake had the sandwiches ready to toast. "I like the outfit." And the smile that had lit her face when she'd seen him. As if she'd half expected him not to return, but he didn't voice that last one. She'd changed into leggings and a voluminous white business shirt. Jake couldn't be certain without a much closer inspection, but the leggings appeared to be decorated with penguins, and the urge to trace the outline of one had him pushing his hands into his pockets.

"Tessa had an accident." She waved towards her legs. "She likes the penguins."

"So do I." Jake had stayed for a specific reason. He wouldn't spill his guts about Drew. He would warn her to surround herself with friends. *But not until after dinner.*

She sat opposite him at the table. He poured the wine, waited while she swirled the contents and sniffed delicately before tasting it. "That's better than the average house red." Her eyebrows lifted in appreciation.

"Let's pretend the weekend never happened."

"Then you wouldn't be here," she pointed out with unarguable logic.

"I might." Jake wanted her. Warm, soft, incredibly

generous. He'd had the craziest sensation of her pouring her soul into the kiss when her body had curled into his on the bed. The heat had been lightning-fast, his lips burned now at the memory, but beyond the flash fire was something deeper, something special. They'd each taken, but she'd shared something precious. He wanted much more than the few seconds of abandoned pleasure they'd shared. "The world will press around us again tomorrow, Eleanor."

She studied him for long seconds, the silence crowded with questions. She asked one. "You're offering a moment in time? I can do that. Tell me how you met Tony."

"He hasn't said?" Jake chuckled. "We met in my last year at school—a prep course for law."

"Yeah, yeah. You went to law school together, bonded over women and song and various illicit substances." She circled her hand as if saying "get on with it."

"No illicit substances. Neither one of us wanted to sabotage our future licence to operate." He transferred the cooked sandwiches to plates and set them on the table. "You could say Tony introduced me to the Australian countryside."

"It's a dream of his. To have a hideaway in the mountains."

"He's brought the twins to see Bron and Peter a few times."

She took a bite of the sandwich. Cheese spurted onto her fingers, and she grabbed for a serviette.

"My fault." Taking her hand, Jake nibbled the gooey cheese off her fingers, knowing touching her was a mistake, knowing it would make it harder to walk out her door tonight. "I overloaded the sandwiches."

"Tell me amore bout the great Australian outdoors." She withdrew her hand from his.

"Holidays with Peter and Bron usually involved cities and art galleries and museums and orchestral concerts. I can see you rolling your eyes."

"I envy you the art galleries. That's all."

Who knew Eleanor Jane Anderson was a secret art lover? "Tony convinced me to go diving. Being underwater introduced me to a whole different world. The perfect escape from classes and late-night swotting for exams. We were diving buddies. One time down the south coast, early in our diving days together, my tank malfunctioned. We had to rely on his and each other to get up safely."

"Tony meant it literally when he said he'd trust you with his life." She licked a dribble of cheese off of her fingers, and the action was ridiculously erotic.

Down boy! "It's the kind of experience that cements or destroys a relationship. It's lucky we'd bonded before he unleashed his uncle's pet pig on me. He treated the damn animal as if it was a member of his family."

She giggled. "In her teens, Grace had a pig as a pet. Clancy. He followed her everywhere. He would have slept with her if I hadn't put my foot down."

"Have you got a pen and some paper?" he asked. Afraid if he stayed longer, he'd share more memories, yield to the temptation to create new ones.

"How old-fashioned." But she collected a notepad from the kitchen bench. "For my shopping lists."

"How practical. Here's another list. Your parents, your sister, Mrs. P, Tony Baldwin, your GP," he recited names.

"Why do I need this list?" She returned to her seat.

"Ring them all." He couldn't explain the urgency driving him, but he wanted an army at her back. "Tell them you and Drew are proceeding with the DNA test tomorrow. Tell them your plans."

"Why before the test?"

"Take someone with you, Eleanor." Jake reached across the table to grip her wrist.

She tilted her head to one side, considering him. "Will you come?"

"It's better if I don't." He released her wrist and sat back.

"Better for whom?"

"Better for Tessa if you and Drew don't have me as a

bystander. Drew was initially reluctant. I don't think he'd be comfortable having me there. He'd see it as pressuring him." Drew would see it for what it was, Jake supporting Eleanor, and he wouldn't take the risk of further exposing her to Drew's evil genius. "That's not my role."

"What is your role, Counsellor?" She picked up her glass and stared into it.

"Bluntly. It started out as protecting Bron and Peter from emotional and financial exploitation. With paternity confirmed, and like you, I think we'll find Drew is Tessa's father, my role is to ensure Bron and Peter get to spend time with their granddaughter and, like any grandparents, are allowed to make a financial contribution to her upbringing."

"You're still thinking of a contractual arrangement." She looked up with a frown he made no move to rub away.

"Contracts can protect the rights of both parties."

"Would you insist on a pre-nuptial agreement before marriage, Jake?"

His heart raced. If Eleanor loved a man—him?—enough to marry him, a pre-nuptial agreement would be as brutal as a backhander. He leaned closer until they were nose to nose. "What's that got to do with Tessa?"

"It's about whether you can tell the difference between trust and carrying a big legal stick. My father still does deals on a handshake, even though Smithhouse abused the deal he made. When I give my word, it means something to me."

"Was Robert Hill your only lover?" He hadn't known the question lurked inside him.

"That's not pertinent to our business relationship." She flopped back in her chair.

"I don't think of business when I look at you." *I stop thinking when I look at you.* Which made him useless to them both.

She took a slow sip of wine. "I dated a few men in Melbourne."

"But no one serious? Robert hurt you." He pushed because he needed to know.

"He made me cautious. So, I make the decisions to start, to end, to control the pace." Her honesty revealed more doubt about him than she'd probably intended.

Jake didn't have much control over what was happening between them. Fascination, desire, the helter-skelter chemical reactions she triggered in him when they touched. "That's a good lesson to learn."

Stopping before he was in too deep was a rational choice. When custody was confirmed and Drew returned to the UK, Jake could take the time to explore what was between them. Not love. He didn't do love anymore. Spontaneous combustion more like. Although describing what they shared as pure lust diminished their connection. He cared what happened to her and Tessa. Adopting her caution would give them both a chance to work out what was happening. *Bullshit, Taylor.*

* * *

Ella scanned her living room, crossed to straighten the chintz spread on the sofa, and plump up the cushions. Tessa had been settled and asleep when she'd checked, Tootles tucked under her chin. She straightened the photos on the mantelpiece. Jake's car hadn't been waiting when she arrived home. Two weeks since she'd seen him. She moved restlessly around the room. Maybe he wasn't coming. She checked the time again. Her buzzer sounded.

"Thank you for coming." Ella leaned against her open door, a smile she couldn't contain spreading across her face when he rounded the corner in the stairwell in his classy suit and bad-boy ponytail. She'd called, and he'd come.

He held up a carrier bag. "I took a punt and picked up some food. I'm guessing you haven't eaten yet."

"I'm just home from the centre."

"Do you need to check Tess?" There it was. Simple understanding. An awareness of the needs of others. Which made his abandonment more incomprehensible.

"Why haven't you called, Jake?"

"You wanted to get to know Drew, work out the lay of the land," he said carefully, stopping on the top step.

"And talking to me—about anything in the past fifteen days—would prevent that from happening?" Her annoyance snuck through.

"I didn't want to muddy the waters."

"How bloody reasonable of you!" *And it hurt like hell to find herself questioning his answer.*

"Can I come in?" He waved the carrier bag.

Ella stepped back. Fragrant Italian herbs mixed with tomatoes teased her nostrils when he strolled past her to hoist the bag onto the kitchen benchtop. He started unpacking containers.

"What's it to be? Do we eat while it's hot, or do you want to fight first?" He turned to her with a rueful smile. "The daggers are sticking out of my back, Eleanor."

"We'll eat. I'll serve. What's that?" She pointed at the bottle he pulled from a brown paper bag bearing the logo of the local bottle shop.

"Champagne."

"Very good French champagne." Her gaze drifted from the Pol Roger label to his face. "I didn't know they stocked that."

"Neither did the kid on the register. He found it at the back of the fridge."

"It's a bit early to celebrate, isn't it?" Ella peered into the containers and found penne arrabiata, a green salad and a creamy, decadent tiramisu. He'd remembered her favourites. "Drew delayed providing his sample for the first week."

"You called."

"You expect me to believe you were waiting for me to call you." Ella snorted.

"Not exactly." He opened a cupboard and lifted down two crystal champagne flutes. "Same jumble sale?"

"What does 'not exactly' mean?" *Had he been waiting for*

her to call? "Four white wine, four red wine, four flutes and four whisky glasses. A job lot." She babbled to hide her nervous excitement at his admission being with each other was a celebration of sorts.

"Drink much whisky?" He popped the cork and filled the glasses.

"I've been known to." She tipped the salad into a bowl and carried it to the table.

"To drown your sorrows or another reason?"

"In my experience, sorrows don't drown. They're there in the morning along with a deadly hangover."

"You must tell me about that experience sometime." He smiled tentatively, but "*sometime*" implied tonight wasn't a one-off.

"What does 'not exactly' mean, Jake?" She placed her hands on her hips, determined to get a straight answer.

"Let's eat while it's hot."

"I expect an answer." Ella set plates and the food containers on the table. "Can you grab the cutlery please?"

He passed her a bundle of knives, forks and spoons, grabbed some paper serviettes from the bench and handed those to her before bringing the champagne to the table. Watching him take off his jacket, hang it over the back of his chair, and remove his tie started a flutter low in Ella's belly. When he undid the top buttons on his shirt and rolled up the sleeves to expose strong forearms, the partial striptease had her wriggling in her chair.

The pasta made up for another missed lunch, and, for a few minutes, she concentrated on eating. "Thanks for this," she said. "It's my favourite pasta dish. They add the right amount of chilli to the sauce."

"Glad you're enjoying it. Unlike last time."

"I had things on my mind last time." *Like her fear of Taylor Law's misuse of power.*

"You've always got things on your mind. How's Tessa?"

"Your cousin never asks that." Ella sat back in her chair. That's what she'd missed. "You always do. Is it because you're interested in her, or know that it's often top of my mind?"

He pushed his plate away and leaned back in his chair, copying her pose.

"Having observed you over a number of encounters, I'm guessing both," she mused, waving her glass in his direction. "You genuinely like children, and whatever your suspicions of me or the situation are, you wouldn't blame a child for adult shenanigans."

"Innocent until proven guilty," he offered the lawyer's mantra. "And children are more innocent than most."

"Bullshit. I was guilty until proven innocent."

"Lust blurred my judgement." He toasted her briefly, a tender smile playing around his mouth.

"I doubt it!" Ella said. She was tempted to lean forward and take him. Test if he tasted as rich, as satisfying as every other time they'd kissed. Addictive enough for a lifetime. "I've seen a bit of Drew in the last two weeks. His parents as well. He brought them for a visit last weekend." She regarded him over her glass.

* * *

"How was that?" Jake noted the colour in her cheeks. He liked seeing her flustered. He'd missed her like hell, but his cousin's behaviour towards her wasn't so different to Drew's pursuit of Julia. Drew's random calls and visits to Jake added to his worry, reinforcing Jake's conviction that pretending they barely knew each other and never spoke was the best way to protect Eleanor from Drew's malicious mischief-making.

"Didn't they tell you?"

"I've kept out of their way too."

"And lost your phone?" she asked sceptically. "Drew loves social media. Sharing photos, happy snaps."

"I must remember to check Drew's feed some time."

"Bronwyn loves having her granddaughter and son

together. It shines out of her. Peter"—she searched for the right word—"Peter is anxious. I'm not sure why. Concern about Bronwyn overdoing it? He's fallen for Tess as well."

"And Drew?" he asked. Her wariness about Drew, her readiness to talk to Jake about her concerns, settled the uneasiness he'd carried in his gut for the last few weeks.

"Drew." Her lake-calm eyes met his. "Provided an almost plausible excuse for his delay on providing a DNA sample. He studies us all. Still hasn't really asked about Tess. Baulks if there's a suggestion he pick her up. And Tessa knows it. Children do."

"What's Tootles take on it?" he deadpanned.

"She hasn't voiced an opinion yet. Would you like dessert now?"

"Later. Why did you ask me to come, Eleanor?"

"Why did you stay away?" She sipped the champagne, then studied the wall over his shoulder when he stayed silent. For distraction or Dutch courage? He wasn't sure. "I've been furious with you until Drew told me a story."

"Tell me."

"It niggled at me, reminded me of a conversation just out of reach. I checked with my parents and sister." She propped her chin on her hand, her clear gaze pinning him to the chair.

"What was it about?" Jake should have expected she'd turn her forensic skills on him.

"The woman Drew hooked up with after Chrissy."

"Drew talked about her?" Jake kept his eyes on her, not prepared to defend or explain himself. Trust was a fragile flower.

"He told me a different story. An older story, he said. About his fiancée. You destroyed his relationship because you can't bear to see him happy. Have always been jealous of him because his parents lived and yours died." She had a beautiful voice, even when she was repeating Drew's poison.

"What are you asking me?" His logical mind told him

that demanding trust without any explanation was unreasonable. He accepted he was unreasonable.

"The odd thing about his story," she continued as if he hadn't spoken. "The thing that niggled and niggled at me was the name of the woman you deliberately and callously seduced from him. His words, *"deliberately and callously,"* not mine. Julia. You see, when I first arrived in Sydney, Chrissy was a mess. She told a jumbled tale of her boyfriend, who we now know is Drew, hooking up with his cousin's fiancée. His cousin—that would be you. Unless there's another cousin?"

"Finish the story, Eleanor."

"I told you some of this the day I couldn't get a babysitter and Bronwyn turned up at your office with Peter. I couldn't remember the details, couldn't remember the name of the woman. Grace did. *Julia.* Odd, don't you think, that Drew had a fiancée with the same name as your fiancée?" She frowned as if trying to unravel a puzzle.

"Are you asking me to confirm or deny his story?" Jake studied the bubbles in his champagne flute as Eleanor inched her way towards the truth. His mouth went dry waiting for her to decide his guilt.

"I know the answer to that. It's why Chrissy asked you to fix things. Drew left Australia with your Julia." She presented her judgement.

"You're sure." Light pushed into the dark places in his mind.

"Dating another woman was a simple way to show Chrissy it was over between them. Dating your fiancée is harder to understand."

"But you've worked that out?" He lifted his head, freed of a burden.

"I've met men like Drew before. They tell slanderous stories or assume confected outrage at others, but the bad behaviour is all their own. I'm guessing the motives he attributed to you are his. He doesn't want you to be happy. He's jealous of you. He'll hurt you if he can. Am I right?"

Long-held tension leaked out of Jake's body. Eleanor's clever guesswork absolved him of disloyalty to his family. He merely had to confirm the truth. But in inviting him here and telling this story, she'd given him something Julia never had: the benefit of the doubt.

"Julia comes from a big, boisterous family. When she saw Drew and I didn't get on, she decided to engineer a reconciliation. I wouldn't discuss it, so she talked to Drew. He was happy to talk about our relationship, his grievances. He told her I was intent on destroying his life. Ultimately, he convinced her, making her question our marriage. She told him of her doubts." He'd never told this story before, but he couldn't stop now. "Drew said it freed him to tell her of his love."

"You booked the room at the hotel that night," she said slowly. "For you and Julia. Did you find them in bed together?"

"Classic cliché, Eleanor." He couldn't hide his grin.

* * *

"How did Chrissy get there?" Ella bit her lower lip as she considered possibilities, examining this new piece of the jigsaw puzzle of her sister's love life. "Drew called her?"

"I don't know the answer to that."

"She wasn't worth years of regret, Jake." She waved her champagne flute, chastising him.

"Are you referring to Julia here, or Chrissy?"

"Now I know you better, probably both. I'm not blind to my sister's flaws. You would have sympathised with Chrissy's betrayal." That's why her sister had spent the night at the hotel. Even dealing with his own shock and betrayal, he'd had space to consider her sister's distress. His compassion was bone-deep.

"Julia came back to me," he said matter-of-factly. "Drew dumped her after six months. He wasn't really interested in Julia."

"Was he punishing you, or trying to get rid of Chrissy? Or did he get lucky and kill two birds with one stone?" Thinking aloud, Ella found the answer. "That's it!"

"Didn't your mother tell you if you frown like that the wind might change and you'll stay that way permanently?"

"My mother doesn't tell lies," she admonished him. "Did you try to make it work?"

"You mean, did I *want* to make it work? It was beyond fixing, and Julia knew it. But she said something that stuck with me."

"What?" she asked when he hesitated. "I can keep a confidence, Counsellor." If he shared a confidence, it meant he'd learned to trust her a little, and perhaps there'd been value in the lonely weeks spent apart.

"She said if I'd trusted her enough, I'd have told her Drew was jealous of me. Told her my side of the story." He frowned, an admission he was aware of the barriers he erected around himself.

"Fair point. She had a right to believe you'd talk to her, trust her first, last and always. But she made the same mistake. She talked to Drew about her doubts about you. She should have talked to you." Yet if she had, Ella wouldn't be alone with Jake now, learning that loyalty to his family was a formidable obstacle to anyone seeking to get close to him.

"Did Robert ask for a reconciliation?"

"There is no way back from describing someone as boring in bed." Ella discovered that Robert Hall's rejection had lost its sting.

He smiled. "We have lousy taste in lovers."

"I appreciate you respecting my need to make up my own mind about Drew. I respect your integrity in not trying to influence me. You're an honourable man." Attraction, respect, trust gave her the courage to push harder. "Does that mean you can't see me?"

"If I see you, I want to touch you." His voice was a rumbling caress.

Ella let out the breath she'd been holding and reached a hand across the table to take his. "Who's stopping you?"

When a slow, sultry smile spread across his face, the thrumming in Ella's blood became a staccato beat. A knot in her stomach unclenched, then dissolved into a puddle of heat in her lower belly. The fear he might not look at her with that lick of heat in his eyes again had left her listless. She hadn't been able to shake her low spirits, even knowing she couldn't afford to rely on him. He wasn't offering her more than an affair. His deep loyalty to his aunt and uncle drove his silence about Drew. A sense of obligation sealing off part of his heart.

Would he lower his barricades for her? Let her into his life?

"Aren't you going to pounce?" She tried to smile.

"Where's the surprise in that?" He stood, topped off both glasses and walked around the table, keeping hold of her hand. "Bring your glass."

Ella let him lead her to her own sofa, sat obediently and watched him circle the room. A match flickered, and the creamy, slightly exotic scent of the vanilla-soy candles she'd set on side tables filled the space. Then the unmistakable sound of Ed Sheeran—the last track she'd played—crooning *"... people fall in love in mysterious ways,"* rolled over her. The overhead light clicking off cocooned her in a world of Jake's creation. Anticipation skittered through her, and the butterflies in her stomach jostled for room. He joined her on the sofa, his muscled thigh resting against hers.

"One day we'll do this under a real night sky, but tonight we'll have make-believe, with your star-covered ceiling. Sip your drink, Eleanor. Let the French bubbles weave their magic."

"I'm not nervous."

He flashed her a quizzical look.

"Nervous is the wrong word." She sipped, savouring the effervescent alcohol, feeling each bubble pop in her bloodstream. Her body unravelled in steady delight. "Try happy, excited. Okay, I've got a few nerves."

"Let me take that." Placing his glass on the side table, he took hers and set it aside. When he lifted her into his lap, she sighed.

"I want to touch too," Ella confessed, reaching around to tug the thin leather strap from his hair, dropping it behind the sofa, hopefully never to be found again. "Every time I see you, I want to do that. I love your hair, those thick, glossy locks. The perfect anchor for my hands. If I hang on"—she twined her hands in his hair and tugged him closer—"I can do this."

Touching her mouth to his, she sampled texture and taste, then drew back. "You're beautiful, you know." On her second excursion, she traced his lower lip with her tongue, teasing and testing her control. "Such a classically beautiful face." She brushed her lips over one cheekbone, then the other. "Strong bones, fine lines."

"Eleanor."

She paused her exploration. "Mmm."

"Stop talking." He caught her lower lip between his teeth, feasted on it while his hands swept up her sides. He groaned, drawing her with him as he slid down the sofa. She was aware of being nestled between the back of the sofa and his lean length and growing arousal.

Again and again, he dipped into her mouth. Kisses that emptied her mind, drugged her senses, and stirred a craving for more. *Don't stop*, the words beat a tattoo in her brain. *Never stop*. Desperate for his heat, she pushed her hands under his shirt.

"Your hands are cold." His muscles instinctively tightened. "Cold hands, warm heart," he crooned.

The craving to touch everywhere, to taste everything drove her. She strained to get closer—caution had made them wait too long when her heart knew they belonged together.

"Help me, help me, help me." Wriggling out from under his relentlessly tender caresses, Ella knelt on the sofa, her breathing coming in short shallow bursts. Desperate, she'd pulled the sweater over her head, craving closeness. Instead, she'd trapped her hands in her sleeves.

"Let me help," he murmured, still teasing her with his touch. Caught in the blindness of her confining clothing, Ella's awareness narrowed to the fingers tiptoeing across her midriff. Firm, warm, sure in their destination, and still he teased. Pushing her bra aside, he brushed his open palms back and forth across her breasts—tantalisingly light. She cried out with pleasure. "You like that." He sounded entranced before his mouth closed over an erect nipple. He suckled, the pull echoing deep in her pelvis.

"I want to see you." When she flung her sweater aside, he lifted his head, his eyes dark with demand. "Yes," she moaned, seeing her need reflected in his eyes.

"You're lovely," he whispered.

Demand dragged at her loins. Hot, wet, wanting. Threading her hands into his hair, she pulled hard. His eyes were unfocused, his mouth dipping in a sensual curve. "My turn," she breathed, pushing him back on his heels. With urgent fingers, she slipped the first button, moved to the second. Ella purred as the backs of her fingers brushed across his chest. Deep within her, a motor hummed as her body caught the rhythm of his, the steady rise and fall of his chest. She watched their silhouettes dance on the wall opposite—a mating ritual, where she'd found her perfect mate.

"Yes. Please. More," he murmured words of encouragement while she worked on his buttons, his hands resting against his thighs. The heat surrounding her became palpable, burning off him. Anticipation was a firestorm, ignited by the intoxicating scent of arousal. *Heaven smelt like this.* When she drew him up to reach for his belt buckle, he shrugged the crisp business shirt off his shoulders. Seeing his muscled torso made her mouth water.

"Wait." His husky growl stopped her fumbling with his zipper.

"You're kidding." Ella's fingers trembled. *He couldn't*

mean it.

He closed his hands over hers. "Decide now. Here or the bed."

"I won't make it to the bed." She yanked the zipper down the last few centimetres and started pushing the worsted wool off his hips.

"Right answer." He slid to the floor, taking her with him.

They rolled on the thick rug. His trousers caught at his ankles. His fingers skimmed her buttocks, gliding under the leg of her knickers, before sliding into her, then out, enticing her to rise higher, to surrender to her pleasure. She cried out.

He swallowed her cry, then launched a fresh assault on her senses, his tongue mimicking the action of his clever fingers teasing her clitoris. She was boneless, melting over him.

"Jake—" She tumbled into a sharp, sweet orgasm.

"You taste good, Ellie." He sucked her juices from his fingers.

Ella had never felt more powerful. That single erotic action shattered any doubt he might not want her as much as she wanted him. Touch was compulsive, addictive. She ran her palms over his shoulders, down his back, urging him towards her.

"You're more stunning than I imagined." He lavished her with words of praise. "And I imagined a lot." He started a new rhythm. The slip and slide of her leg over his thigh, of his arm over her torso, of his hand over her breast, of her fingers clinging to his as she drew his body to hers.

"You're stunning too." She grabbed his hair to ground herself. Temptation and torture and every moment, every movement, a pleasure more intense than Ella had ever known.

"We're both stunning." He rolled her onto her back. Crouching above her, he trailed kisses from her throat to her core, as if he couldn't get enough of her. *What Jake could do with his mouth was a revelation.* This was how loving should be. Ed Sheeran's voice soared in the background.

"I want—" The words whispered from her lips, but before she could say what she wanted, he'd taken her over the edge again. She stroked a hand down his cheek and smiled.

* * *

Jake raised his head, and the picture she presented shook his confidence he'd ever known what "wanting" meant before her. Her loose curls created a halo around her head on the ancient rug, her eyes were glazed with desire, and her subtle female scent sharpened his need.

"I want you." She beckoned with a come-hither finger and a naughty smile.

Jake surrendered, settling his body over hers. She wriggled. A perfumed shimmy to beguile him. She'd crashed through his defensive walls. All the hot looks and stolen touches had led to this moment, when he couldn't get enough of her. Not sex, but a lovemaking more shattering than he'd ever experienced. "I want to trace each dip and curve. Your breasts"—he caressed them with open palms— "your midriff, your hips." His hands followed his words. When her head fell back, her throat arching in delight, he was there, catching her open mouth with his, pouring his passion into her.

"Please, Jake," she panted.

"I want to please you." He lavished attention on her eyebrows, her cheeks. A kiss here, a caress there. "Wait." He grabbed his trousers, hauled his wallet out of a pocket and flipped it open to find a condom. The throb in his balls matched the throbbing in his temples, an urgent bass while he fumbled the sheath onto his cock. He crawled over her.

"Please." An invitation he couldn't resist.

Jake sampled her full lower lip, stoking her ardour with short hot kisses, building a primitive rhythm. He lowered himself, heartbeat by careful heartbeat, to wallow in the sheer magic of skin rubbing against skin. Her satin softness made him slick and needy.

"Now?" he growled the question.

"Yes." She gripped his forearms.

The air between them hummed. Jake tasted the warmth of her skin, revelling in her instinctive sexuality. With one delicious movement, he buried himself inside her wet heat. Fire and light—sweat-slicked bodies and heated caresses, touching, learning, demanding. Her cry of release tore through the quiet room, closely followed by his. He rolled onto his back, drawing her onto his chest, sucking in oxygen.

What the hell had happened to him?

Before he'd worked out the answer, she propped herself on her forearms, grinned and gave an uninhibited wriggle.

"Give me a minute." Jake slid her off his chest, tucking her into the shelter of his wrapped arm. He pressed soft kisses on her hair while his heart rate returned to normal. Although he doubted it would ever be normal again.

"I may have died and gone to heaven," she murmured.

"Why did we wait?" Jake turned his head to grin at her.

She pushed at his hair, let her hand linger in its thickness. "Because we're sensible, cautious people."

"If we were sensible, cautious people, we wouldn't have started this now." He still hadn't uncovered Drew's end plan.

"I needed this, and you. Now. Do you regret it?" Her gaze was unguarded.

"I could never regret what we just shared, Eleanor. I don't, even though I didn't plan it when I came here tonight." He tucked her closer, pressing a kiss to her temple.

"Did you consider it?" She walked her fingers up his chest, braver than him in her willingness to expose her feelings.

"Let's say the idea's crossed my mind a few times." And until tonight, Jake had fought the temptation. But she'd rung him; she'd confided in him; she'd shown faith in him, and his rigid control had slipped.

"For me, it's been a few hundred." Rising to her feet, she picked up the strip of abandoned condoms and sauntered in the direction of her bedroom, flaunting her nakedness. "Come to bed, Jake."

Even with a head start, Jake caught her before she reached the door, showering her with the petals of a rose he'd snatched from a vase near the sofa.

"Rose petals? How romantic." She studied his interested cock and peeled open another condom. "Allow me."

Jake stoically withstood her exquisite torture, hands clenched at his sides. Once she'd sheathed him, he made his move, lifting her, and holding her against the wall to enter her. He braced to keep the rhythm slow, yet his heart pounded. "Are you looking for romance?"

"True confessions?" Wrapping her legs around his waist, she rocked against him, taking him further into her. "This is romance."

"Let me love you, Eleanor?" With his heart racing, Jake's gaze locked on her as he pushed into her again and again. Her skin was pure silk, her fingers dug into his shoulders, and her eyes glazed over with stunned delight. "Tell me what you feel?"

"Like the firecrackers we had on the farm for special occasions when I was a child. Brilliant colours and flashing lights. Except I'm one of them. The magic's in me and"— she gasped—"about to explode."

Jake staggered to the bed, dropping her on her back and falling beside her, gulping in air.

"You're the one who couldn't wait until we got to bed," she teased.

"You could have run faster." Jake helped her pull the covers over them. When she curled her body around his, he knew what it was to be cherished. She reached for him during the night. She was all soft touches, laughing whispers, and sharing secrets.

"Why do you call me Eleanor?" She cuddled against his

side, her hand linked with his, her warmth inviting confidences.

"It suits you. A bright, shining light. In your work you bring hope to people who are at the end of their tether." The stories his friend, Tony, had told him about EJ had sketched a picture. He'd learned more. "A fire burns in your belly. It warms all in your vicinity."

"You're making me blush, Jake."

"That's what I see when I look at you, when I think of you. Grace and an integrity that never wavers."

In the early hours of the morning, Jake held her close, absorbing the lingering perfume that was a mixture of the fragrance she wore, her scent and the scent of their lovemaking. He hadn't expected this tsunami of feeling. Hadn't had the wit to see that wanting her the way he did had its roots in caring for her. More than he'd anticipated. Maybe more than he was ready for.

He couldn't offer her glamour or mystery or excitement, the trappings of romance. Not when Drew kept a close watch. When Drew had already started planting lies. Peter might be anxious about Drew's next move. Jake was braced for an attack.

* * *

The sounds of Tessa's morning sing-song to Tootles woke Ella. Turning her head, she found Jake missing. Only the indentation in the pillow and the ache in her body told her their lovemaking had been real. She stretched her arms above her head, wriggled her toes and smiled—her marvellous lover, thoughtful, inventive and gloriously thorough. Maybe there was something to be said for studying law if it encouraged such absolute concentration on the task at hand.

She listened for sounds of him in the apartment. When she found none, doubts started to cloud her happiness, and she burrowed further under the covers, seeking comfort.

Why had Jake left her on their first morning as lovers? A morning when they should have clung together, laughing at secret jokes, touching each other, tasting because they hadn't had their fill.

Rolling over in the bed, Ella buried her face in the pillow he'd lain on, surrounding herself with his scent, pretending his body still warmed her.

But Ella had never been big on pretending. Had he really gone without a word?

His note was pinned to the kitchen bench with a coffee cup.

I didn't have the heart to wake you. I've got an early appointment. I changed and fed Tessa and put her back in her cot. —Jake

Not loverlike, but caring. She could work with caring.

"Whoa! Where are you letting your mind go, girl?"

She loved him.

When had that happened? Her heart skidded to a halt. Where had her famed clear-headedness gone? Degree by slow degree, he'd invaded first her mind, then aroused her body, then stolen her wary heart until each breath she took deepened her love.

Snapshots of the pirate king from their first meeting, the caring nephew, the thoughtful man, the sexy male animal rolled through her mind like a video clip, with music rising to a crescendo behind it. She couldn't see the ending.

The sight of the kitchen clock stopped her anxious surmising. "Damn, you'll be late." She had less than an hour and a half to get Tessa to childcare and herself to work.

Warm water cascaded over her head and down her back, following paths Jake's hands had drawn. He hadn't said he loved her.

Neither did you.

He'd been the perfect lover but had made no promises. While they hadn't planned their love-making, he'd come prepared to guard against conception. Caution or distrust? He hadn't actually confirmed that his absence for the last two weeks had something to do with Drew. Hadn't needed to because she'd gone all gooey-eyed when he'd said, *"If I see you, I want to touch you."*

She shouldn't, couldn't expect more. Another woman would be grateful he'd fed Tessa and let Ella sleep in. Eleanor Jane Anderson had learned survival at a tough school. His kindness wasn't in doubt, nor was his skill as a lover. *Was he prepared to share himself?*

CHAPTER TEN

One week of stolen nights and days where Ella allowed herself to dream. One week where she and her pirate hid out in her apartment and talked about everything and nothing, listened to music, squabbled over distant galaxies and took turns making dinner. He arrived after dark and was gone when she rose in the morning, pleading work, but he'd refused an invitation to visit her parents next weekend.

"Not yet."

He'd used the same words she'd used when she refused maintenance from the Brownings. Her secret superstition that accepting money implied an obligation, or could be used against her. She didn't think for a second Bronwyn and Peter had any plans to take Tessa away from her, but an innate caution made her wait until the DNA results were through, until her claim for legal custody was resolved.

What sat behind Jake's *"not yet"*?

Thinking back over the week, she realised they hadn't gone out together. *Anywhere.* Not to see Peter and Bronwyn, not to a restaurant, not even for a walk around the block. A few nights ago, when Tessa had been restless and fretful, Ella had suggested a walk. Jake had taken her place in the rocking chair and sung Tessa to sleep. The sight of her lover soothing her child had tugged at her belly with a longing so intense her knees had given way. Now she tallied it up as another refusal to be seen in public with her.

Yesterday she'd pushed for a lift to his office because of an appointment in the city. He'd hidden it quickly, but his reluctance returned now like thick smog to choke her happiness. When he'd kissed her goodbye, she'd secretly exulted to hear a stranger from a passing car shout, "Get a room."

Something was wrong.

Vague discontent she refused to name prickled under her skin like sharp needles. Her relationship with Robert Hall had started as a secret affair—his choice. When she'd planned outings, he'd coaxed her out of her misgivings by saying he wanted her to himself for a while. Her ego had puffed up like a balloon filled with helium gas. But secrets were hard to keep in small country towns, and theirs was common knowledge long before he ran away with Chrissy.

This wasn't the same. Jake was a loner, fiercely loyal to his family and silent on his cousin's transgressions because of that loyalty. Ella's relationship with him was based on mutual respect. Except without understanding how she'd got here, she was looking for booby traps. The DNA result had come through yesterday, and Jake hadn't visited last night, hadn't called this morning. Checking the silent phone was a teenager's obsessive habit, but Ella was gripped by a teenager's confusion and uncertainty about her lover.

A secret affair? She remembered her unease at his aloofness when they visited his aunt and uncle's house, his disappearance for two weeks when they returned to town. The suspicion he didn't want to be seen with her exposed insecurities she'd thought she'd dealt with. She'd been as clear as she could be that she'd seen through Drew's lies, that she wasn't another Julia. So why did she feel as if they were hiding out, that Jake didn't want anyone to know about their affair—*their clandestine affair?*

Doubts crowded her. He'd been careful to make no

promises. He'd been distant last night when he called to cancel. She hated the doubts, hated more that she couldn't shake them.

* * *

Jake moved towards the door as Drew sauntered into his office. His cousin had demanded an appointment. Jake had agreed. He hadn't spoken to Drew since he'd started staying over at Eleanor's, had pleaded work to avoid contact. His cousin would notice the changes in him that he was only slowly becoming aware of himself. Happiness was the only word for the cocktail of sensations buzzing in his veins.

Drew wandered around the room, selecting a legal tome from the bookcase, flipping through a few pages, returning it, passing on to another, then standing to look out the windows, his hands in his pockets, rocking back on his heels.

"You wanted to see me, Drew."

His cousin spun to face him. "The DNA results are in, but you knew that."

"We all expected the results. I also expected they'd confirm you're Tessa's father." Eleanor had called with the news yesterday, said Drew was dropping by. Jake had made an excuse not to see her. A precaution, because if he'd met his cousin in Eleanor's apartment, there was every chance Tessa would throw herself into his arms for one of their bedtime games, proof he was a regular visitor. Proof Ella and Tessa were important to him.

Jake had missed her last night. *Missed them both.*

"Did Ella tell you?" Drew tapped a forefinger to his lips.

"Chrissy told me in a letter she sent before she died. You confirmed it by agreeing to the DNA test. You wouldn't have taken the test if you didn't know the result in advance." Jake eliminated all emotion from his voice. "Congratulations. She's a beautiful little girl."

"Who looks more like you than me." Drew strolled

towards him.

"Genetics is a complex science," Jake said. His cousin knew Jake had never touched Chrissy, but kept the threat in his arsenal of weapons to needle Jake when he could.

"I've asked Ella to marry me."

A primal roar screamed through Jake. His hands formed fists, and he took a quick step forward, ready to knock his cousin across the room, pound him for daring to think he could lay a hand on Eleanor. A red haze danced in front of his eyes.

His cousin gave an ugly laugh. "Don't like that idea, coz."

"I have no say in the matter." Years of practice allowed Jake to drag his voice under control.

"Been sniffing around her yourself." His cousin tugged on Jake's tie, a small tell he didn't get the answer he wanted from Eleanor. "Does it give you a kick to bed Chrissy and then Ella?"

"Chrissy and I were never lovers." Jake restated the truth.

"But you and Ella are. That's very interesting."

"I was going to say the DNA result rather ends the Chrissy argument." Jake sensed growing edginess in his cousin. "Making the same accusation about Eleanor and I is another unproven assertion."

"I called by yesterday morning, after I got the results. I arrived out front in time to witness a very revealing goodbye kiss." Drew raised his hand and slapped the back of it with his other hand. "You've been a bad boy."

Jake could still taste the kiss that had betrayed them. Eleanor had stood looking at him as if she had a question, nibbled her bottom lip, and he'd forgotten his own name. He'd wanted to hurry her up to his office, lock the door and make love to her for hours. Instead, he'd settled for a kiss that had steam rising from the pavement around them. Her slender body had wrapped around his, her soft moan of delight had rung in his ears and her sweetness had lingered on his tongue. "It's none of your business."

"That's where you're wrong, coz. It's very much my business who the current carer of my child is screwing. You could be a bad influence. In fact, I told her what a bad influence you are. Caught after a night with Chrissy in a hotel room."

"Did she believe you?" He'd had this conversation with Eleanor.

"I wonder." Drew gave a cat-that-swallowed-the-cream grin. "I bet you didn't know Ella's old boyfriend wanted their affair kept secret."

Jake flinched. He remembered the confusion in her eyes when she'd asked for a lift yesterday. She hadn't told him Robert Hall wanted a secret affair, but it fitted. *Shit!*

"Said keeping it secret made it special. A line I've used since. Secret, that is, until he ran away with Chrissy." Drew resumed ambling around the room.

"Get to the point, Drew." Hearing the story from Drew exposed the risk Jake had taken—expecting her to take him on trust when he wouldn't explain his actions.

"Taking my time is more fun." Drew pushed his hands into his pockets with the casual elegance of a male model. "You've been very secretive about your affair with Ella, coz. That makes her uneasy. Still, the silly girl rejected me."

"What do you want?" Jake's body braced for the coming attack.

"Sole custody of Tessa."

The spurt of rage was whiplash quick. If Jake revealed his hand now, he'd lose the game. "Why on earth would you saddle yourself with a child?" Threatening to take custody of Tessa was sheer evil. *Eleanor hadn't called Jake.* His pulse kicked up a beat with the why of that.

"I wasn't told. I was denied the first years of her life." Drew's handsome face filled with regret. "Now she's motherless, and I'm her only biological parent. I can provide her with a secure home, loving grandparents."

The ring of authenticity in his performance curdled

Jake's stomach. Jake was no Robert Hall, but he tasted fear all the same. *What did Eleanor's silence mean?* "She's not motherless."

"Her mother's dead. Ella might have custody, but she's her aunt, and you, even if you're playing house, are technically even further removed." Drew's smile was menacing, but he'd handed Jake an ace. Drew hadn't guessed Eleanor didn't have official custody of Tessa.

"First my parents, now my child. Can't you find your own?" His cousin opened his palms as if seeking divine guidance.

"I was nine. I wasn't the one making the decisions about where I lived." Any remaining sympathy for the boy Jake had followed around as a small child died. He wasn't responsible for Drew's twisted obsessions. Jake's attempts at friendship, as a child, an adolescent and an adult, had been rebuffed. He owed his cousin nothing. "Chrissy loved you. She would have given you a family, shared Tessa with you gladly. Your parents would have been thrilled. That life was yours for the taking."

Drew sneered. "The temptation to take Julia was too sweet to resist. And so easy. Besides, I didn't want a kid then. I had London in my sights and a glamorous new woman on my arm."

In his need to boast, his cousin had let slip his prior knowledge of Chrissy's pregnancy. Hearsay, therefore not admissible as evidence, but Jake filed it away. "I'm assuming you want something, Drew?"

"You bet I do, coz. I'm giving you first chance to represent me. To stitch it up properly."

"That sounds like an ultimatum?" Jake had learned to recognise the signals, the restless hands, the eyes that darted everywhere, and the gleam of malice making Drew's teeth flash white.

"I've already spoken to an old partner of yours ... Rory Davies." Drew crossed to one of the leather chairs, settled into it. "You dismissed him, made it hard for him to get work. He's very keen to take the brief. Feels convinced we can win. He's not too worried about the details." Drew's shorthand for questionable legal practices.

"I'd forgotten you knew Rory." Jake had never understood his cousin's mindless determination to hurt him, but he'd worked out ways to minimise the impact. Wouldn't give a damn now if Drew was taking aim at him instead of Eleanor and Tessa.

"An old mate." A sly smile flashed across Drew's face.

Jake's mind raced, considering and discarding options. He couldn't take the risk Drew was bluffing. Rory would enjoy prosecuting the case. If Drew could maintain his act as the wronged father, there was a chance he'd win.

I love Eleanor. The realisation hit Jake with the force of a runaway truck, a blow strong enough to fell him. He turned away, making a show of walking around his desk and sitting down, taking his time, when pummelling Drew into oblivion held the greater appeal. His cousin might guess he was having an affair with Eleanor, but he couldn't read Jake's heart. *He loved her.* The knowledge came as naturally as his next breath.

"I'm assuming you're looking at living in Australia, with agreements granting access for your parents, for Eleanor and her parents." Jake played dumb, pumping his cousin for his plans.

Drew laughed softly. "If you wrangle attractive enough conditions, I'm prepared to stay in Australia. For a while."

Drew's cockiness was Jake's best chance. His cousin's brand of arrogance convinced him the child Drew had bullied still lived in the man. Jake had worked hard to rid himself of the pattern of frustration, anger, reluctance, and then capitulation to Drew's demands that had shamed him during adolescence. Drew would have more chance of success if he'd got his sleazebag mate Rory Davies to handle this quietly.

Jake pushed to his feet and started pacing his office. "It'll kill any chance I have of getting back in Ella's bed." He threw the words over his shoulder, reinforcing sex as his only interest in Eleanor.

His cousin steepled his hands in front of him, enjoying the show.

"Rory will screw it up," Jake muttered, as he continued pacing, repeating the pattern his cousin expected. "He won't be able to get Bron and Peter on side." Then he came to a standstill, shoved his hands into his trouser pockets and snarled. "What conditions?"

"I'm not as flush as I'd like to be at the moment. Chrissy would have liked the kid raised near the beach. An apartment in Bondi. Big enough so Mum and Dad can stay when they visit."

"What happened to your inheritance?" Jake swallowed his disgust. *His cousin was prepared to mess with multiple lives for money?*

"Living in London is expensive, and there's more competition for my skills there. I'd make more money back here. But"—he lifted a leg to place his ankle on his opposite knee—"I've been to a few of my old haunts. There's a certain reserve from some people. They seem to hold me responsible for the bust-up between you and Julia."

"That wouldn't normally worry you." His cousin was more relaxed now that Jake was ceding him the victory, savouring the moment and pushing for a little humiliation. Relaxed enough to reveal the need for money as well as the fact that hatred of Jake was driving him.

"I need access to that world to work in Sydney."

"And?" Jake kept his expression blank, his body loose, prepared to give Drew any bloody thing, except a hint that he planned to destroy his claim for custody. He'd make sure he never had unsupervised access to Tessa, never had the chance to hurt Eleanor again, and paid twice over for every second of distress this would inflict on her.

"It'll be useful to attend a few parties together, coz, while I ease myself back into the Sydney scene. You can arrange a few invites." Drew brushed an invisible speck of dust from his trouser leg in studied indifference.

"I don't mix with the people you want to meet." But Jake was getting the message. Drew wanted him to grovel in public. He laughed to himself. Being seen smoothing Drew's way at a few social events was a small price to pay for throwing Drew off his scent. Protecting Eleanor was the main game. Eleanor and Tessa.

"You know who does and can get me started. By the time I've got custody of the kid, we should be ready to part company."

"Why ask me? Why didn't you just employ Rory Davies?" Jake was genuinely curious. Rory was better suited to do the job Drew wanted done. Rory could have sued for custody before Jake had even known.

"I know how strongly you feel about your obligations to the family that took in a snivelling orphan." Drew rose to his feet, his smile that of a shark circling its prey. "Mum would be pretty devastated not to see the kid anymore. You always say you owe her."

The hatred in Drew's eyes was chilling but liberating as well. Drew's powerplay was a pincer movement attacking him from two sides, using Eleanor and his parents to blacken Jake's name.

Eleanor would fight, but she'd hate Jake whether she won or lost. If she won, she might think the risk of letting Tessa spend time with Bron and Peter was too great. Bron wouldn't forgive Jake for losing her newly discovered granddaughter. If Eleanor lost, Drew would most likely park Tessa with Bronwyn. Either way, Drew would always hover, a lone wolf ready to strike without warning.

"You should thank me. I'm giving you the chance to pay my mother back by delivering the grandchild she craves. And I've employed Rory. Back-up to keep you on your toes. Make sure you don't start freelancing."

"Then he'll confirm the rules in this state regarding custody. You'll have to attend a mediation session first." Time for Jake to push back a little. "The court looks for agreement between the parties. Compromise."

"What kind of compromise?"

"Eleanor won't give you custody without a fight. Hasn't Rory given you a heads up? Given the situation and Tessa's age, you'll have to agree to access for Eleanor and her family." Jake's knowledge of family law was limited, but common sense was on his side.

Drew shrugged. "She can see the kid sometimes so long as control is mine."

"You'll need a strong case to win custody from her." Jake's only warning to his cousin.

"Then start building it, coz."

"I think you've misunderstood." Jake stood. His cousin's desire to gloat had given him the information he needed. "I can make a few introductions to see you re-established in Sydney. However, representing you in Tessa's custody case would be a conflict of interest." He smiled grimly. "I could be restrained from operating. It's too big a risk when I have no expertise in family law."

"You were prepared to represent Mum and Dad." Drew stared at him, his mouth sagging open in disbelief.

"That's the point. I still do. I'm not sure your interests match theirs." Jake hoped like hell he was right. But it didn't matter a damn. He'd use representing his aunt and uncle as a cover for as long as he could.

"I'll make sure they do," Drew snarled.

Winning sole custody for Eleanor was Jake's real conflict of interest. Rory Daniels would trawl through her past, try to suggest Jake's affair with her made her an unsuitable guardian. He'd probably rake up the old gossip about Chrissy and Jake. Drew would happily destroy Eleanor to punish him.

"I'll win. Don't think hiding behind my parents will comfort Ella." Drew flung the final words as a gauntlet.

Jake sat at his desk, staring into space after his cousin left. Maybe he should thank Drew for bringing him to his senses, for making him see he loved Eleanor. That the magic they made in her tiny apartment, the circle they'd created had become the most important part of his life. Except he'd said the words "let me love you" the first night they'd made love, not understanding the absolute truth of them. Drew enjoyed humiliating him. For the sin of being an orphan who'd moved into his house. But, shit, he'd been nine. Old enough for memories of his parents to give him a hold on sanity.

Tessa was a baby, still making precious memories. She needed Eleanor. God help him, so did he. Keeping secrets from her had been a mistake. Trying to keep their relationship a secret hadn't protected her from Drew.

Slamming a hand on the table, he pushed himself upright. He couldn't afford any more mistakes. The slightest whisper of his real intentions could alert Drew to his plans. He couldn't discount Rory Davies already having him under surveillance. Jake would introduce Drew to any bloody celebrity mover and shaker he named, and secretly build Eleanor's case. When the time came, he'd take Drew down.

He snatched up his phone. Nothing from Eleanor, when texting each other half a dozen times a day had become a habit. *His fault.* Last night he'd pleaded a business engagement. Another text saying he was working tonight would be a denial of all they'd shared. To protect her he'd be a callous bastard. Picturing her shock and distress, Jake despised the boy he'd been, who'd allowed Drew to bully him, and the man he was, unable to see another way out of this mess.

* * *

Ella wrapped her coat around herself, although the chill invading her bones was caused by her own misgivings as much as the brisk wind whistling around the square. Jake's apartment block—a modern, multi-storey security block, professionally landscaped. The top floors would have extensive city views. Jake had an upper-floor apartment. She knew the number, had counted the floors, and the lights were on. She didn't know what had brought her here tonight. A compelling need to see him, a need for him to reassure her that everything was okay, that Drew had been lying when he rang to tell her he was applying for sole custody of Tessa and Jake was letting him?

It didn't make sense. But then nothing made sense at the moment.

Jake's text said he had to work late tonight, yet here he was at barely eight o'clock, home with the lights on. He could be working from home, but she smelled a lie.

A big fat lie, and it was crushing her.

He'd lied once before, hadn't told her Peter and Bronwyn were his aunt and uncle. He'd said it wasn't a lie, just a failure to disclose.

Mrs. P was looking after Tessa for a few hours. Now Ella was standing outside Jake's apartment on an early winter's night afraid of what she'd learn when she rang his bell.

"Hello, Jake. Can I see you?" she asked when he answered. The click of the buzzer opening the front door sounded a death knell.

Another smooth, silent elevator and she remembered the first day she'd met him, when she'd been wary of Taylor Law and the power the company could wield. Tonight she wanted him to tell her Drew was lying, that Jake wouldn't stand by and see Tessa taken from her.

He waited at the open door to his apartment. Bare feet, faded jeans, a figure-hugging T-shirt and the thick locks she loved so much, loose. Bed-rumpled was her first impression, and her legs threatened to give way. Was someone else in the apartment? Robert Hall's betrayal cast a long shadow, undermining her self-confidence as a woman. She'd found Jake out in a lie.

People who lied rarely stopped at one.

"Come in."

The room slapped Ella with its remoteness. Black and white tones, soulless furnishings and an emptiness that dragged at her. He'd told her about it, how he hadn't cared where he'd lived when he'd bought it. She struggled to find her bearings, disoriented by the sterile environment. Did living here tell a truer story about who he was than the man who'd shared her chaos and her bed in recent days?

"Would you like a drink?" He'd crossed to a desk, and held up a glass of whisky.

"Please." She shucked her coat and left it with her bag on the hallstand.

Now that she was here, she didn't know what to do or say. *She loved him.* She wanted him. She trusted him. And was terribly afraid he was going to say something to shatter her certainty. She walked further into the room. The gurgle of liquid leaving a bottle, the splash as it landed in fine crystal, the sound of footfalls on bare boards hammered at her. Then he was at her side, pressing the glass of peaty malt into her unsteady hand. She leaned against his shoulder, and because it was her natural inclination, because she couldn't help herself, she turned and pressed a kiss to the firm, bare skin where the sleeve of his T-shirt ended.

He jerked at her touch. Then whisked the glass out of her hand and swung her into his arms. With a groan, he started kissing her. Desperation leaked from him to her, and Ella was powerless to stop him. She'd been without his touch for two nights now, an eternity.

For an endless time, she floated on a sea of passion, aware his lips had left hers and were trailing along her throat. His busy hands pushed her cardigan off her shoulders. Ella helped him when he tried to free her arms. His fingers raced to the buttons on her blouse and his mouth followed his fingers, sliding down the valley between her breasts. With the buttons free, his thumb slipped the strap from her shoulder, then his warm palm cupped her breast.

They were racing each other, she thought, as if any delay would bring a halt and any halt would be the end of the world.

She surrendered to sensation. He hurried her through a

doorway, tumbling with her onto the bed. They rolled. She pulled at his clothing and he tugged at hers until she was panting, sucking in air, and skin brushed skin. She couldn't deny the slick of heat and need. The scent of his desire was a familiar link between past loving and now. Ella's gaze met his, and she saw her desperate desire to mate reflected before a word could be spoken to shatter the moment. He pulled on a condom, gripped her hips and pushed between her thighs, entering her in an intense movement, claiming absolute possession from both of them. Reaching her peak, she cried out and exulted in his groan as he toppled after her.

When he rolled away from her, Ella accepted the sting of rejection. The wildness of their passion testimony this was to be their last act of loving. She turned her back, overcome by an urgent need to cover her nakedness.

"Were you going to tell me?" Ella sat on the side of the bed.

"I'm assuming Drew called," he said flatly, sliding out the opposite side.

"Drew visited yesterday after the DNA results were confirmed. Do you want me to tell you what he wanted, or do you already know?"

"He said he asked you to marry him." His voice had sharp edges.

"I'm not sure if the word 'marry' was mentioned." Ella's voice echoed in her head, disconnected from her. "He suggested we hook up and collect a motza from his parents." His words had been neither question nor statement, rather a lure to someone he believed would take the bait. The friendly manner of their earlier encounters gone, replaced by hot eyes roaming her body as if he had a right to. She located her blouse and pulled it on, buttoning it up with trembling fingers.

"What was your answer?" Jake's question was a slap in the face.

Had she made love with a man who understood so little about her, who hadn't instantly known her answer?

"I had no answer when he said Chrissy would have been up for it. When he made me see that my sister, who I knew wasn't perfect, would have done it." Drew's covetous appraisal of her body and bold look had made her feel soiled. Ella found her knickers and trousers and pulled them on, stuffing her bra into her trouser pocket.

"Possible. You knew your sister better than me. She might have made a deal with him." He grabbed a robe off the bedside chair, belting it tightly. "But, there's no proof. Chrissy wrote to me, not him, not them. I doubt she had any idea of his parents' true worth."

Ella rose to her feet and turned to face him. His unpitying analysis left her uncertain of her next move. "Drew rang again this afternoon. What is going on, Counsellor?"

Letting him gain sole custody of Tessa had Ella plotting violence. Jake's dull eyes sent a shiver of fear through her. *What was going on?* Why wouldn't Jake tell her?

"Answer me, Jake." Her fingers curled into a fist.

"What did Drew tell you I'm doing?" The half-light of the room left Jake's face in shadow. His mood was unreadable to her from his posture, his expression or his voice—he'd become the shadow.

Ella pushed her feet into her boots and tucked her socks in her other pocket, while her brain stuttered to a halt. "He's suing for sole custody of Tessa. Said he's doing it to give his parents certainty. That you're representing his parents." Saying the words aloud while he watched her made them more real. "You're frightening me, Jake."

"Did he tell you he's using Rory Daniels?"

Her heart stopped. If he'd backhanded her, the shock couldn't have been greater. "The lawyer who helped cheat my parents?"

"I think you should go."

"What did we just do?" Tears stung the back of her eyes.

"We took what we wanted, without considering

consequences." He fisted a hand in his unruly locks, holding the weight off his face. "I didn't make any promises."

"Not in words. Not to me." She scooped up her cardigan as she stumbled towards the bedroom door. But she'd made promises to him. In her heart, with her body. And had failed to reach him. "Is your loyalty to your family so blind, so total you'd destroy everyone else to give them what they want?"

"I won't discuss my family."

She swung back to him. "*We're* discussing you and me."

"You kissed me ..." He halted, lifting and dropping his hands as if he had no idea what came next.

"Silly me. I acted. You reacted." Her bones ached. She'd completely misread his interest in her. Lust, not care, certainly not love. She'd only imagined the love in his touch. The fallout from her error of judgement was more terrifying than she could have imagined. "My kiss was not an invitation to screw me, literally and figuratively." She pushed her hands into her cardigan, but it became twisted.

"Eleanor."

"That makes what we just did the worst kind of lie. You used me."

Ella raced towards the front door, grabbing her coat and bag from the hall. She couldn't breathe, couldn't think past the huge weight pressing against her chest, suffocating her. She couldn't bear to wait for the elevator, pushing into the stairwell and hurrying down several flights of stairs before she collapsed onto a concrete step. Nothing made sense anymore. Their lovemaking had been both tender and tough, as if without speaking, they'd known this would be the last time.

The tenderness had been a lie. If he cared at all for her, he'd never put her through this. If he was helping Drew steal Tessa, she couldn't love him. He'd played her. His betrayal made her want to scream and bite and kick because her heart belonged to him as well as Tessa now. She'd only fight to keep one of them—Tessa.

Another chilly day. Endless cold to match the cold inside Ella as another week passed with no news. The icy wind forced pedestrians to hunch into themselves, to wrap themselves in tight balls to keep the world at bay. If only Ella could. Instead, she trudged from the station to Tony's chambers on Sydney's north shore. With parking at a premium, public transport was the fastest and cheapest option for this lunchtime appointment.

To talk strategy. *Strategy!* The urge to throw back her head and howl at the unfairness of the situation swept over her. A public tantrum would achieve less than nothing, except perhaps a ticket for disturbing the peace. The wheels of justice grind exceeding slow.

What idiot said that?

Three weeks on, and despite Tony's attempts to expedite the mediation hearing, they didn't have a date. The toll on her parents and her sister was mounting. The strain in their voices was clear down the phone. Her fault. She'd allowed herself to be seduced by Jake's charms, by her conviction of his integrity. She'd been wrong.

Tony took his turn reassuring them. The law was there to protect Tessa's best interests. But having Rory Daniels, with tacit support from Taylor Law, as their opponent a second time tested their confidence in the justice system. Her father, more used to doing than talking, had offered to take Jake's restitution money—blood money, he called it— and shove it up Jake's proverbial. Her mother's calmer counsel prevailed. A better revenge was to spend it on Tony and junior counsel to build their case.

Blood money—the urge to violence—revenge. The use of such words in a conversation about Tessa's future made Ella's bones ache.

Every day Ella waited for the guillotine to fall, yet Drew seemed unaware she didn't have legal custody. Unaware of the content of Chrissy's letters. He didn't act as if they were on equal footing, both seeking their first parenting adjudication. Jake knew. She didn't dare speculate on how he'd use the information, the bonus cards she'd given him when she'd judged he was an honourable man. That like her, he was trying to navigate this minefield to find the best outcome for an innocent child.

So many secrets and lies.

Raising her head to get her bearings, she caught the scent of rain followed by a few large drops. She pictured her umbrella where she'd left it, on the table at home, and grimaced. *Terrific.* At least she didn't have far to go. Tony's building was the next one, on the other side of the Sofitel Hotel. Then Ella spotted Jake standing back to allow a woman to precede him down the stairs. His gaze collided with hers before he dropped his lashes, hiding his thoughts.

"Eleanor." He stepped forward. "This is Julia Bennett."

This gorgeous, vivacious, alive-looking woman hanging on his arm was his former fiancée. Another slap at Ella's self-confidence. A real-time lesson in why Jake had never been seen in public with her. With her hair tumbled from the wind, her face pale despite the makeup she'd started wearing to disguise the dark circles under her eyes, and her still-too-large clothes, she was a mess. Replacing her wardrobe was the least of her worries, but she wished her outfit wasn't so ill-fitting and dowdy beside this glamorous woman.

"Julia, this is Eleanor Anderson," he continued.

"Hello," Ella said.

"I must go, Jake." The woman, who'd betrayed Jake and Chrissy, nodded in her direction. Ella searched Julia's face for signs of embarrassment or guilt and found none. "Great to see you." Julia kissed him and patted his cheek before moving gracefully down the stairs on heels so high they'd have crippled Ella.

"Are you going to see Tony?"

Ella inclined her head. "I don't think we're swapping notes anymore, Jake."

"I guess not."

She'd told no one she woke each night with her cheeks damp and her fists clenched. She rarely cried. She did what had to be done. "Although perhaps you can tell me when your 'team' is going to give us a date for the mediation hearing?"

"Rory is leading the case," he said. "Peter tells me it'll be soon."

Ella jammed her hands in her coat pockets, uncaring of the raindrops, heavier now, dancing on the pavement around her feet. "That's what Drew says. He rings me every few days, you know. I'm not sure why. He's like a human poison-pen letter, sharing bits and pieces of dirt he's collected."

"You don't have to answer the phone." He stepped closer.

"But I do." Ella caught a whiff of his scent. Damn him—he still smelled of all things nice. "Tony's advice is not to antagonise him. I assume not to antagonise his legal team. He is Tessa's father." On the rare occasions Ella reacted to one of Drew's snide remarks, his smug satisfaction made her want to slap him. "If I refuse to talk to him, he could say I'm trying to exclude him from her life. It's never been my intention to lock her family out of Tessa's life."

"Soon," he repeated.

"Perhaps you can ask him to stop." Ella shook back her damp hair. "The last time he dropped by the flat he showed me photos he's uploaded for his followers. I don't need to see or hear how he and you are painting the town red, the celebrity events you've taken him to, the gorgeous women you're dating. Like Julia. Why did you even bother with me, Jake? To collect information for the case? Evidence that my morals are suspect and my judgement of men is lousy? What a sacrifice to help your family. Taking pity on a plain Jane."

Her final insults shamed her, berating him about not wanting her in the hope he'd contradict her. In the hope he'd say he was attracted to her, but concern for Bronwyn's health, reconciliation with Drew, or some other family pressure had left him with no choice. The truth was he'd moved on, or maybe back to Julia.

"Tell Tony I'll be in touch." His behaviour baffled Tony as much as it did her.

"Tell him yourself. I won't be your messenger." Ella pushed past him, her back rigid, her eyes hot but mercifully dry.

The return train stalled between stations, leaving her staring at a pocket park. A single leaf scooped up by a light breeze caught her attention. Blown from a nearby tree, across the park, then tossed high in the air to hang suspended above a small pond. It dropped out of sight, and she guessed it was falling, eternally falling. Just like her.

Jake and his ex-fiancée had shared an affectionate goodbye. Ella closed her eyes against the image of him kissing a woman on the steps of the Sofitel for all the world to see. No shame in that kiss. No hiding out.

Ella had been so bloody clever. Believing she was following Chrissy's wishes, that letting Peter and Bronwyn get to know Tessa was harmless, that Drew was playing at being Daddy until something better came along. Positive she'd found the wisdom to satisfy the needs of all the grownups in the room. Weaving daydreams about Jake, forgetting his absolute loyalty to family.

Wealth and power.

She'd feared the combination from the first day but had let down her guard, convinced she'd fallen in love with one of the good guys. Still believed, despite all the evidence to the contrary, there was enough of the nine-year-old orphan in Jake not to give Drew custody of any child. A hope as insubstantial as air.

CHAPTER ELEVEN

High in his apartment, Jake reached for his phone. He'd received three separate phone calls and half a dozen texts over the last twenty-four hours from his cousin, claiming Eleanor had refused access visits, called him an unsuitable father and vowed never to let him near Tessa again. On her last call, she'd denied access to Peter and Bron. Drew was probably mischief-making, but Jake couldn't take the risk Eleanor might provide evidence against herself. At the very least, she needed witnesses to her conversations with Drew.

"Who answered the phone, Eleanor?" he demanded.

"My sister, Grace. Why have you called Jake?"

Her family must be in a state for Grace to leave the farm. Eleanor had reminded him of a willow when he'd seen her outside the Sofitel a week ago. Slender, strong, bending but never breaking. What a bloody stupid comparison. She was dead on her feet. "Drew said you won't allow Bron and Peter to see Tessa."

"That doesn't explain your call," she sounded defeated.

"It won't help your case if you don't allow some access visits." He doodled on his blotter with his free hand.

"Should you be giving me advice when you're representing the people I'm refusing access visits to,

Counsellor?"

"You told me you were following Tony's advice not to antagonise Drew." This was taking too long. Killing her by slow degrees. He'd seen confusion, pain, determination and longing in her eyes on that wet pavement. *Or had he?* He'd wanted to see longing. Missing her was a physical ache.

"I am."

"How does denying his parents access meet that criterion, Eleanor?"

"Don't call me Eleanor," she whispered.

Jake's hand tightened on the phone, his gut clenching at the anguish in her voice. A selfish need to have her look at him again out of glowing eyes had brought him close to confiding in her, confiding in Tony. He'd picked up the phone any number of times since this idiocy began, then dropped it, aware, through Murphy, that Rory Davies was tracking his moves. That Jake needed to hurry.

"If you'd bothered to check further, Counsellor, you'll find Drew didn't give you the full conversation. I won't allow Bron and Peter to see Tessa in the mountains. I've offered supervised visits at our apartment."

"You want Bron and Peter supervised?" Jake repeated, her pain reverberating through the phone. He'd given up all rights to see her, to touch her, to hold her when he'd chosen not to declare his position. *Hell, he was the enemy.*

"Tessa has …"

The catch in her voice walloped Jake. He pictured her white-knuckled fingers grasping the phone, willing herself not to lose control. She'd never cried. Not when he'd accused her of blackmail and greed, not when he'd confronted her in her apartment about trying to exploit Peter, not when she'd discovered his betrayal. Hell, she sounded close to breaking point. Had something happened to Tessa? This was slow torture, like pulling wings off a butterfly. He and Drew were circling from different directions, a ravenous pack hounding a wounded animal. Viciously cruel.

She started again. "Tessa is unsettled. Too many upheavals in too short a time."

"Have you taken her to the doctor?" Jake could have bitten his tongue.

"Looking for evidence of neglect now?" she asked bitterly. "Are you taping this conversation? Because I am."

"I'm not taping this conversation." His eyes burned with self-loathing. "And I don't believe Rory's case rests on charging you with neglect."

"Is that wishful thinking, or do you know for a fact the less-than-scrupulous Mr. Daniels will not argue failure of proper care?"

What had he done to her? He hadn't been able to avoid the confused reproach in Bron's eyes the one time she'd ambushed him in his office. Peter had asked if he'd known what he was doing. His terse response hadn't satisfied the older man, who'd added, "*Make sure you do.*"

"I don't need a doctor to tell me what's wrong, Jake." She hesitated. "Grace is staying with me for a bit. She's offered to meet Peter and Bronwyn. But it appears Drew requires me to be present at all times."

"Have you told Tony?"

"I can't ring Tony with every bloody-minded demand Drew makes."

Someone in that much pain needed to be held. Jake had forfeited the right. "I'll speak to him."

"Tony or Drew?"

"Peter." Jake saw he'd drawn the Southern Cross on his blotter. He closed his phone and poured two fingers of neat whisky, then downed them in a single swallow. His actions and his refusal to discuss any details of the case were confusing Tony Baldwin. Another case of hoping to salvage a relationship when the truth came out.

He didn't know anymore if the end justified the means. If he'd have sold his soul long before they reached the ending. Solidifying his position was taking longer than he'd anticipated. With any luck, Julia was getting the final piece of information he wanted now. Rory Daniels was close to giving the go-ahead for the meeting with the court-appointed mediator.

He stared at the whisky bottle, then pushed his glass away. Two hours later he knocked on Peter's door.

"Come in." Peter pulled him through the door. "What in green bloody blazes is going on?" Peter demanded. "Don't tell me until we join Bron."

Bron was in her private parlour, the fire lit and a book on a small table beside her. She smiled briefly when he entered. "Why haven't you called?"

"I said all I have to say in our last call. I'll support you to gain access to Tessa as her grandparents if you oppose Drew's bid for sole custody." Jake felt weary to his bones. Missing Eleanor was an unceasing ache. "It's up to you now."

"You may have said all you have to say, but we have things to say as well," Bron snapped. Jake couldn't remember her losing her temper in years.

"Do you want a drink? Something to eat?" Peter took the seat beside his wife. A united front.

"No, thanks." Jake shook his head. "I'll head back soon."

"Drew and Rory have promised generous access to Ella and her family. Opposing your son in an open court is a big call to make." Peter's voice cracked, which meant he was considering the possibility.

"I blame myself," Bron said, gripping the hand Peter stretched towards her.

"You of all people have nothing to blame yourself for." Jake crouched in front of her.

"Peter and I were going through a rough patch when your parents died." Bron swallowed. "I was planning to leave Peter."

"I overheard Mum talking about an affair." Jake rose to his feet and backed away.

"I was having an affair," Bron confessed. Peter moved

closer and wrapped an arm around her shoulders. "Your parents' death made me re-evaluate my life. I realised I loved Peter. I resented his work, the imbalance in our life."

"We talked," Peter said. "We made changes. But we never explained ourselves to Drew." He exchanged a look with Bron. "Had no idea we needed to explain ourselves to you."

"I thought my parents were about to break up. I was so confused." Jake sank into the armchair opposite. "Missing them. Wondering if dying was better than divorce."

"But you questioned your mother's loyalty," Bron said with simple perception. "Then Julia left you."

"Drew lied to Julia." Jake had never thought to tell them this story. "He deliberately seduced her to punish me for taking some of your affection."

"I'm sorry." Bron reached for his hand. "I spoilt him because I'd planned to abandon him."

"I was equally responsible." Peter lifted his wife's hand to his mouth, brushing a kiss across her knuckles.

"No one has a monopoly on making mistakes. I remained silent far too long." Jake hadn't told Eleanor he loved her. "You've given me a lot to think about. I've got another question. Have you seen Tessa in the last few days?"

"Drew said Ella has refused permission." Peter sounded wary. A father who still didn't want to believe the worst of his son.

"Tessa's unsettled. Ella asked if you could come to Sydney to see Tessa. She suggested her sister, Grace, be present for the visit." He let that thought drip on his uncle's conscience. "She's offered her apartment."

"Rory confirmed Drew's version of events." Bron frowned.

Jake pushed a hand through his hair, dislodging the queue holding it back. What was his aunt asking? Or was she saying she didn't believe Jake? "Rory and Drew are old friends."

"Rory did his damnedest to destroy Taylor Law's

217

reputation." Peter sounded impossibly old and beaten.

"He did." Jake had nothing left to lose.

"I'm sorry, son." Peter had parented him more than his own father.

"I should head back." Jake kissed Bron goodbye.

Peter accompanied him to the door. "We'll be in touch about our statement."

Jake unleashed heavy rock when he got in the car. Let AC/DC's *Highway to Hell* empty his mind as he started down the mountain, graduated to *Dirty Deeds Done Dirt Cheap*, and then let the silence call him home. Once in the door, he grabbed the whisky bottle and headed for the sofa. He'd tried to be the best adoptive son he could be. He'd walk away and not look back if they hurt Eleanor. A splash of whisky, another single mouthful while he stared at the lights of the city and imagined the ceiling at Eleanor's apartment.

The hope he'd nursed that, somehow, after this was over, he could make it up to Eleanor died. Tessa was suffering. Great. What a big brave hero he was, making a two-year-old miserable, because he hadn't been able to find some other way to stop Drew, except putting Eleanor and her family through hell. Their past experience of Rory Daniels wouldn't inspire confidence he'd play fair.

Fear of failure had invaded Jake's dreams. Or rather nightmares. Nightmares where Tessa was dragged out of Eleanor's arms and handed to a laughing Drew, while Jake stood by and let it happen.

* * *

A standard meeting room, the walls official cream. Or beige? Institutional neutral. On closer examination, they were a kind of white. Ella had recently read there were now one hundred and fifty shades of white in the painter's palette.

Who spent their days creating shades of white?

The furniture was no-nonsense, blonde wood and steel

with barely comfortable chairs. She'd expected neutral, utilitarian, but she'd also expected some welcome. A few landscapes or abstracts to soothe the soul or distract the mind. Instead, the walls were bare. A single narrow window with half-closed Venetian blinds cast faint stripes of winter sun on the carpeted floor. The mediation chairperson had estimated two to three hours for this first session. Just looking at the chairs made Ella squirm with discomfort.

Having Tony Baldwin at her side steadied her. If she stumbled in presenting her case, he'd back her up, restate her arguments logically and calmly, add any she'd forgotten. He touched her shoulder, and she turned her head to meet his tranquil eyes.

"Let's sit, EJ."

For some reason, she'd assumed a circular table—no person able to take a dominant position. Instead, it was rectangular, with the chairperson taking the seat at the top. A whiteboard stood behind her. To summarise competing priorities, if they got that far.

Ella sat, with the mediator on her right and Tony on her left. Ella deliberately took more time than she needed to extract her notes folder from her bag and set it on the table. The delay meant she didn't need to see Jake take his seat opposite her. Stupid, really. The subtle scent of his aftershave had ambushed her when he'd walked behind her to take his place on the other side of the table. Drew sat opposite Tony, with Rory Daniels on his right.

"Good morning. I'm Georgina Bray, your chairperson today. Thank you for coming. I've met Ella and Drew and already have a summary of your respective positions. I see you've brought lawyers today. While I know your names, could you introduce yourselves, please?"

"Tony Baldwin. I'm representing Eleanor Anderson and her family."

Ella focused her attention on the ordinary features of the maternal-looking woman at the head of the table. "I'm Ella Anderson."

"Rory Daniels, representing Drew Browning." He even sounded like a snake-oil salesman.

Ella remembered the self-satisfied smirk on his face when he'd effectively called her a liar. She'd witnessed the handshake and agreement between Smithhouse and her father. Daniels argued it had never happened. Ella had glanced at him when he'd taken his seat. He'd looked through her as if she was equally impotent today.

"Jacob Taylor, representing Bronwyn and Peter Browning, Tessa's paternal grandparents." His cadence was as comforting as when he'd murmured encouragement to Tessa, babbling happily in his arms, her tiny fingers grabbing his cheeks. Ella swallowed the lump in her throat. She had to believe they were equal here, that the name Taylor bought no special rights.

"Thank you. Then I'll confirm what we discussed in our individual pre-mediation sessions. We use first names to talk to each other, and we don't interrupt when someone's speaking. I won't provide legal advice. My role is to mediate. Our aim is to identify options and try and reach a shared outcome. Because your lawyers are present, we can document any agreement you reach."

"Mediation is compulsory, right?" Drew slid a sideways look at Jake.

"It's mandatory in this jurisdiction before custody cases go to court," Georgina confirmed.

"Just checking," said Drew.

In the witching hours, night after night, Ella had paced her small flat, the three essential questions Tony had given her revolving in her head.

Number one was easy: her ideal outcome? Sole parenting rights granted to her. Number two was harder. What would she settle for? A shiver trembled through her for the decision she'd made. A formal sharing agreement where she'd accompany Tessa on access visits until her niece was older and Ella was assured Tessa would be safe and well in Drew's care. Question three stopped her heart even now.

What would she accept to avoid going to court? A formal sharing agreement where she wasn't present for access visits with Drew, but Bronwyn and Peter were. She couldn't give more.

"You understand that whatever is said in this room is confidential. It can't be used in court proceedings if you're unable to reach an agreement here." Georgina looked at each of them in turn. "Ella, would you like to make your statement first."

Her opening bid. Ella opened the folder. The photo of Tessa stuck to the inside grounded her. She brushed a finger down the cheek of the smiling child, then turned her head to address Georgina.

"I'm seeking a parenting order for sole custody of Tessa. She's just two and her mother died a few months ago. Because of my sister's lengthy illness, I've cared for Tessa since she was born. She's comfortable and settled with me. I have strong support structures behind me and steady employment." She paused, her mind a blank. Closing her eyes, she centred herself. "We've only recently discovered that Drew is Tessa's father. My family and I want to include Drew and his family in Tessa's life, but I'd like to do that gradually."

"Tony, do you have anything to add to Ella's statement?"

"Ella's relationship is effectively that of Tessa's mother. Given Tessa's age, taking her away from her primary caregiver could have a negative impact on her psychological health. Ella's proposal shows a willingness to build meaningful relationships with her biological father and his parents. We have affidavits from a number of medical professionals to support our concerns about Tessa's wellbeing if she's removed from Ella's care."

"To sum up, then," Georgina spoke to Ella. "Tessa is secure in your care, you're willing to establish relationships with her biological father, but you believe it's in Tessa's best interests for you to have sole parenting rights."

Ella's hand rested on Tessa's photograph. "Yes."

"Drew, would you like to tell us your concerns?"

"Hell!" Drew threw his hands in the air and then leaned into the table, his telegenic good looks and easy charm focused on Georgina. "I'm a father, and I didn't know my ex-girlfriend was pregnant. I've been robbed of the first two years of my daughter's life. I've left a job in London to be with her. I don't know why her mother didn't tell me, but I want to make it up to Tessa. The only way to do that is to have custody of her."

"Rory, do you have anything to add?" Georgina asked.

"Drew and his family are thrilled to welcome a child and grandchild. She will receive love and great care with her father. While it's not the primary consideration"—Rory paused, Ella was sure for effect—"it should be noted that Drew and his family are much better placed to provide financial security for Tessa. In the future that translates to educational and social opportunities."

Ella lowered her eyes to Tessa's photo, a talisman to guide her through this obscene conversation.

"To summarise your position, Drew. You've had a DNA test to confirm paternity." Georgina checked her notes. "You've just learned Tessa is your child and you want a parenting order in your favour."

"That pretty much sums it up." Drew shrugged.

"At this stage, you're coming from very different positions. Are there any other matters you're concerned about?" Again, Georgina scanned each face in turn. "Ella?"

"Drew hasn't said anything about where he'll live if he was granted sole custody." Ella rubbed her thighs.

"Here," Drew interrupted. "Of course, I'll live here. For the short term."

"What does that mean, Drew?" Georgina asked.

"I have to work. In the future, I may need to travel for work." Drew glanced at Rory, a frown marring the smooth skin of his forehead.

"Drew's mother, Tessa's grandmother, isn't well enough

to travel," Ella objected. "Taking Tessa out of Australia would deny her access to relationships with her grandparents."

"My clients ask for the final written agreement to stipulate that Tessa permanently resides in Australia." Jake entered the lists for the first time. His remark rattled Drew, who angled his body towards Jake to impose his will. *Had Jake just overruled Drew?* Time to do some rattling herself.

"I don't believe my sister intended Tessa to live with Drew." Ella pressed a hand to her chest. "Chrissy and I discussed Tessa's future many times in the last two years. Each conversation ended with a plea for me to look after Tessa. I love her. You don't, Drew."

"That's bullshit," Drew snapped.

"Drew. I must ask you to hear Ella out before you interrupt her. We need to talk to each other in a respectful fashion." Georgina didn't raise her voice.

"She's making stuff up." Drew glared at Jake, who sat quietly. Jake gave Ella the impression of a pirate who'd just boarded a vessel, cutlass between his teeth.

"I have witnesses," Ella said. "I also have witnesses to every meeting you've had with Tessa. You don't look at her. You don't touch her or show any interest in who she is. I'm very concerned about her wellbeing if you are granted custody." Ella took a deep breath. "I think Chrissy told you she was pregnant when she found out. You walked away. You didn't want the responsibility of being a father."

"That's a lie! Jake was present the night we broke up. Did she tell you she was pregnant?" Drew challenged his cousin.

"Chrissy didn't tell me she was pregnant that evening," Jake agreed.

"My sister was confused at the end of her life." Ella hated exposing her sister's greed to strangers, but Ella wouldn't keep silent at the cost of Tessa's well-being. Tony's hand slid into hers and squeezed. "Chrissy dreamed of opportunities for her baby. She wanted your family's money. I believe you see a financial benefit in seeking custody. You don't love her. You don't really want Tessa."

"Can she get away with this crap?" Drew demanded. "Say something, Jake. You're supposed to be speaking for the family."

"The purpose of this mediation is to see if we can find common ground. If that's impossible, then a court will need to decide." Georgina brought their attention back to her. "Can we establish that much?"

Chrissy had pitchforked her into this disaster, but mediation was Ella's area of expertise. Court cases only increased resentment. Often both parties felt they were unfairly treated. Polite conversation was the first casualty. Ella had read all the case studies. Mediation was always better in child custody cases. Less traumatic for the children, less stressful for the parents, cheaper, and in the long term it improved the chances of better relationships.

"I don't want this to go to court." Ella's throat went dry, fearing her admission had handed Drew a free pass.

"If you won't recognise my rights as her father, then this goes to court," Drew snarled.

"Tony, Rory, would you like some time in private with your clients to discuss this?" Georgina offered.

"Ella and I have discussed options that don't involve sole parenting arrangements," Tony replied. "I could outline them here. We're also prepared to table Chrissy's last letter to Ella. It makes it pretty clear, Chrissy wanted money. I understand Jake also has a letter from Chrissy showing money as a primary motivator." Tony had agreed that revealing the existence of the letter was a risk, but insisted complete transparency would ultimately testify to her good faith.

"How is that relevant?" Georgina asked.

"We're here to decide what's in Tessa's best interests. We contend there'd be no issue around custody if Chrissy hadn't asked for money. We also contend that Drew's primary motivation is personal financial benefit through his parents, who have repeatedly offered maintenance. Tessa isn't for sale," Tony said.

"What letters?" Drew turned to Jake.

"It won't be necessary to examine Chrissy's letters." Jake spared Drew a look before turning to the chairperson. "Drew's parents have requested that their rights be considered as part of parenting arrangements."

"Another claim?" Ella touched Tony's sleeve. "Shouldn't we have been told beforehand?" Nausea swirled in her stomach. She bit her lip to remain silent. Bronwyn and Peter loved Tessa. If Ella lost to them, Tessa would be safe and within reach. If necessary, she'd find consolation in that outcome.

"This is most unorthodox, Jake."

"Forgive me, Georgina. For reasons I can't fully explain, this mediation session is the best place to air a number of issues."

"What do you think you're doing, coz?" Drew bared his teeth.

"I'm here, as noted in all the paperwork, to represent the interests of Bronwyn and Peter Browning in the custody matter of Tessa."

"My parents' interests are the same as mine," Drew snapped. "Rory can confirm that."

"Bronwyn and Peter Browning are prepared to petition the court over their interest in parenting arrangements. They, too, became aware of Tessa's existence recently. They've given me an affidavit"—Jake withdrew a document from his briefcase and slid it towards Georgina—"which states they believe their son, Andrew Browning, is unsuitable to have parenting rights for their granddaughter, Tessa, and they give full support to Eleanor Anderson's claim for sole parenting rights."

"He's lying." Drew pushed to his feet, knocking over his chair.

"I have signed statements confirming Drew shared an apartment with Chrissy after she knew she was pregnant."

Jake tabled a second document. "In addition, I have an affidavit from Julia Bennett."

"You bastard," Drew scowled, while Ella stared, and Jake tabled a third document, designed to deliver Ella's greatest wish.

"Rory, you may need to advise your client to watch his language." Jake glanced at his cousin in dismissal. "Julia Bennett went to London with Drew after his relationship with Chrissy ended. Ms. Bennett swears Drew boasted about his breakup with Chrissy. Said the 'stupid woman,' his words, told him she was pregnant and expected him to stick around. He said he didn't want the responsibility of a kid, then or ever. I also have a recent tape recording between Drew and Julia verifying her statement."

"I'll destroy you for this," Drew bellowed.

"I don't care," Jake answered softly.

Drew waved a fist in Jake's face, accusing him of double-crossing him before unleashing a stream of obscenities. When Jake sat, unmoving, Rory caught Drew's arm and hustled him out of the room, leaving a charged silence. Georgina leafed through the documents Jake had passed her, lifting her head occasionally to ask him a question. Ella locked her hands tightly under the table, letting the questions and answers roll around her, scared to hope.

Georgina summed up. "Let's see if I've understood this correctly, Jake. You're tabling documents, which directly contradict Drew's claim to have been unaware of Tessa's existence until recently, and which cast doubt on his capacity and interest in caring for his daughter. In effect, you're undermining his claim for parenting rights."

"That's correct. I anticipate he'll formally withdraw his claim."

"You chose a rather dramatic way to make your case." Georgina frowned. "I'll have something to say to my superiors. A reprimand may be in order."

"I apologise to the court for handling it this way," Jake said. "I received Julia's affidavit last night. Dealing with the matter here, with all parties present, seemed the best way to prevent further escalation. I regret the distress that's been caused."

"What makes you so confident Drew won't pursue the case? Mediation discussions are confidential. A tape recording without his knowledge is inadmissible as evidence."

"His parents and Julia Bennett are prepared to testify. I imagine the people who signed affidavits for Tony are also prepared to testify." Jake raised an eyebrow, and Tony nodded. "Drew wanted a guaranteed victory with him in the role of shining knight. That's not going to happen. While he peddles scandal for a living, it's not in his financial best interests to be the centre of a scandal where he turned his back on the mother of his child when she was in desperate need."

Ella sat slumped at the table, her body turning to jelly. She doubted her legs would take her weight if she tried to stand. Unable to move or think or feel. Tony accompanied the mediator to the door. Tidying up the loose ends, Ella supposed. They'd been in here less than an hour—fifty-four minutes was all it took to relieve weeks of worry. She'd touched Tony's sleeve when everyone rose to leave, indicating she wanted to remain.

Tessa waited at home with her parents and her sister, Grace, who'd fussed over Ella in recent weeks like a nurse on hospital duty.

Tony returned to sit beside her. "Why did he let it get this far, EJ?"

"From Drew's reaction, I'd say he believed he had no other choice. He must have refused to represent Drew, then spent his time convincing Bronwyn and Peter to cross-claim against their son. At least that's what it sounded like, the way he was abusing Jake when they left the room."

"Did you expect it?"

She drew a deep breath and let it out slowly. "You said you'd trust him with your life. That's what I had to do in the end. Trust him with Tessa's life. He knows what it's like to be a motherless child. I didn't think he'd abandon her to Drew's care."

"Then why have you wasted money you don't have employing me?" Tony wagged a finger at her.

"Because this isn't about me and gut feelings." Even in her bleakest moments, she hadn't wavered in her belief Jake wouldn't abandon Tessa, and wondered if loving him had made her lose her mind. "Losing Tessa after losing Chrissy is a grief I don't think my parents would ever recover from. I had no right to take that risk for them. It's my fault we're here today."

"I don't see how you get to that conclusion. Drew's the monster here. What about you and Jake?" Tony asked gently. "If you trust him, can't you be friends?"

"I made the mistake of becoming his lover. That didn't work out. He's got too many demons chasing him to allow anyone near him." She caught sight of Jake walking towards them.

* * *

Jake knew Tony had seen him re-enter the room, knew Tony's questions to Eleanor were designed for him to overhear. Her faith in him was a sucker punch. Until this morning, he'd convinced himself he had no choice. Now his splendid isolation shamed him. He'd been a total bastard, given her no room to hope. She'd trusted him, and he'd put her through hell in return.

He hadn't allowed himself to hope she'd even want to see him again. He'd wagered everything on Julia's recorded testimony enraging Drew enough for him to betray himself during the hearing. It had worked. Drew's abuse sounded far away as the adrenalin keeping Jake focused for weeks drained out of his system, leaving him flat, unable to care. Victory was a reminder he'd lost everything that most mattered to him. Tony was offering a way back.

"Hi, Eleanor, Tony." Jake stopped at the table.

She chastised her lawyer. "Not fair, Tony. You knew he was here."

"You're both friends of mine, EJ. Hard not to see you're both suffering. I'll talk to you later." Tony patted her arm in encouragement.

Tony gave Jake a quick hug on the way out. Jake closed the door behind him, leaning against it for support, the solidness of the timber grounding him.

The meditator had given him twenty-four hours to confirm Drew's claim had been withdrawn. Jake had deflated, like a balloon slowly releasing all its gas. Lethargy had taken its place, a legacy from all the late-night shifts he'd worked. Then nothing, a blind emptiness that he'd won the case and lost the war.

Bloody hell! Ella had trusted him.

Winning the lottery against all the odds must feel like this. Elation fizzed through his bloodstream, a crazy burst of energy urging him to take a risk, to find out how far her trust would take her. "Mind if I take a seat?" Jake gestured to the chair Tony had vacated.

She started to rise. "I'm just leaving. I should let my parents know."

"Ring them." Jake mentally backpedalled. "I mean, can we talk for a few minutes? Can you ring them and let them know you'll be a bit longer?"

She opened her phone. "Dad, a few hurdles still to jump, but she's ours."

He could hear a voice on the other end but couldn't make out the words.

"I'll be home soon. I'll tell you all about it then." She put the phone away. "Thank you."

"For what? Putting you through hell, treating you and Tessa as if you didn't matter?" *When you matter more than my next breath.* Jake pulled the chair away from the table, setting it at right angles to her chair.

"I'm assuming a lot of that had to do with managing Drew." Her generosity was a balm.

"He, with Rory Davies' help, was engineering a large payout from Bron and Peter. In the small print, and using very obscure legal terminology, was a clause where Drew could take Tessa out of the country permanently." He summarised the brutal threat that had driven all his actions.

"I don't understand." She turned her head to look at him. "I wouldn't agree to his schemes, but taking Tessa out of Australia would kill Bronwyn."

A single lapse of judgement on his part, his selfish need to be with her, had tipped them into this hell. "He saw us kissing outside Taylor Law the morning the DNA results came through."

"This is *about* you and me?" Her eyes widened in disbelief.

"Me. It's all about me. And I know that sounds egotistical." Jake couldn't sit, the sharp seesaw of hope and despair driving him to move. He crossed to the window, the slats in the blinds giving him a clear view of the carpark. Tony leaned against his car. Jake knew he was waiting to pick up the pieces. For him, for Eleanor. He spun back to her. "I told you some of this. My childish admiration. He liked it. Until I moved in. I don't know when he started hating me, but I do remember the first time he told me I wasn't welcome in his house. A few months after I arrived. I cried. I ran into the garden and hid.

"He claimed Bron and Peter didn't want me either. I was a charity kid; they felt an obligation." He lifted a hand and caught the back of his neck. His aunt's blistering rebuttal this morning still rang in his ears.

"He lied." Eleanor's voice was as reassuring as an anchor in a turbulent sea.

"I didn't recognise it as a lie at the time, but, yeah. He lied. When you get told something often enough you start to believe it. Insidious stuff really. *'They're pretending to like you, pretending to be kind.*"

"It's obvious they love you like a second son." Her beautiful eyes were crystal clear, and Jake wanted to lose himself in them … and her.

"I worked that out over the years. But by then I'd learned the habit of working hard and keeping quiet. Wanting them to be proud of me. Thinking they loved that studious, serious kid."

"That's why you wanted Taylor Law to succeed."

A knot in Jake's chest started to unravel; she was working it out. Maybe she'd forgive him. Bron and Peter had forgiven him. "You're right about the demons. I owed it to them to make something of myself, and I owed it to my parents."

"That's a big burden for a child to shoulder. Did you also blame yourself for the damage Rory Davies did to the company?" Sadness washed off her.

"I've made a lot of mistakes. Not that one. A hundred cases in two years. That's how many I've found so far. While I have no evidence, and don't plan ever to use this information, he was a mate of Drew's. They spent a lot of time together in the two years Rory worked there before I graduated. Encouraging Rory to trash my inheritance, never explicitly, would suit Drew. If it became public, he could deny all knowledge."

"Did he know about my family's history with Rory Davies?" She tapped her fingers on the table, an irritated drum roll.

"Doubtful. It was enough to remind me of the damage Rory had done to my parents' legacy, to hint at the damage he could do to you and Tessa."

"Did you tell Peter and Bronwyn about your suspicions?" Her direct question told him she wouldn't tolerate any more prevarication from him.

He scratched his chin. "They were dealing with Bron's diagnosis at the time. They didn't need to hear of Drew's petty cruelties from me."

"His behaviour's beyond petty cruelties. He's dangerous. Assuming you had the right to keep the truth from them is arrogant and does them a disservice." She pushed to her feet.

"Yeah. They told me that this morning." They hadn't pulled their punches either.

"You made assumptions about their feelings and never once asked them." Indignation propelled her across the room.

"Right again. And before you dump on me again, in my defence, he is their son." He held up his hands. "They love him regardless of his flaws."

She swirled, her skirt flaring in a wide circle, and marched towards him. "You were afraid to put it to the test," she accused. He caught a whiff of her fragrance as he stepped smartly out of her way. "Your word against his. What if they believed him?" She'd nailed his insecurities.

"I didn't realise how much of the little boy who ran away and hid stayed with me. I was afraid to apply the blowtorch. To see if their love survived having to choose between his version of the truth and mine." Telling her cut Jake's final tie to that little boy.

"Because Julia's didn't? Did Drew tell them some cock and bull story about her? Did they believe him?" she demanded.

"We never discussed Julia." Jake grimaced, remembering how he'd dealt with that betrayal. Retreat into sixteen-hour workdays. And he'd had the work, as one of Rory's biggest scams had blown up in Jake's face about that time. But it had been a useful and timely excuse, and he'd grabbed it with both hands. "Whenever they started to raise the subject, I deflected them."

She stared at him as if he'd grown two heads. "You thought they'd think it was okay for Drew to lie to Julia and steal your fiancée."

"I thought they'd believe she fell out of love with me and in love with him." Jake pinched the bridge of his nose.

"You didn't tell them about the hotel." She pointed a finger at him in disgust.

"Peter told me today he knew about what happened, but I wouldn't let them in." His uncle had called him an idiot and hugged him.

"Male machismo. How utterly pointless." She poured scorn on him.

"Did you and Bron work out a routine?" Jake was beginning to feel irritated. He'd been doing his best. "I was wrong, but I thought I had cause."

"When did you tell them what you planned for today?"

"I spoke to them the day you came to my apartment. I told them I couldn't represent Drew because I didn't support his claim for custody. I said I would continue to represent their rights as grandparents."

"You didn't tell them!" She threw her hands in the air. "You took a huge risk."

"After I put my position, I avoided them. I didn't want to apply undue pressure. It had to be their own decision." Jake had begun to think he'd need to hand the results of his painstaking research over to Tony.

"When did they make it?"

"In the last few days," he admitted. "I got their signature on the document supporting your claim for sole custody this morning."

"They must be devastated." Her instinctive distress on behalf of his aunt and uncle reminded Jake why he loved her.

"They were uncomfortable about the case from the beginning. They asked Drew repeatedly what his plans were. They didn't want to believe he was lying to them. Even so, they'd started investigating what it would mean to make their own application. They don't want Drew to have sole custody of Tessa."

"What convinced them?"

"Drew's last lie about access tipped the balance." He'd intervened when he'd realised his silence had opened the way for constant emotional pressure from Drew. "I told them you'd never denied them access to Tessa."

"Based on Drew's live posts, the one person you didn't avoid was him," she snapped.

"A small concession to throw him off the scent." Another strategy Jake should have explained. "He wasn't getting invites to venues he needed to access if he wanted to work back in Sydney."

"But you could?"

Jake nodded.

"He wanted to humiliate you personally and professionally," she concluded, turning her back on him to look out the window.

Jake wondered if she saw anything when she stared out, wondered what judgement she'd make on his actions.

"It didn't have to be this way." She turned to face him.

"Didn't it?" Jake raised a hand then dropped it.

"You could have confided in your aunt and uncle sooner, in Tony, another person who feels betrayed by your actions. Confided in me. We could have worked together."

"I couldn't take the risk."

"Couldn't or wouldn't? My parents and sister have spent weeks terrified they'll lose Tessa when they've just lost Chrissy." She confronted him across the table. "You've put us through hell to produce a final magic trick. Justice revealed!"

"I couldn't control everything, everyone. Couldn't guarantee the outcome until I had all the evidence. I worked on what I could control. Checking everyone who knew them, anyone who could vouch for movements, conversations." Meticulous fact-checking had allowed him to right the wrongs Rory had done in the past. It was a weapon he knew how to use. "I even studied the details of Chrissy's pregnancy and Tessa's birth."

"Which is how you discovered they were still sharing a flat until that night."

"She told me they were living together. He'd told me it

was over weeks before. Murphy tracked down the taxi driver who helped her move her stuff. Got a date, a journey officially recorded. She stuck in the guy's mind because of what a mess she was. Said he had a daughter the same age. Took her to a Salvation Army hostel." Her unsmiling face had Jake's mouth going dry, panic starting to back up in his throat. "I'm sorry, Eleanor. And those words are hopelessly inadequate for what we've put you through."

"What's his next step?"

"Drew? Back to London, I hope, after I get his signature on a withdrawal of his claim." Jake didn't give a damn now that the threat to Eleanor was neutralised.

"Won't he need to punish you for today?" She cocked her head to one side.

"There's no one on his side. No facts to support false accusations."

"Who needs facts when you've got Rory?"

"You do." Jake admired her essential decency. "But miraculously, you were also prepared to trust me. I wanted you to trust me. Without rhyme or reason, when all the evidence was against me."

"I trusted you'd never hand over a motherless child to someone who planned to use her as a meal ticket." She sounded confused by her own conviction. "I didn't dare say it aloud. My family would have told me I was insane. Almost everything you did supported the idea you'd let Drew take her away from us."

"*Almost* everything?" Jake asked.

"You didn't tell him there'd been no previous custody ruling. You didn't give him copies of Chrissy's letters. You were always kind to Tessa, noticing Tootles, checking what she wanted to eat or drink. You played with her when you didn't have to." She met his gaze, her green eyes clouded. "I believed in that gentle, kind man." Her pain hollowed him out.

She'd trusted Jake to protect Tessa. Not to love Eleanor. "I stayed away from you after he got home. But I couldn't say no when you asked to see me. And I couldn't not touch you when I wanted you so much. I thought he might try to break us up. I swear to God I never dreamed he'd go for custody. The best way to outwit him was to convince him we were through. To convince him I had to convince you, to scare you enough so he'd believe it."

"You were very convincing." Her voice trembled.

Jake tasted defeat in that moment. "I'm sorry."

"Did Julia's role have to be another secret?"

"Drew grilled me about you coming to my apartment that night. I didn't want him to know I was talking to Julia. Murphy worked with her until our final meeting. You gave me the idea weeks ago. You said maybe Drew's new girlfriend knew something."

"He boasted of leaving Chrissy pregnant?" Her body jerked in revulsion.

"He did it to make Julia feel important, prove he'd chosen her. Instead, it was the beginning of her seeing through him." And Julia had wanted Jake's sympathy for being conned.

"She never told you before?"

"Before last week, we'd waved to each other distantly at parties since her return to Australia. She agreed to go and see him, to wear a wire, pretend she wanted him back, wanted to talk about what went wrong between them." The small, soulless room was sucking all the hope out of Jake. "What about us?"

"There isn't an 'us', Jake."

"Because I didn't confide in you?" The earth shifted beneath Jake's feet.

"Because secrets and lies are what got us into this mess in the first place. And we haven't moved beyond them. You repeatedly lied to me, and you kept secrets for Drew. You didn't trust me with the truth, didn't trust me to be able to help you find a way through this. If you'd come to me, confided in Tony, asked Bronwyn and Peter for their support earlier, we might have been able to achieve the same outcome *together*." She collected her bag and coat.

"In that moment I had to put Tessa first." Jake recognised that his learned secrecy, what he called loyalty to his family, was a hollow shell. He'd wanted her unconditional trust, but he hadn't given her his. She'd passed his ridiculous test, and he'd lost her.

"From the bottom of my heart, I thank you for that." She huffed out a breath, steadying herself. "You, me, that was the mistake."

"What if I said the only mistake was not waiting until we'd solved the custody problem before starting a relationship?" Jake wanted to block her path. He remembered his helplessness from the first day he'd met her, when he'd handled the situation badly.

"I'm too numb. Too tired. Too …" She raised her hands, then let them fall. "Too everything to talk about this anymore now. I need to go home to my family. As do you. We were thrown together. You took what I offered, Jake. No need to replay that. No need for more lies."

"Loving you is not a lie."

"But love is conditional for you. A test. You demand incontrovertible evidence. It doesn't work that way. You wouldn't learn the lesson Julia tried to teach you." She turned to the door.

"Wait." Jake was determined to drop all barriers. "Julia's betrayal triggered an old wound. I overheard my parents talking. Before they died. I thought my mother was leaving my father, leaving me."

"Was she?" She paused.

"Bron was having the affair." The knowledge removed the stain from Jake's memories of his mother. "She said my parents' deaths made her re-evaluate her life. Made her work out what was important to her. She blames herself for Drew's shortcomings. Thinks her behaviour then scarred him in some way."

"I'm sorry you carried that hurt alone for so many years. But it's part of the same pattern." She reached for the door handle. "You didn't trust me. I must go. My family needs me."

"Don't we all," Jake murmured inaudibly as she walked through the door. She'd shredded him. By insisting on working alone, he'd lost the woman he loved. "What the hell do I do now?"

CHAPTER TWELVE

A week later, Ella strolled through the gleaming glass doors of the Taylor Law building and crossed to the bank of elevators. The dark flared skirt, cream cashmere sweater and boots fitted her, flattering her still too-slender figure and boosting her confidence. Another jumble sale, but she'd spent money on herself for the first time in months.

A week, a day, a minute can feel like a lifetime. Ella had needed space to think, for the knowledge no one could ever take Tessa away to seep into her bones and sinews and soothe away the constant anxiety. Time for her parents and Grace to feel the same relief and finally return to the farm.

As the disembodied voice of elevator person counted out the floors she practised deep breathing, reaching for serenity when her nerves were stretched tight. She wondered about her welcome. No longer intimidated by the luxury of the outer office, the receptionist's strict adherence to protocol could derail her plans. Jake wasn't expecting her. The doors opened on the welcome sight of Merle at the desk crosschecking diary entries with Miss Not-A-Hair-Out-Of-Place.

"You don't have an appointment, Ella." Merle came around the desk with a smile. "Want one?"

Ella accepted the woman's hug. "I hoped he'd give me a few minutes."

Hoped Jake would give her a chance to say what she'd come to say.

Only a week.

She'd left him in the courthouse and gone home to her family. They'd exclaimed and cursed when she'd explained what Jake had done and why. When Ella had run out of answers to their questions, her father had rung Jake to thank him. They'd had a long conversation and parted friends. For the remainder of her parents' visit, she'd had to periodically listen to her father recounting their conversation, interspersed with comments on Jake's honourableness and how he'd needed the wisdom of Solomon to navigate Drew's sneakiness. Ella couldn't hear herself think.

With the apartment to herself and Tessa, she'd emptied her mind and listened to the silence. Badgered over the years by Drew's malicious sniping, and the insidious poison of being told Drew was the true son and Jake was second best, Jake had chosen to compete with himself to be the best person he could. His random acts of kindness were under the radar—cooking toasted sandwiches when she was too heartsore to feed herself, borrowing a child's seat for his car or doing groundwork to free Peter to spend time with his wife.

He'd deliberately exposed himself to retaliation from Drew by putting her needs before his reputation, and before his family. He could have worked with Drew, and built in clauses guaranteeing shared access for Ella and the Brownings. Instead he'd won sole custody for Ella, given her complete control over who could see Tessa. Forever. He'd protected her and her child, from Drew, from a court case involving Rory Davies.

The hum of joy started deep within her when Ella worked out what he'd done, what it might mean. The hum had become a roar too loud to be ignored. Sincerity had shone in his sombre eyes when he'd said *"loving you is not a lie.*" His sincerity had lured her here.

Merle pressed the switch on the intercom. "Jake, sorry to interrupt, but Ella is here. Can you give her a few minutes?"

Ella didn't hear his answer, but within seconds the door to his office was flung open and he stood there. Her beautiful pirate. Impossibly handsome, impossibly dear, her heart raced in her chest, and her stomach twisted into knots.

His gaze devoured her, checking her all over as if he wanted to assure himself she was still in one piece. Ella's pulse quickened and need pooled in her groin.

"Is Tessa okay?"

"She's fine. She's with Mrs. P." She'd missed hearing his voice. His question eased some of the tension knotting her stomach.

"Mr. P?"

"Much better, thanks." The simple inquiry reassured Ella. He made space in his life for little people, remembered important details like an old man's illness. His compassion alone justified her taking this chance.

"Come in." He turned briefly to Merle. "Cancel all other meetings."

"I don't think …" Ella started to protest.

"Can we have some tea, too, please, Merle?"

Then Ella was inside his stately office. The floor-to-ceiling windows still created the surreal impression his office hung between the arches of the Harbour Bridge, but Ella could no longer blame her light-headedness on vertigo. A potent dose of Jake Taylor up close, and she ceased functioning like a normal person.

He ushered her towards the desk, and Ella glanced over her shoulder at the informal table and chairs where she'd sat for their first meeting. He indicated a straight-backed chair in front of his desk and moved around to sit behind it. That first time she'd considered the leather setting intimidating, now she wished for a chair that didn't hold her spine rigid.

"Is this a formal meeting, Eleanor?"

"Yes." She stared at the patent leather handbag she clasped tightly on her knees, her hands wrapped around the firm, upright handles. Appreciating how ridiculous she must look, she set the bag on the floor beside her. A woman who'd abandoned her defences.

How the devil did he manage to look so beautifully composed when her stomach was rolling like a butter churn? She filled her senses with him, and the loss of the past weeks returned to confound her.

"You don't look like you've been getting enough sleep." His glance was as intimate as a caress. He pushed a hand through his hair, and pulled the leather thong loose. Ella's heart stuttered seeing his hair tumble free.

She'd whispered erotic instructions to him when he'd lain naked in her bed, his hair spread across her breasts. *Did he remember?* Was his action deliberate? Hope stirred. He smelled divine, in person his scent tangier than the faint perfume that had lingered in her sheets after his last visit. She'd been reluctant to wash them, tempted to buy a bottle of his aftershave so she could spray it on a pillow to hug night after lonely night. His firm mouth was creasing in a smile, and his eyes twinkled at her continued silence.

She fumbled her reply. "Neither do you."

A knock on the door, then Merle entered with a tray bearing a pot of tea, cups and chocolate brownies. "Chocolate will increase your blood sugar levels, and you both look as if you need it," she muttered.

* * *

"Thanks, Merle." Jake poured two cups of tea and slid the brownies towards Ella.

She shook her head.

"How can I help you?" Jake considered begging for another chance as she nibbled her bottom lip, then straightened her shoulders.

"I've spoken to Bronwyn and Peter. We've worked out

a routine so they can see Tessa."

"Maintenance?" he asked, watching her.

"We've agreed I won't need maintenance as such, but as her grandparents, they are free to buy her gifts."

"They didn't tell me that." Jake frowned. Peter had explicitly told him yesterday he was pushing ahead with the maintenance offer.

"I told them I was hoping to be more comfortably settled in the near future." She looked away.

"You're moving?" Jake's confidence, sparked by her arrival, drained away.

"It's a possibility. It depends how things pan out."

Panic trickled through Jake's veins. Her composure created a barrier he didn't know how to cross. He'd hoped her visit meant she was prepared to talk to him. She was sounding like she'd come to say goodbye. "Are you going back to the farm?"

"No."

"Possibly moving—not going back to the farm." Jake leaned forward, deliberately shaking his hair loose. She'd given a breathless gasp when he'd released the thong. Her hands curled into fists. He hoped like hell the fists were to stop herself reaching for him. Jake leaned back in his chair, encouraged by the realisation he could still unsettle her as much as she unsettled him. "So, Eleanor Jane Anderson, why are you here? Do you need something from me?"

"I didn't thank you properly the other day. Loyalty to your family, to your parents' company are important." She could be reciting a pre-prepared speech. "I know there've been repercussions."

"What repercussions?"

"Drew's blog." Disgust coated her words. "Tony showed me yesterday. Tony was furious."

"Tony's forgiven me," Jake said, remembering his relief when Tony had called to ask him to meet for a drink. "After blasting me for my idiocy."

"He told me you discussed Julia's evidence with him

before the mediation session. Workshopped whether it was better for you to present her statement rather than him. He would have"— her chest rose on a deep inhalation—"you said it was better if you wore any criticism from the mediator."

"If Bron and Peter hadn't come on side, I'd have given all my evidence to him."

"I know." She pressed ahead, hands neatly folded in her lap. "We were talking about Drew's blog. Drew claims he's updating the record on an old scandal. Some new facts to explain why Julia X broke off her engagement with the CEO of a top Sydney legal firm, the family-owned TL; he didn't bother to spell out Taylor Law."

"He's clutching at straws." Concern meant she liked him, didn't it? He could build on liking.

"With fake news. He accuses you of a grubby affair and fathering a child, whose existence has just become public. He rehashed a few of the corrupt deals handled by Rory Davies and implied the police were looking at a malpractice investigation."

"Is that why you're here? To warn me about Drew's blog." Jake had hoped more than her passion for justice had brought her to him. "It'll be old news in a few days."

"Right now it's prime news. I checked Drew's site overnight. There are loads of hits—people who've shared the item."

More than concerned, she was outraged on his behalf. Maybe some of her passion was for him? "I can handle it, Eleanor."

"Bronwyn showed me the message they're planning to publish to rebut Drew when I was there this morning. An official welcome to their recently discovered granddaughter, Tessa, the child of Drew Browning and Chrissy Anderson, deceased. Bronwyn said it was your idea. You helped them draft it. Including the sentence about Tessa living with me with the support of both families. You're fighting back." Her smile was pure sunshine.

"It's been a long time coming. You were right. I should have called Drew's bluff sooner. Talked to you. I could have gone on the record, presented my own statutory declaration about what Drew intended."

"Why didn't you?"

"I carried that scared little boy inside me without realising it. I've also learned to rely on myself when it's too important to fail." Jake understood her disappointment in him, but Murphy had been positive Rory Daniels was tracking her every move.

"Too important to fail?" she asked carefully.

"Tessa belongs with you." Jake said what was in his heart. "That was the only outcome I'd accept."

"You risked your relationship with Tony." She chastised him. "Potentially you risked your relationship with Bronwyn and Peter if they backed Drew instead of you."

"Old news." Jake came back around the desk and took her hands to draw her to her feet. They stood toe to toe. "Spit it out, Eleanor. Tell me what brought you here."

She was staring at his chest. "Will you marry me?"

Jake tightened his hold, afraid he'd misheard.

* * *

"I didn't mean to say that." Ella met his gaze and tried to back away, inhaling deeply to recover her nerve. A mistake because inhaling meant absorbing the essence of this magical man, remembering everything she'd learned about him. His humour, his thoughtfulness, his sensitivity, and his divine lovemaking.

He released her hands, his gaze narrowing. "What didn't you mean to say?"

"You know what." Ella could feel the heat creeping up her throat. "You won't intimidate me by looming over me."

"We've got about a metre of space between us at the moment, Ellie, and that's a metre more than I like," he muttered. "Let's consider what you didn't mean to say for a bit." His use of the diminutive shimmied down Ella's spine. A disturbing element had crept into his voice, but his expression remained inscrutable.

"Let's not." Ella crossed her fingers behind her back.

"We can treat your proposition as a hypothetical. Are there any obvious advantages in the idea? Would it be an effective way to silence some of Drew's more outrageous claims?" he mused, then shook his head and a damn strand of hair caught in his mouth.

Ella envied his hand brushing it aside.

"Marrying you won't necessarily silence the claims I had an affair with Chrissy." He looked down his nose at her, as if considering an especially tricky problem.

Made reckless by his deliberately provocative words, sure now he'd released his hair to inflame her, she took a swipe at his ego. "I suppose there's some logic in the idea. Tessa needs a father."

"And she's the spitting image of me as a child." He seemed to be weighing up her contribution. And closing the metre gap between them.

"That's a blessing," Ella muttered, wishing he'd say he still wanted her. That desire, affection, love might be part of the proposition.

"But wouldn't it seem to confirm the gossip, not kill it?" His brow furrowed. "Especially now that we've arranged to neutralise most of the damage through Bron and Peter's post. Although"—he paused, as if he'd had an idea—"the post could announce our engagement."

"We've exhausted the possibilities in this hypothetical." Ella was placing her heart in his hands, for a second time, and he was teasing her.

"Are you sure?"

"It's not funny, Jake. I hurt your pride when I walked away in the mediator's office."

"My pride? You're wrong there, Ellie."

"That's really what I came to say. That I'm sorry, and if you'd like, maybe we can have dinner, or go on a picnic, or

..."

He caught her before she reached the door, moving faster than she anticipated, stepping in front of her to block her escape. Tension arced between them.

"Missing our physical relationship, Eleanor?" His voice was low, rumbling through her, raising goose bumps, and demanding the truth.

"Damn you, yes." Ella stamped her foot.

"Lust might not last."

She was sure the sparks flashing between them would ignite whole forests.

"Don't you think marriage needs something more substantial than lust at its base?" He was asking a very serious question.

Ella searched his face, finding more uncertainty than challenge in his eyes. He was unsure of *her* love. He'd made the admission in the mediation room, and she'd thrown it back at him. *Wasn't that why she'd come?* Because she loved him enough to abandon her pride. Because making mistakes is what makes us human. She'd made mistakes as well.

Jake Taylor. He loved the dawn sky. He knew the names and sounds of trees and birds and mountains. He could make little girls laugh and grown up-girls beg.

And he didn't give up—*Taylor's* law.

"What about love? Would that work for you?" Ella took a step towards him and surrendered any advantage she may have had. "I love you, Jake."

"You're incredibly brave, Eleanor Jane." He caught her in his arms and swung her in a circle. Ella gave an involuntary gasp as her body came into contact with his, letting her head fall back so she could see the smile spreading across his face. "I admire that in you."

"Admiration can be a good foundation for marriage." She scrunched up her nose. *Surely, he'd say he loved her now.*

"Don't do that," he whispered, lifting a hand to her face.

"Do what?" The thumb gently grazing Ella's jaw bound her to him as surely as silken threads. His ragged breathing matched her own.

"Scrunch up your face. It makes me want to kiss you."

"Oh." Her mouth dropped open in surprise.

"I want to kiss you when you do that, too. You humble me, Eleanor. You're beautiful, and generous. Be mine?" He lowered his mouth until their lips met, until she was caught in the fantasy he was weaving. Sheer sensation. When he slid a hand into her hair, dislodging the clips holding it off her face, she murmured encouragement. He caressed the nape of her neck while his other arm wrapped her closer.

Ella groaned, welcoming the intensity of darkness, the taste of him. He took more, pulling her against him, running his hands down her spine to tuck her into his body. She belonged in his arms. He drew back, resting his forehead on hers.

"You didn't hurt my pride. You tore out my heart. And I knew I'd brought it on myself."

"You hurt me too," Ella whispered.

"For the record, I've never made love to you out of kindness or pity. I've made love to you because I need you as much as I need to take my next breath. You make me feel invincible. I love you, Eleanor. I always will."

Ella was lost. She knew about his toughness, she understood his loyalty, but his tenderness captivated her. She touched her mouth to his. Her kiss echoed her desire, his passion. Hot, needy, explosive.

"I was going to give you another few days, then I was coming after you," he confessed against her ear.

"Promise or dare?" Ella snuggled under his chin.

"Both. It's been hell not being able to see you, talk to you, touch you. I was planning to ask you to marry me, Eleanor."

"I asked first."

"But you took it back." He grinned, carefree. "So, I think it falls to me. Will you marry me, Eleanor? Will you share Tessa with me? Make a life, a family with me?"

"You put me first." She rested an ear against his chest,

felt his steady heartbeat. "That's what I worked out this week. We've both had to manage alone until now. And we almost lost each other because of it."

"I worked out love is a gift, not a burden," he whispered.

"And you showed me power isn't always used to harm."

"No more secrets." He made the words a vow.

"Only with each other." Ella slipped her hands into his hair and tugged him towards her. "Have I ever told you I dream about your naked body? Naked except for that earring."

"I'll take that as a yes then."

AUTHOR'S NOTE

Many people have contributed to this book, from the individuals who've encouraged me—you know who you are—to the competition judges and critique partners who've challenged me to do better. I'd like to thank my editor, Yezanira Venecia, and Fantasia Frog Designs for the wonderful cover. I'd especially like to thank Melissa Keir, Inkspell Publishing for her professionalism, her willingness to answer endless questions and for taking a chance on a new writer.

Sneak Peek at GRACE UNDER FIRE

CHAPTER ONE

To hell with the naysayers and the doubters, she didn't give a tinker's cuss what they thought. Grace Anderson was slowly winning over the town. Next, she planned to charm the valley. It might have taken the northern New South Wales field day committee a few years to come to the party, but here she was, artisan cheesemaker with her own booth, her own banners and her own prize-winning products. Grace Anderson's farmhouse cheeses were smack bang in the middle of the Exhibition Hall, in the middle of the Northern Rivers Showground, reaping the benefits of the biggest crowds on record.

A single bite of her pale golden cheddar, with its hint of sharpness and people were hooked. Her first experiment in unique cheese, it held prime place in her heart. It'd also won more blue ribbons than her soft cheeses but a few more years and competitions would change that.

Years of hard work were starting to pay off. An announcement cut through the buzz of the crowd.

The video presentation on the removal of woody weeds and revegetation with local native species will start in ten minutes.

Grace's order book was bulging, and she'd made a few solid business contacts today. She didn't mind the work, and the taste of success was sweet. Shoving her hands in the back pockets of her jeans, she rocked back on her heels and allowed herself a grin.

"You look pleased with yourself."

"I am." She leaned across the counter to hug her sister, Ella, placing a hand gently on the baby sling housing her four-month-old nephew. And held on.

"Hug *me*." The imperious demand from below the counter had her drawing back and backpedalling to come around the side of the booth. Ella had nursed their youngest sister Chrissy until her death and adopted her daughter.

Grace crouched to Tessa's height, and the little girl stepped into her arms. Her niece smelled of vanilla and Ella's soap. She wrapped her sturdy four-year-old legs around Grace's waist, anchoring herself in place. Grace grinned at her sister. "When did you get here?"

"About half an hour ago."

"And Jake?"

"Seduced by a ride-on mower." Ella nodded in the direction of the pavilion showcasing farm machinery. "Shiny paint, huge wheels and gargantuan blades. The perfect toy for a hot-shot Sydney lawyer who lives in an apartment."

"How's the house hunting going?" Normal chitchat when her sister's visit was anything but normal.

"We've found a bungalow with wide verandas and a large garden." Ella's hand cupped her baby's bottom. "Perfect for the kids. Jake's put in an offer."

"Fingers crossed." Grace held crossed fingers in front of Tessa, who mimicked her action.

"A bit higher than the budget we planned," Ella confessed.

"Budgets rarely match dreams. I've fallen for a German curd vat." Grace winced. "Much more than the budget I planned."

"Are you hurting?" Tessa caught her chin, turning Grace's face towards her.

"Kiss it better?" Grace pointed to her cheek, and the child planted a sloppy kiss.

"How much longer will you be here?" Ella gestured around the Hall.

"A few hours. Packing up will take another hour. I should be at the farm by about seven."

"Any clues why Mum and Dad called the meeting?" Ella's inquiry was laced with concern.

"You know what they're like," a united team—Grace had never known a time when their love wasn't strong and real—an aura tangible enough to reach out and touch, "a

family meeting only starts when all the family is present."
　"But?"

ABOUT THE AUTHOR

Australian Jennifer Raines writes contemporary romances set mainly in Australia, but not exclusively—think Malta, Finland, New Zealand or ?. A dreamer and an optimist, her stories are a delicious cocktail of mutual respect, passion and loyalty because she still believes in happily-ever-afters. Jennifer loves those days when words flow and the joy of writing makes the hard slog worthwhile. She's always made up stories about strangers in the street, in a café or strolling through an airport terminal; finding inspiration in snippets of conversation, news items and the sheer puzzle of human interactions.

Jennifer is a member of Romance Writers of Australia and is a three times finalist in the Emerald competition,

2017, 2018 (Taylor's Law) and 2022. She's a member of Romance Writers of New Zealand, winning the Pacific Hearts competition in 2017 and 2019 (Grace Under Fire). She's also a member of Romance Writers of America and has been a finalist in chapter competitions in 2019, 2020 and 2021 (Taylor's Law).

Jennifer lives in inner-city Sydney, Australia, with the requisite number of partners (1) and animals (2). Her desk overlooks a park which nourishes her soul when she raises her head from her keyboard. She gets some of her best insights during long yin yoga poses or walking—anywhere. Jennifer adores historical romance but chose to write contemporary because she thought (wrongly) it needed less research.

Jennifer can be reached through her webpage https://jenniferrainesauthor.com and via Facebook https://www.facebook.com/jenniferrainesauthor

Her book(s) are available through major providers.